I0688682

BE MY VALENCRIME

THE JUNIPER JUNCTION HOLIDAY MYSTERY SERIES: BOOK THREE

AMY M. READE

PAU HANA PUBLISHING

BOOKS BY AMY M. READE

THE JUNIPER JUNCTION HOLIDAY MYSTERY SERIES

The Worst Noel

Dead, White, and Blue

Be My Valencrime

THE LIBRARIES OF THE WORLD MYSTERY SERIES

Trudy's Diary

Dutch Treat (Coming soon)

THE MALICE SERIES

The House on Candlewick Lane

Highland Peril

Murder in Thistlecross

STANDALONE BOOKS

Secrets of Hallstead House

The Ghosts of Peppernell Manor

House of the Hanging Jade

PRAISE FOR AMY M. READE

The Worst Noel: "This is such a light and fun holiday mystery that I just could not put down! I am hooked and can't wait for the next one! It reminds me of the books they made into movies on the Hallmark movies and mystery channel." From Amazon reviewer

Dead, White, and Blue: "I really enjoyed this book and how the characters evolved. As a mother of two boys, I could relate to the teenage characters in the book and the story line kept me interested in turning the next page. A fun read and would highly recommend!" From Amazon reviewer

Trudy's Diary: "The narrative of present-day Daisy alternates with nineteenth-century Trudy after she starts reading Trudy's diary, and it kept me reading late into the night. The plot, full of twists and turns, and the memorable characters made for a fascinating read. I love mysteries and loved this one! I highly recommend it." From Amazon reviewer

Secrets of Hallstead House: "Thank you, Amy, for taking me to a new place and allowing me to imagine." From Phyllis H. Moore, reviewer

The Ghosts of Peppernell Manor: "If you're a fan of ... novels by Phyllis A. Whitney, Victoria Holt, and Barbara Michaels, you're going to love *The Ghosts of Peppernell Manor* by Amy M. Reade." From Jane Reads.

House of the Hanging Jade: "House of the Hanging Jade is a suspenseful tale of murder and obsession, all taking place against a beautiful Hawaiian backdrop. Lush descriptions of both the scenery and the food prepared by the protagonist leave you wanting more." From The Book's the Thing

House of the Hanging Jade: "I definitely see more Reade books in my future." From Back Porchervations.

The House on Candlewick Lane: "As in most gothic novels, the actual house on Candlewick Lane is creepy and filled with dark passages and rooms. You feel the evil emanate from the structure and from the people who live there ... I loved the rich descriptions of Edinburgh. You definitely feel like you are walking the streets next to Greer, searching for Ellie. You can feel the rain and the cold, and a couple times, I swear I could smell the scents of the local cuisine." From Colleen Chesebro, reviewer

Highland Peril: "This is escapism at its best, as it is a compelling mystery that whisks readers away to a land as beautiful as it is rich with intrigue." From Cynthia Chow, Kings River Life

Murder in Thistlecross: "Amy Reade's series has a touch of gothic suspense, always fun, and this particular entry has the extra added attraction of the old Clue board game (later a movie that was equally delightful) wherein the various suspects move around the castle and the sleuth has to figure out who killed who, how and where." From Buried Under Books

Copyright © 2020 by Amy M. Reade.

Cover design by http://www.StunningBookCovers.com

All rights reserved. No part of this publication may be reproduced, distributed or transmitted in any form or by any means, including photocopying, recording, or other electronic or mechanical methods, without the prior written permission of the publisher, except in the case of brief quotations embodied in critical reviews and certain other noncommercial uses permitted by copyright law.

Publisher's Note: This is a work of fiction. Names, characters, places, and incidents are a product of the author's imagination. Locales and public names are sometimes used for atmospheric purposes. Any resemblance to actual people, living or dead, or to businesses, companies, events, institutions, or locales is completely coincidental.

Pau Hana Publishing

Print ISBN: 978-1-7326907-6-9

Ebook ISBN: 978-1-7326907-7-6

Printed in the United States of America

In memory of Sharon Aguanno

CHAPTER 1

Valentine's Day was Lilly Carlsen's least favorite day of the year, followed closely by the day the clocks spring forward. Both days left her tired, grumpy, and in need of chocolate. In the case of Spring Forward, she usually settled for strong coffee. In the case of Valentine's Day, though, nothing but chocolate would do.

She had been forced to buy her own chocolate beginning the year she married Beau. He wasn't much of a romantic and didn't like chocolate, anyway. And from the time he had left her and their two toddlers fifteen years previously, she hadn't had a boyfriend who would buy her chocolate for Valentine's Day.

Until now.

Lilly had been dating Hassan Ashraf for over a year. This would be their second Valentine's Day together, but the first one didn't really count because Hassan had been on a gem hunting trip in Sri Lanka and hadn't even been able to get in touch with her via telephone. He had given her a box of chocolates, a bouquet of roses, and an apology when he returned from his trip.

But this year was going to be different. This year he would

be in Juniper Junction and they already had reservations at their favorite restaurant, The Water Wheel. He knew how much Lilly loved chocolate, so she was pretty sure she could look forward to a gorgeous box of gourmet treats from her favorite chocolatier.

Her only dilemma was what to give Hassan for Valentine's Day. He didn't need jewelry, so a watch was not an option. He didn't usually wear ties, so that wasn't a good idea, either. She had been browsing online to find leather-bound travel journals, but she wasn't sure he would use one of those.

Valentine's Day was fast approaching and she needed to make a decision.

The weeks leading up to Valentine's Day were among the busiest of the year at Juniper Junction Jewels, Lilly's shop on Main Street in the small Rocky Mountain town. It usually started getting busy midway through January with romantics looking for the perfect gifts for their Valentines. Lilly had always thought it interesting that women tended to do their shopping early—men tended to wait until the last minute.

Her favorite days in the shop were when men came in looking for engagement rings. Though some of them had ideas for precisely the ring they wanted, the majority of them were unsure of themselves and needed some gentle guidance through the process of buying such an important piece of jewelry.

That was where Harry, Lilly's shop assistant, came in handy. Harry wasn't just a darling man—he was also a natural when it came to knowledge of different gems and stones, and many of the men who came into the shop in search of an engagement ring seemed to relax under his capable attention.

It was early February and Juniper Junction Jewels had been bedecked in pink, red, and white gauze, cupids, and hearts since mid-January. Lilly hated the sickly sweet look, but it was necessary.

Toward the end of the day, Harry and Lilly were taking the

pieces of jewelry from their light pink velvet displays and placing them in the vault until the next morning. Harry lingered over the rings, paying special attention to one with a pale pink sapphire in a white gold setting.

"Isn't that a gorgeous ring?" Lilly asked, noticing that Harry had slowed his pace in dismantling the displays.

"Mm-hmm," he answered, staring at the bauble.

"Say, how's Alice these days?" Lilly asked. Harry had been dating Alice for many months, and the young woman was every bit as sweet as Harry. The two were a perfect match.

Harry's head snapped up and he gave Lilly a suspicious look. "Why do you ask?"

Lilly smiled. "I just happened to think of her when I saw you mooning over the pink engagement ring. If I remember correctly, Alice's favorite color is pink."

Harry blushed four shades darker than the ring.

"She's fine. Just studying hard. Midterms will be here before she knows it," he said, sidestepping the elephant in the room— was he was looking at the pink ring with the intent of buying it for Alice?

Lilly grinned and dropped the issue. It was obviously making Harry uncomfortable.

"Let's get these pieces put away and go home. It's been a long day," she said. Harry turned his attention away from the dazzling ring and picked up several bracelets to take to the vault.

"Have you heard the forecast?" he asked over his shoulder. "It's supposed to storm tonight."

Lilly glanced outside the big plate glass windows in the front of the shop. It had already been dark for almost an hour.

"I heard that. The clouds rolled in this afternoon."

"I can't wait for spring," Harry said. Lilly smiled, but didn't answer. She loved winter, with its moods and its snowfall and its cold temperatures. Fall was her favorite season, but winter was a close second.

When they had locked the vault and triple-checked it, they both left. Snowflakes were already falling thickly.

"Be careful getting home," Harry said, then drove off.

Lilly stood looking at the sky for a moment before getting into her own car. She loved watching the snow fall through the darkness. She shivered just a little and followed Harry out of the alley behind the shop and onto Main Street.

* * *

Barney, the Carlsen family's soft-coated wheaten terrier, greeted Lilly, as usual, with a frenzy of barking and tail-wagging when Lilly walked into the kitchen through the back door.

"Hi, Barn!" she said, laughing. The big lug of a dog jumped up and placed his paws on her coat, trying to lick her face. She bent closer to him to accept his kisses.

"Hi, Mom," Laurel said as she came down the stairs and into the kitchen.

"Hi, honey. How was school?" Lilly was finally getting used to having only one child at home. Tighe had been away at college since the previous August, and though Lilly had been sure she would never adjust to the situation, she was getting accustomed to it. She brushed away the thought that Laurel, a senior in high school, would be following her brother out of the nest in another six months.

"It was good." Laurel opened the refrigerator door. "What's for dinner?"

"Leftovers," Lilly said. "Can you grab the jar of soup in there?" Laurel handed her mother a large jar of *zuppa Toscana* they had made over the weekend and Lilly emptied it into a pan on the stove. While the soup warmed she cut slices of Italian bread and placed them on the table with olive oil for dipping.

"Can I go over to Nick's tonight?" Laurel asked as they sat down for dinner.

"I don't think you should. There's a storm coming and I don't want you out driving in it," Lilly warned.

"All right. I'll just call him and tell him I can't come."

Lilly looked at her daughter. She had expected a barrage of whining and eye rolling, but there was nothing. Lilly wondered what was going on.

She got her answer a couple minutes later.

Laurel toyed with her bread, breaking it into tiny pieces and arranging them in a circle on her plate. "Vanessa is going shopping for her prom dress this weekend."

"Oh?" Lilly suspected Laurel would want to accompany her best friend.

"I think I'm going to go with her," Laurel said.

"That sounds fun," Lilly said. "Isn't it early to be shopping for a prom dress?"

"Not really. Lots of girls have their dresses already."

Lilly had a hunch about where this conversation was headed.

"Maybe I'll look for a dress while I'm out with Vanessa," Laurel suggested.

"Has Nick asked you to prom?" Lilly grinned.

"Not yet. But it can't hurt to have a dress picked out, right?" Laurel's grin matched her mom's.

"No, it can't hurt."

"Depending on the price, do you think you could help me pay for it?" Laurel asked.

Well, that escalated quickly, Lilly thought. *So that's why she didn't give me a hard time about staying home tonight.*

"I suppose I could chip in some," Lilly said. "Um, how much are you thinking of spending on a dress?"

Laurel shrugged. "Five hundred dollars, maybe."

Lilly almost choked on her bread. "Five hundred dollars?" she wheezed. "For a prom dress?"

Laurel must have sensed her mother's disbelief. Anyone with a pulse would have sensed it.

"I'm just throwing a number out there," she hastened to explain. "I have no idea how much the dress will cost."

"I don't mind helping to pay for a dress, but for heaven's sake, Laurel, my wedding dress didn't even cost five hundred dollars."

"That was ages ago, Mom. I'll look for something cheaper than that, obviously," Laurel said, her tone taking on just a hint of snippiness.

"Good." Lilly unclenched her jaw. "Where are you going to look for dresses?"

"Ruby Red's," Laurel said. Lilly glanced at her daughter out of the corner of her eye. Ruby Red's was the most fashionable dress shop in town. Also the most expensive.

"I doubt you'll find a prom dress under five hundred dollars at Ruby's."

"We'll look at other places, too." Laurel hurriedly pushed the rest of dinner into her mouth. "I have a lot of homework to do. I'll come down and do the dishes in a little while."

I raised a smart girl, thought Lilly. *She knows how to make a quick exit and she knows that by mentioning the word "homework" I won't give her grief. Well played, Laurel. Well played.*

CHAPTER 2

*L*illy ate the rest of her dinner in silence. It was times like this she missed Tighe the most. Her stress-inducing conversation with Laurel had left her feeling sorry for herself. But Tighe was at school and he wouldn't be home until spring break, so there wasn't much point in moping at the kitchen table. Lilly figured the best course of action would be to buck up, clear the table, and do the dishes. If Laurel really did have a lot of homework, she would—probably—appreciate her mom doing the dishes for her.

When Lilly let Barney into the backyard later that evening, the wind had picked up and was making an urgent *whooshing* sound as it blew through the treetops surrounding the house. Snow was coming down heavily, joining the six inches that had already fallen since she arrived home from work. She couldn't even see Barney at the rear of the yard, but she knew he was enjoying his romp in the snow.

She let him in as soon as he returned to the back door and he promptly shook all the snow off himself and onto her and the floor. She laughed and grabbed a towel. She rubbed him down as best she could and wiped up the mess on the floor; then he accompanied her into the living room.

Lilly had come up with several new jewelry designs and she wanted to get them down on paper before they disappeared, like a snowflake, into the whirl of other things that cluttered her mind.

She and Barney sat on the couch, Lilly with her sketch pad and Barney curled up next to her, half asleep. She had worked for over an hour when inspiration hit for Hassan's Valentine's Day gift. She would come up with a new design in Hassan's honor, and she would donate the proceeds from the year's sale of the piece to an Afghan charity. And she knew exactly the design she would make—an XO with onyx crystals in a sterling silver setting. The symbol, which stood for "hugs and kisses," made her think of Hassan, with its suggestion of love and warmth. She drew up several sketches, then smiled to herself and closed her notebook.

"He's going to love this, Barney." She leaned over to kiss the dog's snout. Just then the phone rang, startling her. "Hello?"

"Hi, Lilly, it's Nikki." Lilly's brow furrowed. Nikki was her mother's in-home nurse and though she stayed later in the evenings once in a while, she generally left for home shortly after Bev finished dinner.

"Hi, Nikki. Is everything all right?"

"Your mom is insisting that you're out in the storm, stuck somewhere, and in trouble. Can you talk to her? Maybe if she hears your voice she'll calm down."

"Sure. Do you want me to come over?" Lilly asked.

"Let's see how this works first. I'd hate to have you come out in this storm if you don't have to." Lilly didn't answer, but she was relieved to hear it. She didn't like being outside in hazardous conditions, especially in a car. "Besides," Nikki continued, "I'm going to spend the night because of the weather."

"Good. It's not a pleasant night to be out driving."

Lilly waited a few moments while Nikki took the phone to Bev.

"Hello, Lilly?" Bev asked.

"Hi, Mom. I'm just sitting here at home in the living room. Barney and Laurel are here in the house with me. Are you all right in this storm?"

"Of course, dear. Why did you call?"

Lilly was confused. "I didn't. Nikki called me. She just wanted me to let you know that I'm all right."

"That was nice of you, Lilly. Now I've got to go. Nikki and I are watching television."

Lilly said goodbye and waited for Nikki to get back on the phone.

"Your mom made a liar out of me," Nikki said in a rueful tone. "Sorry to have bothered you. As soon as she heard your voice, she must have forgotten her worries."

"That's no problem," Lilly assured the nurse. "Call anytime. It's good to know that Mom still knows who I am."

"Oh, she definitely knows who you are. She talks about you all the time," Nikki replied.

"She does?" Lilly asked, her heart sinking. She wondered what family secrets Bev might be spilling to Nikki.

Nikki must have heard the dismay in Lilly's voice. "Don't worry," she said with a laugh. "It's all good stuff."

They hung up and Lilly sat back on the couch with a feeling of relief. Ordinarily she wouldn't mind her mother's nurse being let in on private family matters going back decades, but Nikki was Beau's girlfriend. And as much as she liked and respected and appreciated her, Lilly had an understandable desire for Nikki to know only the good things about the family.

Her thoughts turned to her mother, who was becoming more confused of late. It didn't surprise her that Bev thought she might be stuck somewhere out in the storm, but she didn't want her mother worrying unnecessarily about things that weren't real. She remembered the days when her mother could juggle a dozen things on the to-do list and keep track of her kids' schedules, her husband's travels for work, and her own myriad responsibilities. Those days were long gone, but they brought a nostalgic smile to Lilly's lips. Her mother had been quite a dynamo in her younger days. It was sad to see her decline like this, but luckily there were many things from years and years ago that Bev could remember with crystal clarity.

Which brought up another worry. Nikki had been spending seven days a week with Bev, bless her, and she hadn't had a day off in quite a while. Lilly was on the hunt for someone who could relieve Nikki for a day or two a week, but the search wasn't going well so far. Nikki didn't seem to mind and she was being well-paid for her dedication to Bev, but Lilly was pretty sure she wanted a day to herself once in a while.

Hassan called as Lilly was getting into bed and they talked for several minutes. They had gotten into the habit of calling each other late in the evening, and Lilly found that it was easier to relax and go to sleep when she had spoken to Hassan before bed.

The storm reached a fever pitch in the middle of the night. Lilly woke up to the sound of Barney whining and lay in bed for several minutes, listening to the wind rage outside. Barney usually slept at the foot of her bed, but on nights like this, he curled up closer to her.

After a few minutes, Lilly could have sworn she heard some-one's voice. At first she thought it was the wind, but the wind didn't say things like "school" and "snow day." She got out of bed and padded down the hall to Laurel's room, where she stood outside the door, listening.

Sure enough, Laurel was talking to someone. Lilly knocked on her daughter's bedroom door. "Laurel?" she called softly.

There was silence on the other side of the door. "Yeah?" came Laurel's voice after a few seconds.

"Who are you talking to? It's three o'clock in the morning."

"Just a friend from school. I must have lost track of time. Sorry."

"Hang up and go to sleep, honey. You have to be up in three hours."

"They'll cancel school in the morning. I'll be able to sleep in."

"Don't argue with me, Laurel. Hang up and get some sleep. Goodnight. Love you."

"Love you," Laurel grumbled. Lilly shook her head and returned to bed, where Barney hadn't budged.

Sure enough, school was cancelled the next day because of the forecast for continued blowing snow and near-zero visibility. The new president of the Chamber of Commerce, Lilly's replacement, had also issued a recommendation that stores in Juniper Junction open an hour late to allow the public works department extra time to clear the roads.

Even though she left the house an hour later than usual, it took Lilly much longer than she expected to get to work because of the driving conditions. Snow blew across the road, obstructing her vision, but she was grateful that the plows had been out and the roads were clear of accumulated snow. Harry was already inside when Lilly arrived at the jewelry shop.

"Wow! What a morning!" Lilly exclaimed as she walked into the store. Harry was arranging displays in the glass cases. "You probably didn't even need to come in today, Harry. I would be surprised if we get a single customer."

"I don't mind," Harry replied. "Besides, there's something I wanted to ask you."

"What is it?"

"We've never discussed this before, so I was just wondering if I get an employee discount on jewelry."

Lilly struggled to keep a grin from taking over her whole

face. "Of course. You and I pay the wholesale price if we buy anything."

Harry smiled. "Thanks."

"Any particular reason you're asking?" Lilly asked, allowing herself just one nosy question.

"Well, you know I was looking at that pink sapphire ring yesterday..." Harry began. Lilly smiled broadly, knowing where this was headed.

"Yes," she prompted.

Harry took a deep breath. "I'm going to ask Alice to marry me."

CHAPTER 3

*L*illy let out a squeal. "I knew it! I'm so happy for you!" She was beaming. If they had been anywhere but work, she would have hugged him.

His face matched hers. "I'm happy, too. I just hope she says 'yes.'" His smile disappeared, replaced in an instant by a worried frown.

"I have no doubt of it," Lilly said. "I've seen how she looks at you. I'm just so thrilled." She gave Harry a fond smile and took a sip of the coffee in her travel mug.

"So when are you going to ask her?"

"Valentine's Day." Harry's grin had reappeared.

"How romantic," Lilly gushed. "Do you want the day off?"

"No, no, I don't want the day off," Harry was quick to reply. "We're going out to dinner that night and I'll ask her then. If I have to stay home all day, I'll go bananas."

"I see what you mean. Then I'll be happy to have you at work." Lilly smiled again and bustled to the vault in the back to carry more pieces of jewelry to the display cases in front.

The morning passed slowly, with not a single customer braving the biting wind and snow to buy jewelry. A few people made their way quickly up and down Main Street, but they obviously had destinations in mind and Lilly suspected they were headed to places like the pharmacy or the bank for reasons that wouldn't wait for the weather to get better.

Around lunchtime she called Laurel to see what was going on at home.

"Hi, Mom," Laurel answered.

"Hi, honey. What time did you get up this morning?"

"Around ten."

"You're not going anywhere today, are you?" Lilly asked.

"No. Vanessa's coming over to hang out this afternoon." Vanessa lived only a block away, so Lilly was pretty sure she would make it to the Carlsen house in one piece.

"Okay. Be good. Love you."

"I'm always good, Mom. Love you."

Lilly dialed her mother next. Nikki answered.

"Hi, Nikki. How's Mom doing today?"

"Okay, I suppose," Nikki said. It wasn't the boundless enthusiasm Lilly had hoped for.

"What's wrong?"

"Your mom was furious with me this morning for making her breakfast," Nikki said in a low voice. "I make her breakfast most days and normally she doesn't mind, but today she was angry. She said she's perfectly capable of making her own meals and that if I'm going to keep interfering with her independence, she'll fire me."

"Hmm…. That doesn't sound like Mom. She's usually non-confrontational with everyone but me." She could hear Nikki chuckle. "I'll try to stop by after work if this wind ever lets up. In the meantime, I guess you should just let Mom fix her own lunch and dinner. If she wants help, she'll ask for it."

Lilly hung up with Nikki and went back to the office, leaving Harry in charge of the shop. There was paperwork to catch up on and she wanted to look at her XO design sketches again. She kept colored glass crystals in her office to use in making design templates, so she arranged a number of black crystals in an XO pattern and stood back to admire it. The pattern could be used for anything—pendants, cufflinks, earring, or tie tacks. She couldn't wait to show it to Hassan.

When mid-afternoon arrived and not a single customer had come into the store, Lilly decided to close up for the day and send Harry home. They put the displays in the vault and went their separate ways, Harry to his house and Lilly to her mother's house. The wind had let up a little bit, so visibility had improved enough to make the drive easier than it had been that morning.

Lilly climbed the front steps of Bev's house and knocked before opening the door. At first, she was pleased by what she saw.

Bev sat in her armchair, giggling helplessly. Nikki sat in the rocking chair opposite Bev, also laughing. She looked at Lilly and winked. Fred, Bev's cocker spaniel, ran up to Lilly and danced around her feet.

"Well, what's going on here?" Lilly asked, beginning to laugh herself.

Bev wiped tears from her eyes and leaned her head back. "Oh, Lilly," she gasped. "You've missed the funniest thing."

"What was it?" Lilly asked, looking from her mother to Nikki.

"Fred had an accident in the kitchen and Nikki slipped in it and when she did, she knocked a whole five-pound bag of sugar off the counter! There's sugar everywhere! You should have seen it!" Bev's voice rang again with peals of laughter.

Lilly gave Nikki a confused look. It didn't sound funny. Nikki glanced at Lilly and shook her head just enough so Lilly would know not to put a damper on her mother's hilarity.

"I have to go to the bathroom," Bev said, pushing herself up from the armchair. "I'll be right back." She left the room with Fred in tow. Lilly looked to Nikki for an explanation.

Nikki stood up and headed for the kitchen. Lilly followed her. The nurse said over her shoulder, "There's wet sugar—five pounds of it—all over the kitchen floor. I'll clean it up. Your mom thought it was so funny that I didn't want to ruin her good mood. I don't think I've ever seen her laugh like that. It must have been like watching one of those home video shows where people trip or fall and everyone thinks it's hysterical."

Lilly's shoulders fell when she saw the mess on the kitchen floor. "Nikki, I'll clean up the mess. You go sit with Mom. It's bad enough you suffered the indignity of slipping in dog urine without having to clean up the sticky mess left behind. Are you hurt?"

"I didn't even fall. I just slipped on the wet spot. I don't mind cleaning it up." Nikki chuckled. "You know, it must have been pretty funny to watch."

"You go." Lilly shooed her out. "I'll get to work in here."

Cleaning the kitchen floor took almost a half hour because so much sugar had spilled everywhere. When Lilly wandered into the living room after she had finished, Bev and Nikki were sitting on the sofa, looking through old photos.

"And here are Lilly and Beau's wedding photos," Bev was saying, pointing to a spread of pictures over two pages. Lilly didn't mean to groan out loud, but she couldn't stop herself. There were about a billion reasons she didn't want anyone looking at those photos.

Nikki smiled. "What's the matter with these?" she asked. "I think they're cute!"

Oh, God. Not "cute." Wedding photos are not supposed to be "cute."

"That was a long time ago," Lilly said.

"That Beau. What a darling," Bev enthused.

Lilly squinted at her mother. If Nikki hadn't been dating Beau, Lilly would have spoken up. *Beau? Darling? He left me with two little kids and disappeared without a trace, Mom. There's nothing darling about that.*

She let it go. Since Beau had come back to Juniper Junction over a year ago, her mother had been under the mistaken impression that he was some charming handyman sent straight from God Himself for the benefit of the old ladies of Juniper Junction. Sure, maybe he had helped Bev around the house, and sure, maybe he had helped her friend Mildred with chores around her house, but that didn't make him a saint. There was still the matter of abandoning his family and disappearing for a decade and a half.

Nikki seemed to sense that Lilly was growing agitated. She put her hand on the photo album so Bev couldn't turn the page. "What are you going to have for dinner, Bev?" she asked. Lilly let out a quiet sigh of relief.

But Bev was having none of it. She gently pushed Nikki's hand away. "I want to look at these photos first," she said. "Wasn't Lilly's wedding dress pretty? A neighbor made it for her. She got a good deal." She looked up at Lilly. "How much did that dress cost?"

"About three hundred dollars," Lilly answered. Her mind immediately turned back to the discussion about Laurel's prom dress. Between the urine-soaked sugar in the kitchen, her mother's insistence that Beau's ex-wife and Beau's present girlfriend look through Beau's old wedding photos together, and the thought of having to shell out five hundred dollars for a prom dress, Lilly was afraid she might stop breathing.

To her relief, Nikki came to the rescue again.

"Bev," she said, taking the album from her lap and standing up, "I'm sure Lilly has things to do at home. We really should get your dinner started."

"What are you making?" Bev asked.

"You told me you wanted to make dinner yourself," Nikki reminded her.

"Oh, pooh. I was kidding," Bev said. She looked like she really meant it.

"Why don't you come out and help me?" Nikki suggested.

"All right, dear. That would be fine." The misunderstanding from earlier that day seemed to have been forgotten as quickly as the photo album. Lilly put the album in its rightful spot before saying goodnight to her mom and Nikki, then she left.

She shook her head as she descended the front steps. It was always an adventure going to her mom's house. As Bev's dementia progressed, Lilly never knew what to expect when she went over there. Thank goodness for Nikki—even if she was dating Beau.

CHAPTER 4

When she got home, Lilly walked into the kitchen, tossed her handbag on the counter, and hung up her coat wearily. She wanted nothing more than to get into pajamas and go to bed. Barney raced in to greet her, his nails slipping and sliding on the kitchen floor. Lilly grinned as she rubbed his ears.

"Laurel?" she called, going to the bottom of the stairs. She could hear Laurel's bedroom door open.

"Hi, Mom."

"What are you doing?" Lilly looked up at her daughter, who was standing at the top of the stairs.

"Just hanging out."

"Is Vanessa still here?"

"No, she had to go home about an hour ago."

"Are those other people I hear upstairs?" Lilly asked.

There was the briefest hesitation.

"Laurel, is Nick up there with you? He'd better not be." Lilly's jaw clenched.

"No, Mom. Just a couple of my friends from school."

"Oh. Who are they?"

"Karley and Bella." Lilly remembered them from Laurel's soccer games in middle school, but she hadn't seen them since then.

"Okay. Are they staying for dinner?"

"Nah," Laurel answered. "They just came over to say hi. Why are you home so early?"

"Not a single customer today. The weather kept most people indoors."

"I'm sorry," Laurel said.

"Tomorrow is another day. What do you say to frozen pizza tonight? I'm tired."

"Sounds good to me. I'll be down soon."

Five minutes later the three girls came clattering downstairs.

"Hi, Mrs. Carlsen," Karley and Bella said in unison.

"Hi, girls. I haven't seen you in a long time," Lilly said.

"I guess about five years, right?" Karley asked.

Lilly nodded. "That's probably right. How have you both been?"

"Pretty chill," Karley said.

"It's all good," Bella said simultaneously.

Lilly smiled. *Typical teenage girl response.*

"Bye, Mrs. Carlsen. See you later," Bella said.

"Bye, girls. Get home safely."

Just a half hour later, Lilly and Laurel were sitting down to a dinner of pizza and tossed salad. "I'm sure school will be open tomorrow," Lilly said. "Make sure you don't stay up until all hours on the phone tonight."

"I won't. I'll turn off my ringer so I don't hear it if anyone calls."

"Who would call in the middle of the night?" Lilly wondered aloud. It was a rhetorical question.

"I'll do the dishes tonight," Laurel offered.

"And I'll let you," Lilly said with a tired grin. "Thanks, honey."

While Laurel cleaned up the kitchen, Lilly went into the living room with her cell phone and called her best friend, Noley Appleton.

"Guess what," she said when Noley answered the phone.

"What?"

"Don't tell anyone, but Harry is going to ask Alice to marry him on Valentine's Day," Lilly said.

"That's so romantic!"

"I know, right? They're just perfect for each other. Anyway, it's time to start planning the engagement party. What do you think?"

"I love the idea, but shouldn't we wait until they're actually engaged?" Noley asked.

"Sure, we can wait, but just be thinking about it. You're the magician when it comes to parties." As a recipe developer, cook, and nationally-syndicated food columnist, Noley was Lilly's go-to person whenever food was involved. She could cook everything from heavy roasts to dainty finger foods.

"I'll start making a list of possibilities. Say, how's your mom? Bill said she was mad at Nikki about something." Lilly's brother, Bill, had been dating Noley for a little over a year.

"She's having an up-and-down day," Lilly said with a sigh. "I closed the store early this afternoon because of the weather and I went over to see Mom. She was in hysterics because Nikki had slipped on the kitchen floor and she thought it was the funniest thing in the world. This morning she was mad at Nikki for making her breakfast, but by late this afternoon they were friends again and she wanted Nikki to make her dinner."

"I hate to see her like that," Noley murmured.

"Me, too. But I guess it's part of the disease. There are some days Mom is just like her old self, and some days when she can't remember what year it is."

"I suppose the best thing to do is to enjoy the good days," Noley said.

"You're right. Listen, I have an idea. Why don't you and Bill and Hassan and I take Mom out for dinner the weekend before Valentine's Day? She would enjoy that."

"Sounds good," said Noley. "I think Bill is off Saturday night." As a member of Juniper Junction's police force, Bill had unpredictable hours, depending on what was going on in the decidedly small criminal underbelly of the town.

"Are you two doing anything for Valentine's Day?" Lilly asked.

Noley sighed. "I don't know. Bill hasn't mentioned it."

"Don't wait for him to mention it," Lilly advised. "He's not always the brightest when it comes to stuff like that. Remember that awful teddy bear he gave you last year?"

Noley laughed. Lilly had called Bill on his way home from work the previous Valentine's Day to remind him that it was an important day. He panicked. He stopped at a drugstore that evening and picked up one of the only Valentine's Day items left in stock, a small red teddy bear holding a pink plastic flower. A white vinyl heart on the bear's stomach read "Happy Valentine's Day." Noley had shown the appropriate appreciation, but later confided to Lilly that it would have been better to have nothing at all, since she now felt obligated to display the hideous little bear in her house. They still laughed about it.

"You think I should plan something?" Noley asked.

"Definitely. It's got to be better than last year." Lilly chuckled.

"I'll get to work on it." The women hung up and Lilly dialed Tighe's number.

As usual, he didn't answer, so she left him a message asking him to text her to confirm that he was still alive. Then she curled up on the sofa with a good mystery and read until bedtime. When Hassan called she asked if he would be in Juniper Junction the weekend before Valentine's Day.

"I'm afraid I can't get there before Valentine's Day," he said.

"Rats. I was hoping you could join Bill and Noley and me to take Mom out to dinner on Saturday night."

"I'm sorry, Lil. I've got so much to do here."

"Here" was Minnesota, where Hassan kept an apartment near his parents. He had bought a house in Juniper Junction not long after meeting Lilly, so he had a nice place to stay when he was in town. Luckily, that was often.

CHAPTER 5

The days that followed were clear and cold with little wind and no extra snow, and they sped by as more and more people visited Juniper Junction Jewels looking for the perfect Valentine's Day gift for that special someone. Lilly was happy for the customer traffic, not only because it was good for business, but because it kept Harry busy almost constantly. He had been getting increasingly agitated at work and Lilly knew it was due to nerves over his Valentine's Day plans.

On Saturday morning, two days before Valentine's Day, Vanessa and her older sister picked up Laurel to go out for breakfast, then prom dress shopping. It was something Lilly had hoped to do with her daughter someday, but Laurel informed her that Vanessa's mother wasn't going, either, so it would be "weird" if Lilly went. So Lilly watched them go, having made Laurel promise not to put any money down on a dress until Lilly could see it, too. If she was going to pay for at least part of it, she had no intention of having absolutely no say in the choice of dress. In her mind's eye, she could see Laurel picking out something with a neckline down to her navel or a dress that had sheer material all the way up her legs, making underwear a non-issue. She shuddered at the thought.

The jewelry shop was open on Saturdays, so Lilly went in to work after Laurel left. She and Harry were setting out displays when there was a knock on the window.

Lilly turned around to see who was there. "Hassan!" she cried. He stood outside the window in a long wool overcoat, carrying the biggest bouquet of roses Lilly had ever seen.

She ran to unlock the door for him and threw her arms around his neck before he could even get inside the shop. He laughed. "What a welcome! I should arrive in Juniper Junction like this every time."

Lilly grinned and accepted the flowers, then hurried to the back office, where she kept vases on the off chance she had fresh flowers to display.

"I don't know if this vase is even big enough," she exclaimed, carrying it to the front of the store. Hassan had taken off his coat and was talking to Harry. His handsome Middle Eastern features were heightened in the early morning light coming in through the window. He looked tired, though.

"What time did you get in?" Lilly asked, arranging the flowers in the vase. It looked like they would just fit.

"I got the earliest flight out of Minneapolis and drove here from Denver as soon as I landed," he said with a wink. "I wanted to surprise you."

"This is the best surprise ever." Lilly gazed at him. Harry walked quietly into the back office and Hassan gathered Lilly to his chest and kissed her properly.

After several seconds she stepped back. "You look exhausted. Why don't you head to your house and get some sleep?"

"I am pretty tired," he admitted. "I'll give you a call when I wake up and I'll see you tonight."

"Sounds good. I hope you're able to get a good rest. No coffee this morning," she warned as he pulled his coat on.

He kissed her again. "No coffee, I promise. All I needed was to see you and now I'll be able to relax."

He left, hurrying down the sidewalk in the cold, and Lilly watched him go with a smile on her lips. Harry returned to the front of the shop.

"That was really nice of Hassan," he said. "I'll have to watch him to pick up some of his moves."

"He doesn't have moves," Lilly said. "That's just the way he is. And I have a feeling you don't need to take notes from anyone."

Harry chuckled.

Saturday was shaping up to be a good day.

Lilly closed the store early on Saturdays, so she went home with plenty of time to get ready for dinner. Laurel came home with a phone full of pictures and a head full of excitement over the prospect of getting one of the dresses she had tried on. She and Lilly sat on the sofa next to each other and Laurel swiped through all the photos. There must have been a hundred of them.

Laurel pointed to one, tapping to enlarge it. "This one was my favorite," she gushed. "Isn't it gorgeous?"

Lilly took the phone and looked closely at the photo. She had to admit it was a beautiful dress, and Laurel looked beautiful in it. The dress was a stunning fuchsia satin with wide straps at the shoulders, a reasonable V-neck, and a full, sweeping skirt.

"That is beautiful," Lilly agreed, handing the phone back to Laurel. "Do I dare ask how much it costs?"

Laurel looked down at her phone. "I think that one was about eight hundred dollars," she said, clearing her throat.

"You're kidding."

Laurel looked at her mother with a mixture of sadness and frustration and heaved a loud sigh. "I wish I was kidding. Too much?"

"I think it's too much," Lilly said. "We've got college to think about, and if you want a car you're going to have to figure that into the budget, too."

"It was at Ruby's."

"In that case, I bet we can find one that's just as nice without spending so much."

"That would be great."

"Did Vanessa find anything?"

"She found a cream-colored dress that makes her look like a Greek goddess," Laurel said wistfully. "If she puts her hair up, she'll look just like she stepped out of ancient Greece."

"How much is that dress?"

"Only six hundred dollars."

Only six hundred dollars. Lilly shook her head almost imperceptibly. *Where is Vanessa getting that kind of money?*

As if sensing what Lilly was thinking, Laurel spoke up. "Vanessa's parents are paying for half and she's paying for the other half." Lilly nodded. Once they had looked at all the photos and Lilly had agreed that Laurel's favorite was, indeed, the best of the bunch, Laurel went upstairs, her steps a little slow and her shoulders slumped.

Lilly wished she could buy the dress Laurel wanted, but it was out of the question.

Laurel spent the rest of the afternoon moping around the house until Lilly finally couldn't stand it any longer. "Laurel, please take Barney for a quick walk outside or read a book or do something. You've got to stop obsessing over that dress."

Laurel scowled, snapped the leash on Barney, threw on a winter coat, and left the house, slamming the door behind her. Lilly heaved a sigh and longed for the days when Laurel's biggest problem was how to figure out the area of a rectangle. Had that really been only three years ago?

It seemed longer than that.

CHAPTER 6

At four thirty that afternoon, Hassan knocked on Lilly's back door and let himself in. Lilly greeted him with a kiss and a glass of wine. They sat and talked for a little while, then at five o'clock they left for Bev's house. Bill and Noley were already there. Bev had decided the day before that she wanted to go to Treetops, so Nikki had made sure that Bev was dressed up and ready to go. Lilly had invited Laurel to join them, but Laurel had declined, saying she was too tired to go anywhere.

Treetops was a small, posh restaurant located just outside Juniper Junction. It was called Treetops because it was a three-story bed and breakfast situated on a bluff overlooking a deep gulch. Tall pine trees grew in the gulch and the restaurant of the bed and breakfast was on the third floor, above the tops of the trees. It commanded a gorgeous view of the mountains surrounding it.

The group was shown to a table near a plate glass window, as Lilly had requested when making the reservation. Normally such a coveted spot would be hard to reserve, but since they were eating pretty early, the table had been available.

It was a round table, so conversation would be easier. Unfortunately, it started out on a sour note.

"You really should have invited Nikki and Beau," Bev scolded Bill and Lilly. Bill looked at Lilly as if to say *You're in charge here.*

"Mom, the last person I want to share a Valentine's Day meal with is my ex-husband."

"You're just bitter, Lilly. He's really a fine young man."

He's neither fine nor young, Lilly wanted to say. Hassan gave her a sympathetic look.

Lilly tried a different approach. "Well, we all wanted this evening to be just about you, Mom."

"If it was all about me, shouldn't you have invited other people that I'd like to have here?" Bev asked, sticking her chin out.

"No." Lilly wasn't going to spend the evening arguing about why Beau hadn't been invited. "Mom, why don't you take a look at the menu?" She buried her face behind her own menu so her mother would stop talking.

Bev pushed the menu away from her. "I already know what I want."

"What would you like, Bev?" Hassan asked.

"I'll have cottage cheese and pineapple."

For this we came to the most expensive restaurant in three states? Lilly thought. Her mother had made her grumpy and she immediately regretted her ill-mannered thought.

"Wouldn't you like something more than that?" Bill asked.

"No, I'm not very hungry," Bev replied.

"Maybe you'd like to order something to take home and you can have it tomorrow night for dinner," Bill suggested.

"That's a good idea. Maybe I'll be hungrier tomorrow night. Can we get something for Nikki to eat with me?"

"Sure, Mom. What do you think she would like?" Lilly asked.

Bev picked up her menu. "Maybe some chicken," she said. "I'll have chicken, too." She chose chicken *cordon bleu* and when everyone ordered, Bill ordered the chicken to take home after dinner.

All attention was focused on Bev, as Lilly had hoped it would be. As the meal progressed, Lilly became less and less grouchy over the spat with her mom and tried to enjoy their time together.

They were halfway through dinner when Bill's phone buzzed. He answered it quickly and excused himself from the table to take the call in the lobby of the restaurant.

When he returned everyone looked at him expectantly. "No big deal," he said. "Just someone from the station to let me know what I've got on tap for my shift tomorrow morning."

"They couldn't let you have dinner in peace with your family and your lovely wife?" Bev asked in disgust.

Everyone froze. Bill looked like a deer caught in headlights. It was Noley who spoke up after several seconds of uncomfortable silence. "Bev, Bill and I aren't married, remember?"

"Oh, nonsense." Bev leaned toward Noley and asked in a loud whisper, "When are you two going to start having babies? I'm not going to live forever, you know."

Bill cleared his throat. "Not appropriate, Mom." She seemed to take the hint and changed the subject.

"So why can't they leave you alone and let you have dinner with your *family*?" Bev winked at Noley. Bill closed his eyes and shook his head. Lilly watched Noley try to keep a straight face.

"It's okay, Mom," he explained. "Sometimes they let me know what to expect so I go to a different site in the morning instead of to the station. That's all."

Bev reached for her purse and drew out a deck of cards. Lilly looked at Hassan in a panic, wondering if Treetops had ever seen a guest do that. Bev looked around at her fellow diners brightly.

"Does anyone want to play Texas Hold 'Em?" she asked.

Bill had adopted the deer-caught-in-headlights look again.

He really needed to work on his facial expressions, Lilly thought. Noley gave Bev a curious look, clearly not understanding that Texas Hold 'Em was a poker game.

Hassan, thankfully, came to the rescue.

"Bev, I would love to play once we get back to your house, but I was hoping to hear some stories from you about when Lilly and Bill were kids." Lilly sighed in relief. Hassan's request had been perfect. Not only would it likely stop Bev from playing poker in a fancy restaurant as if it were an Old West saloon, but Bev was good at remembering stories from the long-ago past and would probably relish the chance to tell stories about her kids.

Bev laid her cards aside. "Boy, do I have stories!" She spent the next half hour, all through dessert and coffee, regaling the table with stories of when "Billy and Lilly" were little. She seemed to forget about the poker game and Lilly found herself wondering if poker would have been preferable to Hassan and Noley knowing about all the stupid things she and Bill had done as kids.

Bev didn't mention poker again once she got back to her house, so no one else mentioned it to her. Nikki had gone home after Bev left for dinner, so she wasn't there when Bev got home. Lilly and Hassan waited in the living room while Bev got ready for bed, then as she was drifting off to sleep they left, locking the front door behind them.

"What a night, huh?" Lilly asked. "I'm always so exhausted after I spend time with Mom. I don't know why that is. We were just sitting there. And yet, I know I wouldn't be able to sleep if I went to bed right now."

"It's because mental anxiety is as hard on the body, if not harder, than physical stress," Hassan said, "and you're anxious when it comes to your mom."

"I suppose you're right." Lilly took his hand. "Want to go for a quick walk? Maybe that would help me to relax a bit."

They joined hands and struck off down the street. Since Bev's house was close to the house Hassan's parents had bought the previous summer, they walked in that direction. Following an arsonist's strike on the house just before closing, Amir and Basra had decided to go through with the sale, then they fixed up the home and made some improvements to it. Their first stay in the house had been over Thanksgiving, and their whole family had come to help celebrate. Now, when Hassan and Lilly walked by, they had wonderful memories of the Ashraf family's first Thanksgiving there. The house looked quaint and charming from the street—lights were set on a timer inside, so it looked like someone was home. Curtains hung in the windows and winter greens in a large galvanized bucket graced the front porch. One of the neighbors had promised to keep an eye on the house when Amir and Basra were in Minnesota.

When they walked back to Bev's house to get in the car, all was quiet. Lilly turned to Hassan. "I worry about Mom at night. I've become really dependent on Nikki being there for her."

"Your mom doesn't seem to mind being by herself, so that's what's important right now," Hassan said. "There may come a time when she'll need care at night, too."

"And we can't get Nikki to do it, because she's already there all day. We really need to get someone to relieve her once in a while," Lilly fretted. "She needs a life too, even if it is with Beau."

Hassan grinned. "His loss is my gain." He squeezed Lilly close to him. "Nikki can have him." Lilly looked up at Hassan and kissed him.

"How did I get so lucky?" she asked. He squeezed her closer.

"I probably won't see you tomorrow," he said when he dropped her off at home a few minutes later. "I'll be on calls overseas most of the day. I'll talk to you tomorrow night between calls."

She kissed him again and went inside. Only Barney came to

greet her, so she hoped Laurel was asleep. That girl had not been getting enough sleep lately.

Lilly let Barney out, then got ready for bed. She peeked into Laurel's room to check on her before she went to her own room.

But Laurel wasn't there.

CHAPTER 7

*L*illy's heart raced. She knew she hadn't gotten a text from Laurel telling her she was going out, but she checked her phone just to be sure. Nothing.

"Laurel?" she called out. No answer. She went downstairs and looked in the living room, thinking perhaps Laurel had fallen asleep on the sofa. But she wasn't there, either.

Lilly opened the door to the basement and called out Laurel's name again. No answer. She hadn't expected to find her daughter in the basement, since it scared the hooey out of her, even when Lilly was home. She wouldn't have gone down there when Lilly was out.

Lilly whipped out her cell phone again and called Laurel. Laurel's phone went straight to voicemail. Next Lilly tried the Find My Family app on her phone, but Laurel must have had the phone turned off, since the feature wasn't working.

Lilly had Nick's number. Should she call him? She didn't want to wake him up if Laurel wasn't there, but this was too important for texting. She dialed Nick's number and his sleepy voice answered.

"Hlo?" he mumbled.

"Nick, it's Mrs. Carlsen. I'm sorry to wake you up," Lilly said hurriedly. Now she felt bad for calling him. "Laurel isn't home and I thought she might be at your house. I guess not?"

"No," he said, a little more clearly. "I went out with my brother and didn't see her tonight. Do you want me to make some calls, see if I can find out where she is?"

"Do you mind?" Lilly asked. "I don't have the numbers of any of her friends besides Vanessa, so you might have more luck than I would."

"Sure," he said. "You call Vanessa and I'll start calling some other people. I'll let you know if I find out anything."

"Thanks, Nick." Lilly hung up and quickly dialed Vanessa's number.

She, too, answered the phone with a sleepy voice.

"Vanessa, it's Mrs. Carlsen. I don't know where Laurel is. Have you seen her? Is she at your house, by any chance?"

"She's not here, Mrs. Carlsen. I didn't see her tonight. Do you want me to call some people to see if they've heard from her?"

"No, that's okay. I've got Nick making some calls. Thanks anyway, Vanessa. If you hear from her, will you tell her to call me?"

"Sure, Mrs. Carlsen."

"Thanks." Lilly hung up and dialed Tighe next. She doubted Laurel had gotten in touch with her brother, but it was worth a try.

"Hi, Mom," Tighe said when he answered the phone. Lilly had known he would be awake.

"Hi, honey. Listen, I'm looking for Laurel. Have you heard from her?"

"No. But don't worry, Mom. You worry too much. I'm sure she's out with Nick."

"She isn't. I just talked to him."

"Vanessa?" Tighe suggested.

"No. I talked to her, too. Have you talked to Laurel lately?"

"Not in about a week. Why?" Tighe asked.

"I was just thinking she might have mentioned something to you. She wasn't happy with me earlier today because I gave her some pushback about the cost of the prom dress she wants and I thought she might be staying away from the house just to upset me."

"I doubt it, Mom. She might have been mad, but she gets over stuff. I can call her if you want."

"I've tried. Her phone goes right to voicemail. It's either off or the battery is dead." Lilly swallowed hard.

"Call Uncle Bill. Maybe he can help."

Bill. Why hadn't she thought of calling him?

"Good idea. I'll talk to you later, honey."

"Call me when you hear from her," Tighe said. Lilly hung up and dialed Bill. He answered on the first ring.

"What's up?" he asked.

"I don't know where Laurel is."

"Have you tried calling her?"

"I'm not stupid, Bill," Lilly said testily.

"I know, I know. I was just asking. Sometimes people don't think to do the most obvious things when someone is missing. How long has she been gone?"

"I don't know. She wasn't here when I got home from dinner, and the Find My Family app isn't showing me anything, and her phone is going to voicemail."

"Do you think she would have gone to Mom's house?" Bill asked.

Lilly spun around as the kitchen doorknob rattled and the door swung open. Laurel walked into the kitchen, shaking her hands from the cold.

"Never mind, Bill. She just walked in."

"Where was she?"

"I don't know. I'll figure it all out and let you know tomorrow. Thanks."

She hung up and swung around to face her daughter.

"What?" Laurel asked.

"Where have you been?" Lilly tried to keep the anger out of her voice and to remember how worried she had been just moments before, but it wasn't easy.

"At Nick's."

"You don't say."

"What?" Laurel asked again. "Sorry about my phone. The battery was dead. I really need a new phone."

"I'm surprised to hear you were at Nick's," Lilly said, ignoring the comment about a new phone. "I talked to him a few minutes ago. Woke him up, in fact. He said he hadn't seen you tonight because he spent the evening with his brother."

Laurel stared at her mother for what seemed like ten minutes, but was really only a few seconds. "He's lying."

"One of you is," Lilly said. "Go upstairs and get ready for bed. We'll discuss this in the morning, once I've had time to calm down and think this over."

Laurel stomped up the stairs.

"And don't storm around here like that!" Lilly yelled up behind her. "You're not three years old!"

Laurel slammed her bedroom door in response.

Lilly took a deep breath. "Come on, Barn. Time for bed." The dog, who had sat watching the exchange from the corner of the kitchen, apparently decided everything was all right and bounded up the stairs ahead of Lilly.

Lilly was in a foul mood the next morning. And since it was Sunday, the shop was closed and she had the whole day to ruminate over the previous day's events. She didn't know who was lying to her, Laurel or Nick. She wanted to believe that Nick had lied, but she was pretty sure he had been asleep just before he answered the phone. She didn't want to believe that Laurel had lied to her, but she had to admit that it was the more likely scenario.

When Laurel came downstairs, she said a tentative "good morning" to Lilly.

"Morning," Lilly replied. "Laurel, have a seat. We need to talk about a few things."

Laurel heaved only half a sigh before she stopped herself. She probably figured it wasn't the wisest way to begin a conversation with her mother.

Lilly set a plate of Noley's blueberry muffins on the table and sat down across from Laurel.

"You know, whatever you were doing last night, you can tell me," she began. "It's better to tell the truth now, even if it's bad, than it is to be caught in a lie later." She waited for Laurel to say something, but when there was nothing but silence, she asked a question. "Were you really with Nick?"

Laurel shook her head.

"I didn't think so. Where were you?"

"At a coffee shop."

"With whom?" Lilly asked.

"Karley and Bella."

"So why didn't you just tell me that?"

Laurel looked down at her hands. "Because I didn't think you liked them."

"Really?" Lilly asked. "I barely know them. They seem like nice girls. Why would you think I don't like them?"

Laurel shrugged. "I dunno. That's just what I thought."

"If you had just left me a note saying that you had gone to the coffee shop with Karley and Bella, this entire mess could have been avoided. I was in a panic, I woke people up, I had your friends looking for you. There will be consequences for this, you know."

"I know." Laurel's response was barely audible.

"You'll give me your phone for one week. And you're grounded today."

"That's not fair," Laurel whined.

"I'll tell you what's not fair." Lilly pushed her chair back and poured herself another cup of coffee at the counter. "It's not fair to cause me to worry the way you did just because you didn't feel like telling me the truth. It's not fair that I woke up Nick and Vanessa last night to ask them to help find you."

"All right," Laurel snarled.

"And don't you dare use that tone with me. You can head right upstairs and do some studying today."

Laurel didn't stomp up the stairs as she had the night before, but Lilly was pretty sure she wanted to.

CHAPTER 8

That afternoon Lilly went over to Bev's house with some cleaning supplies. Nikki opened the door with a surprised look on her face.

"What's all that?"

"I'm having a bad day. I thought cleaning Mom's house might calm me down."

Nikki laughed. "If you say so." She helped Lilly carry a bucket of supplies inside.

"Lilly, dear, what are you doing?" Bev asked from her armchair in the living room.

"I came over to clean for you, Mom." Lilly grunted as she set the rest of the supplies on the floor.

"You don't have to do that," Bev said.

"I know, but I want to."

Bev shrugged. "All right, then. Suit yourself." She turned her attention back to the television, where a black and white movie was playing.

"Do you want some help?" Nikki asked.

"No, I'm good. But thanks, anyway."

Nikki settled onto the sofa to watch the movie with Bev.

Lilly was heading up the stairs to start in her mom's bathroom when the front door opened. She turned around to see who was there.

Bill stood in the foyer looking at the cleaning supplies. He looked up at Lilly. "What's all this?"

"I'm cleaning."

"Oh. I'm on a lunch break, so I thought I'd come over to say hi to Mom. How did things go last night with Laurel?"

"She's grounded for one day and she lost her phone for a week. She went to a coffee shop with a couple of girlfriends."

"That sounds pretty harmless. Why is she grounded?"

"Because she didn't tell me where she was going and she knows that's the rule." Lilly closed her eyes and looked at her mother. "Mom, do you mind if I get a cup of coffee? I'm starting to get a headache."

"Sure. Just help yourself." Bev used the remote control to pause the movie and invited Bill to sit down. Lilly went into the kitchen, where there was already half a pot of coffee in the coffee maker on the counter.

"How's work going today, Billy?" Bev asked.

Bill settled into his favorite armchair. "Not bad. I'm working on a vandalism case over by the town square."

"Like what kind of vandalism?" Lilly asked, returning to the living room with her coffee.

"Someone threw a brick through a back window of a store."

"Was anything stolen?"

"No. Just property damage."

"How are you ever going to figure out who did it?"

"We'll just get some security camera footage from a few of the shops around the area and nab the people who did it in no time."

Bev shook her head and Lilly walked toward the stairs. "I'm going to get started upstairs." She turned around and looked at

Bill. "Do you need help with Valentine's Day this year? It's tomorrow, you know."

"I know," he answered with a smirk. "Just because you had to remind me last year doesn't mean I'm totally incompetent. I'll have you know that I got Noley something really nice."

"What is it?"

Bill shook his head. "No way. I'm not telling you before I tell Noley."

"Come on, please?" Lilly was wheedling now.

"No way."

"Just give us a hint." Lilly took in her mother and Nikki with a hand gesture. "We all want to know, don't we?" She looked at the other two women to encourage them to pester Bill with her. They both nodded.

"All right, but it doesn't leave this room." Bill grinned. "It's a cooking class." He glanced around at his sister, his mother, and her nurse. Lilly frowned and Nikki screwed up her mouth with a confused look. Bev shook her head again.

"You know she already knows how to cook, right?" Lilly asked finally.

"Sure I do. But this is Italian food taught by an Italian woman. It's authentic."

"I don't know, Billy," Bev said in a skeptical tone.

"No? Should I have gotten her something else?" Worry now creased Bill's features.

Lilly grimaced as sympathetically as she could. "Maybe she would like something that the two of you can do together. Valentine's Day is about love and togetherness, after all."

"I could offer to take the class with her," Bill suggested.

"I'm sure she could teach you how to cook Italian food and it wouldn't cost you anything," Nikki spoke up. Lilly nodded.

"How about making a baby for me?" Bev chimed in. Everyone turned to stare at her.

"Inappropriate, Mom," Bill said. "Besides, I'm too old to have kids."

"Mom, they're not married," Lilly reminded her.

"If you say so. But that doesn't mean they can't have a baby." Bev let out a long sigh.

"That's really up to them, Bev," Nikki said gently. Bev scowled in response.

"Well, I don't want to get her another teddy bear."

"God, no." Lilly hadn't meant to sound so horrified.

"What do you mean by that?" Bill asked.

"Nothing. I just think you should get her something from the heart," Lilly answered. She hoped she hadn't hurt his feelings.

"What do you suggest? I'm running out of time."

"How about a weekend getaway?" Lilly suggested.

"That's a great idea," Nikki agreed. "That's what Beau and I are getting for each other."

Spare me, thought Lilly.

Bill gave both women a dubious look. "That sounds like more than I can afford," he said.

"It's surprisingly affordable," Lilly said. "All you have to do is go online and find a weekend rental. There are tons of places right here in Colorado, I'll bet."

"Can you help me?" Bill asked. "I've got to work and I won't be off duty until late tonight. I don't even know where to start looking."

"I'll go online and try to find some places for you later this afternoon," Lilly promised. "As soon as I finish cleaning, I'll get right on it. Just text me some possible dates so I can put them in the websites and get accurate prices."

"I'll do that. Thanks."

Lilly went upstairs with her now-tepid coffee and got started on her cleaning chores. It wasn't long before she had finished—Nikki was doing a great job keeping Bev's house clean.

When she went home she was pleased to see that Laurel was sitting at the kitchen table with books and notebooks spread out in front of her.

"You look so studious," Lilly said with a grin.

"I'm studying for a test I have this week. I think I'm going to get a good grade on it."

"That's what I like to hear."

"What are you and Hassan doing for Valentine's Day?" Laurel asked, setting her pencil aside and stretching.

"We're going to dinner at The Water Wheel," Lilly said. "What are you and Nick doing?"

"I don't know yet. We might just go to the movies."

When Laurel returned to her studying, Lilly busied herself on the computer. She spent over an hour perusing vacation rentals that would be perfect for Bill and Noley.

When Bill finished his shift that night, he called Lilly. She told him to sit down at his computer while she forwarded to him all the places she had found. He opened them one by one and it seemed to Lilly that each place impressed him even more than the previous one. She had limited herself to fifteen places, figuring that even that number might overwhelm her brother.

She was right.

"How am I ever going to choose? I'll be up all night." He let out a groan.

Lilly made some suggestions and Bill hung up feeling a little more in control. While she was getting ready for bed just a short while later, he texted her that he had chosen a place and made reservations. She didn't ask which one so she wouldn't be tempted to spill the beans to Noley.

She crawled into bed and called Hassan. They didn't talk for long; He was exhausted from days and nights of mixed-up schedules. When he had a lot of calls with suppliers, vendors, guides, and other gen hunters in Southern Asia, his hours became topsy-turvy due to the time differences between those places and the United States.

"I'm looking forward to seeing you tomorrow," Hassan said just before they hung up. His tone was warm, just like the way he made Lilly feel.

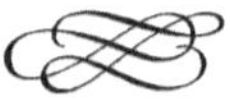

CHAPTER 9

*L*illy awoke to sunshine and blue sky on Valentine's Day. *A great start*, she thought.

Harry was already at work when she got there. They unlocked the vault and began setting out the displays. Before Lilly unlocked the front door, Harry picked up the pink sapphire ring he had had his eye on.

"I'm ready to get this," he said. Lilly smiled.

"I'll write up the receipt," she said. When she was finished and he had paid for the ring, she reached under the counter for an empty velvet box. She placed the ring in it with great care and handed it to Harry.

"Are you excited about tonight? Or nervous?"

"A little bit of both," Harry said. "I'm meeting Alice for dinner at seven. I'm taking her to Treetops and I'm going to ask her just as we finish dinner. I've talked to the people at the restaurant and they're going to serve dessert if she says yes. If she says no or she doesn't know, they're not going to serve the dessert. I'll want to get out of there fast."

Lilly shook her head affectionately. "She'll say yes, Harry. I know she will. You'd better have a look at that dessert menu before you go."

He reddened and turned away. "I already did," he said with a shy smile. "I'm having the chocolate mousse if she says yes."

Lilly gave him a broad grin. "That's the spirit."

They unlocked the front door and were practically run off their feet all day with customers who needed last-minute gifts and weren't hesitant about cost. When she finally locked the door after the last customer, she leaned her back against it. "I think that was the biggest crush of people I've ever had in here."

"Well, I'm glad it's over. I've got somewhere to be." Harry tried to smile, but he swallowed hard instead and started coughing.

"Let's just get things put in the vault and you can get on with your plans," Lilly said. She took two pieces of jewelry from the display case and headed to the back. Harry followed, but when he reached to put a necklace and matching bracelet into the vault, Lilly noticed his hands shaking.

"Harry, look at me."

He took a deep breath, put the jewelry on the vault tray, and turned to face Lilly.

"This should be one of the happiest evenings of your life," she told him. "I'm going to finish putting the jewelry away and I want you to go home and take some deep breaths and maybe have a glass of wine to settle your nerves. She's going to say yes, I just know it. You have nothing to be nervous about."

"Thanks, boss."

"You know I can't stand it when you call me that," Lilly chided.

"I know." He grinned and took another deep breath. "Okay, I'll let you know how it goes."

"I can't wait to hear all about it."

Harry left, tripping as he went out the back door. He turned around to look at Lilly with a sheepish grin and she shook her head. "Maybe two glasses of wine," she called after him. He gave her a thumbs-up and slid behind the wheel of his car.

Lilly chuckled to herself. He was such a good guy. Alice was lucky. And she seemed like such a nice person the few times Lilly had met her. Harry was lucky, too.

She turned her attention to putting away the rest of the jewelry displays, then went home to change her clothes for dinner.

Lilly took her time getting dressed that evening. She had a beautiful coral-colored flare dress that she paired with a vintage coral necklace she had found at an antique store. She slipped on a pair of nude pumps and was ready to go.

A few minutes before she had to leave for The Water Wheel, she went through the mail in the kitchen. Laurel came in from walking Barney, her cheeks red and her eyes bright.

"Do you know yet what you and Nick are doing tonight?" Lilly asked.

"He's going to pick me up and we're going somewhere quiet. That's all he said."

"Sounds romantic," Lilly said with a smile. "I don't need to tell you to make good choices, right?"

Laurel rolled her eyes. "No, Mom."

"Good. I'm meeting Hassan at The Water Wheel. I'll see you later. Have fun, honey." She leaned over to kiss Laurel's cheek.

"I will." Laurel walked to the back door to close it behind her mother. Lilly went down the steps and Laurel called behind her, "Make good choices, Mom!" She laughed and Lilly shook her head, waving.

Lilly drove to The Water Wheel and found Hassan waiting. As usual, he opened her car door, offered her his hand, and closed the door behind her. Lilly was all for equal rights and equal pay for equal work, but this bit of chivalry always made her smile. She hoped Tighe would treat a young woman the same way on a date.

Hassan kissed her and took her hand. "Are you hungry?" he asked.

"Starving. I didn't even get time for lunch today."

He grinned. "And I slept through lunch, so I didn't eat, either. I hope the portions are big tonight."

The restaurant was doing a bustling Valentine's Day business. All the tables were taken by couples. There were no children in sight, and no tables with groups of friends and family. This was a night just for people in love.

A server led the way to their table and pulled out Lilly's chair. Hassan waited to sit until she was seated. They ordered two glasses of wine and looked at the menu.

When their wine came they placed their orders. After the server disappeared, Hassan picked up his glass and raised it. "Here's to many more Valentine's Days together." He smiled at her.

Lilly blushed. She picked up her glass and clinked it against his. "To many more Valentine's Days together." She couldn't stop smiling.

As she took a sip of the wine, it struck her, not for the first time, that he was talking about a long-term future. After all, wasn't that what he had in mind when he bought a house in Juniper Junction? She set her glass down and looked at him, wondering why she hadn't thought of this before. Was it possible he was going to propose tonight?

She had thought about marriage to Hassan, of course, but always with a feeling that something like that was in the distant future. Now her heart beat faster as the thought of marriage to Hassan zinged around in her head like a pinball.

Was she ready for such a step? Her first marriage had ended with such a dull thud that she wasn't sure she could handle a second marriage. Why hadn't she given this some thought before now?

She was in a panic. What would she tell him if he proposed? She didn't want to say anything that would hurt him, but she wasn't sure she was ready to accept, either. She took a deep, ragged breath.

Hassan's brow wrinkled. "What's wrong?"

"Nothing."

"You look pale."

"Do I? It's probably because I'm drinking wine with no food in my stomach."

"Don't drink any more until we at least get you some bread," he cautioned. She nodded, her neck tight.

He looked around for their server and, catching his eye from across the room, motioned him over. He asked for a basket of bread and the server brought it immediately, along with bruschetta and a crock of soft butter.

Hassan broke a piece of bread and handed it to Lilly. "I'm worried about you," he said. "Here, eat this."

He watched as she chewed slowly. "Feel any better?"

Lilly nodded. "Thanks." She could have died from embarrassment. She couldn't tell him why she had felt so shaky all of a sudden.

"Eat a little more, then I have a gift for you."

The lightheadedness came on quickly. She stuffed more bread in her mouth, hoping it would stave off a fainting spell. Anyone watching her would have thought she hadn't eaten in a month.

"Lilly, are you sure you're okay?" Hassan asked, tilting his head.

She nodded, swallowing the giant hunk of bread. She took another sip of wine so she wouldn't choke to death.

"I'm okay," she finally said. If he pulled an engagement ring out of his pocket, she would just say yes. That's what she wanted, after all. They would just choose a wedding date far in the future, when she was ready.

"If you're sure," Hassan said. His voice was filled with skepticism.

"I'm sure, really."

"If you say so. I want you to close your eyes now." He reached into his breast pocket. Lilly took a deep breath and closed her eyes. She opened one eye a tiny bit and peeked.

"No peeking," he said with a laugh. She closed her eye again.

"Now hold out your hands." She did as she was told.

She could feel a box being placed into her palms. It was about the size of a postcard and an inch tall.

Engagement rings don't come in boxes like that, she thought.

"Open your eyes."

She opened them and he was smiling expectantly.

"Open it," he urged.

She looked at the shiny red box. It wasn't wrapped in paper, but it had a white grosgrain ribbon tied around it. She was confused.

She untied the ribbon and lifted the lid off the box. Nestled inside cotton batting was a folded piece of paper. She took it out, unfolded it, and read it silently to herself.

She smiled as it dawned on her what the gift was. It was a weekend getaway for two at a five-star hotel in Aspen.

How embarrassing. Here she was, expecting an engagement ring and not knowing how to respond to a proposal, and all he wanted to do was take her to Aspen for a couple days. She grinned at him, hoping he didn't sense her relief.

"What do you think?"

"I already can't wait to go!" she exclaimed in a quiet voice. "Thank you. This is a wonderful gift."

"You're disappointed, I can tell."

"No, no. I'm really not. I'm actually thrilled."

"You're not acting like yourself," he said. Then his eyes

widened and he covered his mouth with one hand. "Oh, my God. You thought I was going to propose."

She didn't say anything. What could she say?

"Lilly, it's…." He stopped and looked like he was searching for the right words. His mouth opened and closed several times, but no sound came out.

"I'm so sorry. I wouldn't propose without talking to you about it first. I'm so sorry," he repeated.

"Hassan." Lilly leaned forward and grasped his hand. "It's okay. Really. I was in a panic because I didn't know what to say if you proposed. I wanted us to talk about it first, too."

He heaved a sigh of relief. "I can't believe I didn't think this through."

"I didn't, either," she admitted. "It never occurred to me until I had that first sip of wine."

"And that's why you turned pale suddenly." He shook his head. "We will talk about it, I promise. I don't want to do anything until you're ready. You've just had so much going on in the past year or so that I was afraid I would overwhelm you if I proposed."

Lilly nodded. "And I made such a failure of my first marriage that I don't know if I'm the type who should be married."

He caressed the back of her hand with his thumb. "I think you're the type. But we can talk about it later. For now, let's enjoy dinner and talk about when you can get away for a few days in Aspen."

Just then, as if on cue, the server brought their entrées. Lilly had picked up her fork to take a bite of her chicken when her phone buzzed in her purse, which lay across her lap.

She didn't answer it. She wanted to enjoy Hassan's company in their favorite restaurant and have a romantic Valentine's Day. The buzzing stopped, but it started up again just a moment later.

She sighed. "Someone's calling me and they've called twice in the last minute. It might be important."

She reached for the phone and checked the caller ID. Laurel was calling from the house.

"Hi, honey," she answered.

Hysterical sobbing erupted on the other end.

CHAPTER 10

"*L*aurel? What's wrong?"

Lilly couldn't hear Laurel's response through the muffled weeping.

"I can't understand you, Laurel. You have to calm down. Are you hurt?"

"... broke ... up...," Laurel answered, gasping for air.

"Who broke up?" Lilly was starting to get a tingly feeling along her arms. She had a hunch the evening was about to go downhill fast.

"Me ... and Nick," Laurel cried.

"Oh, I'm so sorry," Lilly murmured. "Just a sec, honey." Lilly covered the speaker on her phone and looked at Hassan. "Laurel and Nick broke up. I really should get home."

"Oh, I'm sorry," he said. "Sure. I'll tell the waiter that we'd like our meals to-go. You go home to be with Laurel and I'll wait here for the food. I'll drop yours off on my way home."

"Thanks." She uncovered the phone. "Laurel, I'm coming right home. Just give me a few minutes."

"I don't ... want to ruin ... your night," Laurel said through her sobs.

"You're not ruining anything. I'll be there soon." She hung up and gave Hassan a sad smile. "I'm sorry about this, but she really needs her mom right now. Thanks for dropping off dinner." He came around the table and pulled out her chair for her, then kissed her and shooed her toward the exit.

Lilly drove home quickly, hoping Laurel wouldn't hyperventilate before she got there. She had visions of Laurel lying on the kitchen floor, unconscious, and she drove faster.

When she got home Laurel was lying face-down on the sofa in the living room. Barney stood watch next to her, probably wondering what was going on.

Lilly tousled the fur on his head and sat down next to Laurel, placing her hand gently on Laurel's back.

"I'm home."

Laurel slowly turned over onto her back. Her face was red and puffy from crying. A river of mucus ran from her nose and across her cheek. She was still crying, but not as hard as she had been when they talked on the phone.

"What happened?" Lilly asked.

Laurel took a deep breath and told her story between the tears that were beginning to flow more slowly.

"He picked me up and we went to one of the diners outside of town. I thought it was weird because last year for Valentine's Day he got me flowers and we went to a fancy place on Main Street. So we sat down and ordered and then he said he wanted to talk to me about something. Then he said he didn't think we should see each other anymore."

At this point the tears fell faster again and Lilly leaned into Laurel to put her arm around the girl's shoulders.

"It's okay," she said softly. "Cry it all out."

"I don't know why he just couldn't tell me here or in the car or something," Laurel finally said. "I mean, who takes someone out to dinner to break up with them? It was stupid. Did he think

I wanted to eat after that? So I told him to take me home and then I called you as soon as he dropped me off."

"And you don't know why he thinks you shouldn't see each other anymore? I mean, did he give you a reason?"

"He says that we're just different people than we were a year ago. That's all. What does that even mean?" She threw her hands up in the air and let them fall into her lap.

Lilly didn't have an answer.

"And the prom dress! I guess I'm not going to prom." Laurel's face crumpled again.

"You don't know that," Lilly said. "Maybe you can get a group of girls to go together. I bet that would be even better than going with a date."

Laurel shrugged. "I don't know. I thought I would be going with Nick." She sniffled loudly. There was a knock at the back door.

Lilly went to open it and Hassan stood there holding a paper bag. "Here's your dinner," he whispered.

"Who's that?" Laurel called from the living room.

"It's Hassan. He just came to drop something off and he's headed home."

Laurel appeared in the kitchen doorway. "Hi, Hassan. I guess you know what happened?"

He nodded solemnly. "I'm very sorry to hear about it, Laurel."

Laurel looked down. "Me, too."

Hassan turned to leave. "You can stay," Laurel said. "I know I interrupted your dinner. I'm sorry."

"Don't be sorry," Hassan assured her. "This is much more important."

"Is that your dinner?" Laurel asked Lilly, nodding toward the bag.

"Yes. Want to share it with me? It's fancy chicken."

Laurel shrugged. "I don't know if I can eat. I feel like I'm going to throw up."

Lilly turned to Hassan. "Why don't you get your meal from the car and eat it here?" Then she faced Laurel. "You need to eat. You didn't have dinner, and you're under a lot of stress right now. You don't have to eat a lot, but you should eat something. Sit down and you and I can share the chicken."

"Are you sure it's all right with you if I stay?" Hassan asked Laurel.

She nodded. "Yeah. I want you to stay." He went out to his car. Laurel pulled out a kitchen chair and slumped into it. Lilly poured her a glass of milk, swirled some chocolate sauce in it, and took it to the table. Laurel gave it a dejected look. "I wish I was dead."

"I know you feel horrible right now." Lilly sat down next to her daughter. "But it will get better with time, I promise. The pain will eventually go away."

"How do you know?"

"Because, believe it or not, I was your age once and I had boyfriends, too. There was one in particular who broke up with me right before Christmas and I thought the world would end. In fact, I *hoped* the world would end. But I got over it, the world didn't end, and I moved on."

"What kind of a guy breaks up with his girlfriend on Valentine's Day?" Laurel asked, tears tracking down her cheeks again.

"Not a very nice one, that's for sure," Lilly said, putting her arm around Laurel's shoulders and squeezing.

Hassan knocked once at the back door and came into the kitchen carrying his own dinner. "Laurel, you can share my dinner, too. It's Fettuccine Alfredo."

"I love Fettuccine Alfredo," Laurel gulped. "You're so nice, Hassan." A loud sob broke forth. Hassan glanced at Lilly with a look of horror. Clearly, he was not accustomed to dealing with issues affecting teenage girls. Lilly almost chuckled, but she managed to check herself.

"Everything is going to work out, Laurel. You'll see. Someday you'll look back on this and not feel sad at all," she said.

Laurel could only nod and sniffle. Lilly popped her chicken into the microwave and served it to Laurel, piping hot, just a minute later. "Eat some of this. Just a few bites. Please?"

Laurel did as she was asked while Lilly heated up Hassan's meal. He passed his plate to Laurel before he ate any of it. "Here, take some of this, too." Laurel swirled some of the pasta with her fork and put it on the plate with the chicken.

"This is going to make me fat. Then who will want to go out with me?" she asked in despair. Hassan got that look in his eyes again.

"Of course it's not going to make you fat," Lilly said. "You could eat three plates of this and not gain an ounce."

"Not true," sobbed Laurel.

Lilly's phone buzzed, but she ignored it. She convinced Laurel to eat a little bit of both the pasta and the chicken while she and Hassan shared the rest of both meals. For the second time that evening, the phone buzzed twice within the space of a minute and Lilly sighed with exasperation.

"What now?" She reached for her phone.

It was Harry.

"I'll let that go to voicemail," she said. The last thing she needed tonight was to have a conversation with a jubilant Harry about his upcoming marriage to Alice while Laurel was in the throes of misery.

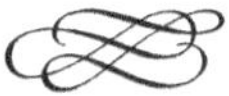

CHAPTER 11

*L*aurel went upstairs after dinner. Hassan was about to leave when he turned around and reached into his coat pocket. Lilly smiled broadly when he withdrew a small chartreuse box embellished with brown ribbon and a sprig of greenery. She recognized that box.

"I was going to give this to you after dinner at the restaurant, but it didn't work out," he said.

"These are my favorite chocolates in the whole world." She kissed him. "Thank you." Then she gasped. "I forgot about your gift!" She had taken a photo of the XO template and she had planned to show it to him at dinner and explain the gift.

But before she could suggest showing him the picture, he smiled and said, "Spending the evening with you was gift enough." *Could this guy get any better?*

"Tell you what. Come to the shop tomorrow and I'll give you your gift," she said.

"Deal. See you tomorrow."

Laurel asked Lilly to lie down with her in her bed until she fell asleep that night. Lilly obliged, of course, because that's what mothers do when their children are upset. Even their teenage children.

When Laurel was finally sleeping, Lilly tiptoed into her own room and finally remembered to check her voicemail.

"Hi, Lilly. This is Harry. I just wanted to tell you that Alice stood me up for dinner. I don't want to talk about it, so I thought I'd tell you now so that you don't ask any questions about it tomorrow at work. See you in the morning."

His voice sounded raspy and tired. Lilly knew he had shed tears that evening, too.

This had been the worst Valentine's Day ever.

The next morning Laurel begged to stay home from school, but Lilly refused to let her give in to her emotions.

"You go into school with your head held high and you don't even look at Nick," she told Laurel. "Find Vanessa and Karley and Bella and the three of you hang out together. Eat lunch with them today."

Laurel's eyes were red and puffy from crying that morning, but she put on some makeup and went to school with a scowl. "I hate Nick," were the last words she uttered before walking out the door.

Lilly didn't like to see Laurel upset when she left for school, but angry was better than sad under the circumstances.

Now to face Harry, she thought. It was going to be awkward with his unspoken catastrophe hanging over them at work, but she supposed they could both be professional about it.

 Harry looked terrible. He obviously hadn't slept at all the night before, and it looked like he might not have showered that morning, either.

"G'morning, Harry." He had gotten to the shop before her and it looked like he had stopped for fast food and was already on his second cup of coffee, judging from the detritus on one of the display cases.

"Morning."

"Thanks for getting the displays set up already."

"Welcome."

She couldn't think of anything else to say, so she went back to her office. She left the door open and could see Harry moping around the front of the shop as if his shoes and his heart were filled with lead. She couldn't bear to see him like that.

When she went to the front of the shop to unlock the front door, he was standing still, staring out the front window as if in a trance.

"Harry? You okay?"

He closed his eyes and shook his head like he was clearing the cobwebs. "Yeah. Sorry, boss. I just hope we get a lot of customers in here today."

Lilly didn't have the heart to tell him that the day after Valentine's Day was always one of the slowest days of the year, since people had spent so much money on Valentine's Day gifts. He would figure it out for himself soon enough, anyway.

There were a few stragglers who came into the shop to browse during the day, but it wasn't until late afternoon that two people came in and caused Lilly and Harry to take special notice.

They were police officers, dressed in uniform and clearly not there to look at jewelry.

Lilly walked up to them. "Can I help you, officers?"

"We're looking for Harry Montrose."

Harry, who had been standing off to the side, stepped forward. "I'm Harry Montrose. Is something wrong?"

"Mister Montrose, do you know an Alice Davenport?" one of the officers asked.

Harry glanced sideways at Lilly, who glanced sideways at him. "Yes," he said, a little bit of hesitation in his voice. "Is she all right?"

"That's what we need to find out, sir. Her family has reported her missing."

* * *

"Missing?" Harry spoke the word as if it were unfamiliar to him, as if he didn't understand its meaning.

"Yes, sir. We understand that you were supposed to have dinner with her last night. Is that correct?"

"Yes."

"And did you have dinner with her?" the officer asked.

"No. She stood me up," Harry replied. He still seemed to be utterly confused by what the policemen were saying.

"So she did not meet you for dinner?"

"No."

"Were you supposed to pick her up?" the officer continued.

"No. She was going to meet me at Treetops."

The first officer nodded to the second, who wrote something down in a notebook. "We'll have to confirm that with the restaurant."

"Are you saying that no one knows where she is?" Harry asked. It seemed like the situation was finally beginning to dawn on him.

"Her family doesn't know, so they filed a Missing Person report. Do you know where she is?" the officer asked. He seemed to be doing most of the talking.

"No. I don't know. I called her to see if she had forgotten our dinner, but her phone went right to voicemail."

The officer nodded to the partner again. "Let's get the phone records, too."

"Check my phone records?" Harry asked.

"Yes, sir. We'll also be checking Miss Davenport's phone records."

"Am I in trouble?" Harry asked. "I don't know where Alice

is." His eyes widened as the realization finally hit that the police were questioning him in connection with a missing person.

The officers chose to ignore his question and instead the first officer asked more of his own. "Do you know where she might have gone? Do you know of any other plans she may have had last night?"

Harry shook his head. "As far as I know, she was going to spend the entire evening with me." He paused. "I was going to propose to her."

Lilly winced inwardly, thinking that Harry probably shouldn't have offered that information.

She was right. The officer pounced on it.

"So you were going to ask her to marry you and she didn't show up. You must have been upset. What did you do when she didn't show?"

It was obvious that Harry immediately recognized his mistake in telling the police about the proposal. He closed his eyes and ran a hand over his forehead.

"I went home," he said dully.

"Do you live with anyone?"

"No. I live alone."

"Can anyone confirm that you went home after Miss Davenport didn't show?"

Harry shook his head. His eyes wore a frantic look. Lilly supposed his feelings were at war with themselves. For one thing, he must have been worried about Alice's whereabouts. He also might be feeling just a little bit of relief that he might not actually have been stood up. And finally, he must be afraid that the police wondered whether he had something to do with her disappearance.

Harry finally looked at Lilly. "Should I call a lawyer?"

Lilly watched the police officers exchange glances. "Probably," she said quietly.

"I don't know any lawyers." His voice was becoming higher

and more strained.

"I'll call my lawyer," Lilly said in a soothing tone. "She's good."

CHAPTER 12

*H*arry nodded. "What else can I tell you to help find Alice?" he asked the policemen.

Then, without waiting for a response, he continued talking. "I can't believe this. I don't know where she could be." He raked his hands over his face. "Now I'm sorry I was upset with her for standing me up. What if she's in trouble somewhere? What if her car broke down and she's stuck in snow? What if her phone is dead and she can't call for help?" His voice rose with every "what if" until he had to stop and take a deep breath. The officers were just watching him, not saying a word.

"The first thing you need to do is try to calm down, Harry," Lilly said gently. "I know that's easier said than done, but you won't be any help to anyone if you're so upset you can't think straight."

He nodded and took another deep breath.

Finally the first officer spoke. "Okay. Now you need to concentrate, Mister Montrose. Do you remember Alice telling you anything about what she was doing yesterday? Was she going to school? Was she staying home? Anything at all that you can remember?"

Harry looked up as he thought.

"I can't even think straight," he said finally.

"That's okay. If she told you anything, it'll come to you. Just give it some time."

Harry snapped his fingers. "Wait. I remember now. She told me she had a class and then she was going to the library on campus to study for her midterms. I don't think she said where she was going after that."

"That's a good start. We'll check with her professor to see if she was in class yesterday. And maybe there are security cameras at the library, so we can find out if she went there afterward."

"What should I do?" Harry asked.

"Try to think of anything else she might have told you," the officer said. "And stay local." With that, he and his partner left. Harry pulled his cell phone out of his pocket and called Alice's parents. Lilly couldn't hear what they were saying to Harry, but she wondered why they hadn't called him to ask if he knew where Alice was before contacting the police.

Finally Harry hung up and heaved a long sigh. "Alice's mother is a piece of work," he said, shaking his head. He didn't elaborate and Lilly didn't ask.

She did, though, decide to give voice to her thoughts. "Why didn't her family call you before they called the police?"

Harry looked sheepish. "I don't know them very well. I've only met them once or twice, and it was quick both times. Alice says they're very strict and don't approve of our age difference, which is five years, so she doesn't want them to know the extent of our relationship. They didn't have my phone number."

"But you have theirs?"

"Yes. Alice gave it to me once in case I couldn't get in touch with her."

"So why didn't you call them when she didn't show up last night?" Lilly knew she sounded nosy, but she also knew the police would be contacting him again to ask those same questions.

"And tell them she stood me up? No, that would have been embarrassing. Plus, like I said, she's trying to keep our relationship off their radar."

"But they obviously know about you, since they knew where to send the police to look for you."

Harry sighed again. "It's complicated. They know about me, of course. But they only know the basics, like how old I am and where I live and where I work."

Lilly nodded, grateful once again for her warm relationship with Hassan's parents. She and Hassan were older, of course, but even her white skin and her Christianity didn't matter to his parents. They were open and welcoming to her.

It was then she remembered Hassan was supposed to visit the shop to see her Valentine's Day gift for him. She texted him, asking him not to come and promising to explain later.

"I'll call Bill and see if there's anything he can tell me," Lilly said. "Do you want to come over and have dinner at my house? It's just me tonight. Laurel is watching a play practice at school."

Harry thought for a moment. "Thanks, Lilly, but I think I'd rather just be by myself tonight. I need to think this through. I mean, what if she left because she suspected I was going to propose and she couldn't handle the pressure?"

"I don't know Alice all that well," said Lilly. "But she doesn't really seem like the type to be scared off by much. She's sweet, but she's strong, you know?"

Harry nodded. "That's what I love about her, among all the other things."

Lilly put her hand on his arm. "You could probably use some rest, Harry."

"I know. I didn't sleep at all last night because I was so upset. I have a feeling it'll be more of the same tonight." His shoulders were slumped and his eyes were bloodshot. He really needed sleep.

"Don't bother coming in tomorrow if you feel like you'd rather sleep," Lilly told him. "I can manage just fine here."

"Thanks, boss. But I think coming to work will be good for me. I'll call you if I hear anything or if I decide to sleep in tomorrow morning."

"Okay, Harry." After putting away all the jewelry, they left the shop through the door in the back office and each drove off in separate directions.

Once Lilly got home she called Bill.

"I know why you're calling," he said in greeting.

"Alice?" she asked.

There was a momentary silence, then Bill spoke. "No. I meant Mom."

It was Lilly's turn for silence. She gripped the phone a little harder. "What about Mom?"

"She wandered off today."

"Is she back home? How did that happen? Where was Nikki?"

"She's back home. She left when Nikki ran upstairs to make the bed," Bill said. "We're going to have to do something. Maybe something as simple as telling Nikki not to bother with any work around the house. Her whole job needs to be to keep an eye on Mom."

"You're right. Nikki doesn't need to be doing those things, anyway. That's not why she's there."

"She just does them to be helpful." Bill said.

"I know. I'm not blaming her. I'll just talk to her and tell her that I can do those things. I'll just make a stop over there before or after work each day and do a little light housework." *Just what I need in my life,* thought Lilly. *More stuff to do.*

"I can help you," Bill said. "We can split the work. That house doesn't get very dirty."

"Let me call Nikki right now. I'll call you back after I've talked to her." Lilly hung up and called her mother's house.

"I'm so sorry about your mother wandering off this morning," Nikki said when she answered the phone. "I should have known better than to leave her alone downstairs."

"That's why I'm calling. Bill and I want you to know that we don't blame you for anything. But we think you should probably just stick to Mom like glue from now on. Let us worry about doing the dishes and making beds and cleaning the house."

"That sounds like a good plan," Nikki said. "I'd love to help her out around the house, but I agree that she can't be left alone."

"How's she doing this evening?"

"She's in a great mood," Nikki replied. "We're watching a game show and she knows most of the answers. She amazes me."

Lilly chuckled. "She's a trivia queen. How her mind can be so full of useless information but not realize where she is when she leaves the house is beyond me."

"Speaking of leaving the house, I'm a little concerned about her going out when I leave for the night. I think I'll stay tonight, if that's all right with you."

"That would be great. But the alarm is on at night, isn't it?"

"It is, but what if she opened the door to leave, the alarm went off, and she ran off because she was spooked? There's no telling where she might go. That's the scenario I'm worried about."

"You're right. Feel free to stay whenever you want. And thanks, Nikki. I'll talk to you tomorrow."

They hung up and Lilly called Bill back.

"Everything's straightened out. Nikki is going to make Mom her only priority and she'll stay there tonight. You and I are the new cleaning crew."

"That's okay. Thanks for calling. I feel much better knowing Nikki is not going to let Mom out of her sight."

"Me, too." Lilly said.

"Why did you call me earlier?"

"Oh. Once you told me Mom went missing, that's all I could think about. The police came to the shop today to talk to Harry about his girlfriend, Alice. No one knows where she is. She stood him up last night for dinner and no one has talked to her since then. Well, at least Harry and her parents haven't talked to her. I was wondering if you know anything about it."

"I haven't heard anything, but I'll check around."

"Thanks."

Once Laurel came home, Lilly went to bed, exhausted. The last thing she did before falling asleep was to call Hassan. She explained everything that was going on with her mother and Alice and apologized for not giving him his Valentine's Day gift.

"I told you, just being here in Juniper Junction with you is enough of a gift for me," he said.

How did I get so lucky? she wondered as she drifted off.

CHAPTER 13

Not only was Harry at work the next day, but he was there early and he brought coffee for Lilly.

"Any word on Alice?" she asked as soon as she saw him.

"Nothing."

"You look better today." She took a sip of her coffee.

"I managed to get some sleep last night," he said. "I didn't think I'd ever be able to sleep again, but my body and brain must have been exhausted."

"I talked to Bill last night and he didn't know anything about the search for Alice. He was going to try to get some information for you today."

"Thanks, Lilly. I've thought so hard about where she could have gone, but I can't come up with anything. She doesn't go out very much. I phoned a few of her friends last night when I got home, but none of them have seen or heard from her, either."

"She'll turn up, Harry. Think positive thoughts."

He nodded absently.

Easy for you to say, Lil, she thought. *It's common knowledge that the longer a person is missing, the worse the outcome is likely to be.*

And she's been gone now for over twenty-four hours. Lilly didn't voice her concerns to Harry. He watched the news. He knew the statistics as well as she did.

But Lilly's own mother had gone missing just a day ago. True, Lilly didn't find out about it until her mother had already been found, but how would she have reacted if the missing person were her mother?

Suddenly things looked a little different. But Lilly couldn't help thinking that there was something more sinister about Alice's disappearance.

About an hour before closing, Bill called Lilly's cell phone.

"I talked to the officers in charge of Alice's case," he said. "There was nothing they could tell me yet. They're waiting on phone records and a callback from the manager of Treetops to confirm that Harry was at the restaurant waiting for Alice to show up on Valentine's Day."

Lilly sighed. "I was hoping they had found some other information."

"These cases usually move quickly once there's a solid lead and once they've started eliminating suspects," Bill said. "They just need one tip to start making progress. It'll happen. Tell Harry they're working on it."

"I will."

"One interesting thing has come up," Bill noted. "Another young woman went missing the same night as Alice. Same age. Works in Lupine as a stripper. The officers in charge are looking into it to see if the two are somehow related."

"That sounds ominous," Lilly said. Lupine was a town not far from Juniper Junction and was known for its nightlife. "Two women go missing on the same night from adjoining towns. That can't be good. The big difference, obviously, is that Alice is a student and the other woman is a stripper. Not exactly running in the same circles, I would think."

"I agree, but don't tell Harry about the other disappearance right now, okay? He doesn't need to know about it until we have more information."

"Got it."

When Lilly hung up she told Harry that Bill hadn't been able to gather any additional information for him about Alice. He leaned on the glass jewelry display case and put his head in his hands.

"I was hoping he could get some inside information." His voice was thick with emotion.

"Me, too. But don't lose hope. He said that all they need is one good lead and things will start falling into place. It only takes one lead, Harry. They're good at what they do."

"Do you think someone has her?" Harry asked, looking up. His eyes were strained and he took a shaky breath.

It was the first time anyone had mentioned the possibility aloud. Really, there were only two possibilities: either Alice had disappeared on her own or she disappeared at the hands of someone else. Lilly hoped it was the former, since Alice would probably be in less danger that way.

But she had to admit that Alice wasn't the type to go running off without telling anyone.

It was looking more and more likely that someone else was involved.

"I hope not, Harry," she finally said.

That night Lilly stopped at her mom's house on her way home from work to do a quick round of housework. Then she went home to have dinner with Laurel.

"How was school?" she asked as they sat down at the table.

"Awful."

"Why?"

"Because I saw Nick three times." Tears started trickling down Laurel's cheeks. "He wouldn't even look at me."

"I'm sorry, honey," was all Lilly could say. Alice's disappearance weighed heavily on her mind and she needed to think about something else for a while.

"Want to go to a movie?" she suggested.

"Not really," Laurel said. She was staring into space with a look of utter dejection on her face. She hadn't touched her dinner.

"How about bowling?"

"Nah. The shoes make me look stupid."

"But that's part of the fun!"

Laurel rolled her eyes.

"How about making cupcakes?"

"Just what I need. Cupcakes. So that I get fat and no one will ever ask me out again."

"Of course boys will ask you out again," Lilly said. Laurel was a vivacious girl—usually—with a generous heart and a friendly smile. She was pretty, too. Lilly could see the obvious, that this was only a temporary situation, but she knew it was much harder for Laurel to see the big picture from the pit of the funk she was in.

"Want to watch television? Your choice," Lilly said.

Laurel sighed and pushed herself to her feet with an effort.

"All right. I'll see what's on." She trudged off to the living room with Barney in tow.

A few minutes later she was settled on the sofa with Barney's head on her lap. When Lilly peeked into the living room to see if she had found something to watch, she was pleased to see Laurel smiling at something on the screen.

"Popcorn?" she asked.

"Sure."

Lilly made a bowl of popcorn and joined Laurel in the living room.

The show was dumb, but funny. It was the type of slapstick

comedy that can elicit laughs even from the grumpiest grump. It was just what the doctor ordered for Laurel's mood.

They had watched several minutes of the show when the phone rang. It was Bill.

Lilly left Laurel laughing on the sofa, stroking Barney's head, and took the call in the kitchen.

"I hope you're calling with good news about Alice and not bad news about Mom," she said.

"Neither, actually. I wanted to ask you a few more questions about Alice. Right now two guys are on their way to Harry's house to question him again and I just wanted to get some information from you."

"Is he in trouble?"

"They just have some more questions for him," Bill said.

"You didn't answer my question."

"I don't know if he's in trouble, to tell you the truth. I'm not able to keep up with every detail of the investigation. I've got a vandalism spree to investigate myself."

"More trouble with brick throwers?"

"Nah. Someone stole all the twinkly lights hanging over a couple shops by the town square last night."

Lilly shook her head. "Okay, so what do you want to know? I've only met Alice a few times, so I don't know how helpful I can be."

"Do you know what she studies at the community college?"

Lilly thought for a moment. "I think she majors in social work."

"Do you know how she met Harry?"

"I think they met at the coffee shop where Harry picks up his coffee every morning. It's an expensive place, so I never go in there. Good coffee, though."

"Did it ever occur to you that the coffee shop Harry goes to might be too expensive for a student?" Bill asked.

"No. It's none of my business how Alice spends her money," Lilly said in an exasperated voice. "Bill, these questions make no sense. What are you getting at?"

"We think Alice *is* the stripper who went missing from Lupine."

CHAPTER 14

*L*illy was too surprised to say anything for a moment, but finally she found her voice.

"That can't be right, Bill."

"Unfortunately, I think it is. It's taken a little time to figure it out because the stripper's name is Cotton Candy and she wears contacts and a black wig."

"And Alice wears glasses and has blond hair," Lilly said.

"I know. But it makes sense that someone named 'Alice' would change her name in a gentlemen's lounge, doesn't it? I mean, 'Alice' isn't exactly a common stripper's name."

"I just can't believe this. She's so sweet and unassuming," Lilly said. Then she had a horrifying thought. She gasped.

"Do you suppose Harry knows about this?"

"He will very soon if he doesn't already," Bill replied.

"Should I call him?"

"I would wait. I don't know what or when the guys are going to tell him. And don't forget, it's possible that he knows about her, um, job."

"I can't imagine he knows," Lilly said, her voice heavy with skepticism.

"Listen, take it from me. You wouldn't believe the secrets some people keep. Being on the force has a way of opening your eyes to all kinds of things that people do that would shock anyone else."

"But Harry is so sweet and innocent. He can't possibly know about this."

"We'll see."

Lilly hung up and returned to the living room, lost in thought.

"What's wrong?" Laurel asked.

"Harry's girlfriend is missing," Lilly said. No sense in sharing the sordid details with Laurel.

"I wish Nick was missing," Laurel grumbled.

"If he were missing, you'd be worried about him."

"I'd be celebrating. I hope Harry's girlfriend turns up. He must be worried."

Lilly nodded, wondering if Harry would tell her about Alice's secret in the morning.

As it turned out, she didn't have to wait that long. An hour later, after Laurel had gone up to her room, Lilly's cell phone rang.

"Lilly, you're not going to believe this," Harry began.

"What?" she asked, her heart sinking. The way he spoke made it clear he hadn't known about Alice.

"I've just found out something ... something...." She couldn't stand waiting until he found the right words.

"I know about it already," she stated flatly.

There was silence on the other end.

"You knew?"

"I probably found out about it around the same time you did."

"How did you find out?" Harry asked.

"Bill called and told me. I'm really sorry about it, Harry."

"I had no idea. How could I not have known that? I was

going to ask her to marry me! You'd think I would know every-thing there is to know about her. I can't believe she'd deceive me like that."

"Let's not jump to conclusions, Harry. There are lots of reasons that young women take jobs in strip clubs ... er, gentle-men's lounges."

"Yeah, I get that. Reasons like income. But there are other places to get jobs, places that don't require women to take their clothes off."

"Like I said, Harry, let's not jump to conclusions. Let's wait and find out what the police uncover and—"

"Don't say 'uncover.'"

Lilly almost laughed at her inadvertent choice of words, but she didn't because she knew Harry would be hurt.

"Sorry, Harry. I didn't mean that."

"That's okay." There was a long pause. "Where do you think she is, Lilly? This puts a whole new spin on things. I obviously didn't know her as well as I thought I did. Maybe she took off and just left town."

"I wish I had the answers for you, Harry."

Again, she was exhausted when she called Hassan that night. She brought him up to date on Alice and he was as surprised as everyone else had been.

The next day when Lilly opened the store Harry hadn't arrived yet. He was usually there at least half an hour before opening. She called his cell.

"Hmm?" he answered.

"Did I wake you?"

"Yeah. I'm sorry, boss. I don't think I can make it in today." He cleared his throat.

"That's okay. You get some rest and let me know if there's anything I can do. Take all the time you need."

"Thanks." He hung up.

She waited on the few customers who came in during the

day, surprised at how much she missed Harry. She loved having him as an assistant, but she hadn't realized how much she had come to depend on him for conversation and camaraderie.

That evening as soon as she closed up the shop she hurried home and rifled through her old recipe file. She knew there were some casserole recipes in there. She was looking for something to make for Harry that would be tasty and comforting. She finally found the three-by-five card she was looking for.

Macaroni and cheese. Perfect.

She did a quick inventory and was pleased and a little shocked to find she had all the ingredients. In contrast to Noley, she rarely had her pantry well stocked and found herself at the grocery store more often than she liked.

It didn't take long to prepare the macaroni and cheese and get the casserole dish packed into a box, along with cooking instructions, to take over to Harry's house. She threw in a bagged salad (Noley wouldn't have forgiven her if she had known), a pint of cherry tomatoes, and some cookies.

When she arrived at Harry's she found that she hadn't been the only one with the idea of making comfort food for her friend. There were several people inside, all of whom had brought gifts of food. There was a pot of tomato soup, homemade bread, a pan of lasagna, a bucket of fried chicken and a side of mashed potatoes from a fried chicken joint, and a chicken pot pie, among many other things that had been dropped off by well-wishers.

Two conclusions were obvious: Harry had a lot of friends and he wasn't going to have to cook for months.

Lilly set her dish of macaroni and cheese on the countertop along with some of the other offerings. Harry was encouraging people to eat, since he had more food than he could handle. He was standing in the kitchen, looking a little bewildered by the number of people and the amount of food in the kitchen.

"Harry, sit down. What can I get you?" Lilly asked.

He shrugged. "Some lasagna, I guess."

She opened his cupboards until she found the plates, stacked neatly just like everything else in the kitchen. Somehow she wasn't surprised to find that his kitchen was well organized.

She slid a spatula full of piping hot lasagna onto his plate. Next she found the sharp knives and sawed two pieces of the homemade Italian bread from the long loaf and put them on a plate next to the lasagna.

She put the plate in front of him. "Can I get you something to drink?"

He nodded. "Thanks, Lilly. There's coffee in the coffee maker on the counter."

"Are you sure you want something with caffeine?" she asked.

He nodded. "Even if I don't have caffeine, I'm not going to be able to sleep. I might as well be alert if I'm going to be awake all night."

Lilly poured him a cup of coffee and set it on the table. Several people sat down with him, but nobody ate anything.

Harry made introductions in a listless voice. "Lilly, this is Mack, a friend of mine from the gym. This is Wayne, my next-door neighbor. This is Mary Louise, a friend from way back, and this is Stu, who goes to school with Mary Louise and also happens to live up the block."

"How do you do," Lilly said, shaking the hand of each person in turn around the table.

"I'm not going to stay unless you want me to, Harry," she said. "I hope you're able to get some sleep tonight."

"We'll make sure he goes to bed, don't worry," Mary Louise said. She fixed Harry with a look of concern. "That coffee's not helping." She reached for the cup, but Harry held onto it.

"I feel like I need it. What if something happens while I'm asleep?"

"We'll take turns staying with you," Mary Louise suggested,

and the others around the table nodded. "We'll stay awake and let you know if there's a call or a text for you."

Harry gave her a skeptical look. "Promise?"

She nodded. "Of course. Right, guys?" She looked around the table at Harry's other friends. Mack and Wayne nodded their agreement, but Stu shook his head sadly.

"I wish I could, but I can't. I have to be at home for the dog."

"That's okay, buddy." Harry clapped Stu gently on the shoulder.

"That's so nice of you," Lilly told Harry's friends. Then she looked at Harry. "So you'll go to bed?"

Harry nodded glumly.

"Have you talked to Alice's family?" Lilly asked.

"Yeah. I stopped over there earlier. I expected there to be a lot of people milling around, but there was no one. I mean, no one except her parents."

"Does she have siblings?"

Harry nodded again. "A brother."

"So what did they have to say?" Stu asked.

"Just that they're working with the police to find Alice," he said. "They don't know any more than I do, or if they do, they're not telling me." He looked down at his hands, which had dropped into his lap.

"Her parents must be distraught," Lilly murmured.

Harry shrugged. "What parents wouldn't be? But they're pretty emotionless people, so they didn't open up and tell me how upset they are or anything."

"And what about the brother?" Lilly asked. "Have you talked to him since Alice went missing?"

"David? Yeah. David and Alice don't get along. He doesn't like me, so we didn't talk for long. He thinks Alice has gone off somewhere for attention and is going to reappear any day now."

It seemed a pretty stupid stunt, and Lilly felt sure Alice

hadn't taken off just for attention. It was obvious from the tone of Harry's voice that he felt the same way.

"Harry, you've got a lot of people here for support, so I'll get going. Laurel is waiting for me to have dinner. Don't hesitate to call if you need something, you know that. And let me know if you hear anything."

"I will, boss. Thanks for coming by and thanks for the mac and cheese. I love mac and cheese." Lilly placed her hand on his arm before she left.

"They'll find her, Harry. I just know it."

CHAPTER 15

When Lilly got home Laurel had dinner on the table. Probably as a result of spending so much time with Noley over the years, Laurel was a great cook for someone her age. She had prepared a pork tenderloin with roasted vegetables and pork gravy.

"This is delicious!" Lilly exclaimed, taking a bite of her food.

"I made it because Nick hates pork. I'm making stuff he doesn't like to remind myself of how stupid he is."

"If that works for you, go for it," Lilly said.

"Can I go over to Vanessa's for a little while after dinner?" Laurel asked.

"If your homework is done."

"It's done."

"Okay. I'll do the dishes and you can head out. Don't be late. It's a school night." Lilly kissed her and Laurel left.

The days of chauffeuring her kids were nothing but a memory, and Lilly was thankful for it. She hurried to wash the dishes, then went over to her mother's house to do some cleaning.

When she got there Bev and Nikki were collapsing with laughter over something on television.

"What's so funny?" Lilly asked.

In between gasps for air, Bev answered, "Oh, Lilly, there's the funniest show on! People take home videos and they get shots of people falling, walking into walls, banging their heads, and the funniest things!" She could hardly breathe she was laughing so hard.

"Let me get the bathroom cleaned upstairs and I'll join you," Lilly said. Her mother nodded, wiping the tears that were streaming down her cheeks. Lilly hurried to gather the supplies she would need, and headed upstairs to clean.

When she returned to the living room, Bill was there. He was standing behind Bev's chair, laughing along with her and Nikki.

"I love these shows," he said to Lilly.

"What brings you here in uniform?" Lilly asked.

"I thought I'd just stop in to see how everything's going. I was hoping Mom had something in the fridge I could snack on."

"I have cheese and fruit, dear," Bev said. Bill went into the kitchen and Lilly followed him to put the cleaning supplies in the closet.

"Any word on Alice?" she asked.

Bill shook his head. "Not yet. The parents are trying to cooperate, but they're weird. So is the brother, from what I've heard."

"Harry told me that Alice and her brother don't get along well."

"Apparently there's always been a lot of sibling rivalry and it doesn't help that the two of them are close in age," Bill said. "The guys doing the investigation say the mother hadn't even shed a tear about Alice. At least not when they've been at the house."

"Alice lives in an apartment, doesn't she?"

Bill nodded. "She lives by herself. That's the other thing—her purse, car keys, phone, and credit cards were in her apartment. All the things you'd assume she'd take with her if she were planning to go somewhere."

That didn't sound good.

"Lilly, I don't need to tell you to stay out of this, right?" Bill gave her the eye.

"Of course you don't." She didn't look at him.

"Lilly...."

She looked at him then, her eyes challenging. "I told you, you don't have to say a word. I know enough not to get involved."

"Good. Don't go visiting any strip clubs." He smiled.

She gave him her best smile in return. She hadn't promised not to interfere; she had merely told him he didn't need to remind her not to.

Just then Bill's radio squawked. Every time she heard that radio, Lilly thought it was completely unintelligible. Somehow Bill was able to decipher what was being said.

He pushed a button to talk. "I can be there in five," he said. He turned to Lilly. "Gotta run. There's something going on down on Main Street."

Immediately Lilly thought of her jewelry shop. "It's not my shop, is it?"

Bill gave her an exasperated look. "Wouldn't I tell you if it were your shop?"

"All right, you don't have to get testy."

Bill grabbed a cheese stick and an apple from the fridge and left. Lilly returned to the living room to watch television with her mother and Nikki.

It was so good to see her mother laugh. Lilly hoped this show would be on the air every night. It was one of those shows that had been on for years, so there were about a million reruns. After a half hour of watching people flip off trampolines, get yanked off docks, and fall into kiddie pools, Lilly bid her mom goodnight and headed home. Nikki accompanied her to the door.

"I'm thinking about spending a few nights a week here, if that's okay with you," Nikki said.

"That's fine. I'm so sorry I haven't had a chance to interview anyone to spell you at Mom's house."

"It's no problem, really. I think your mom is great, and I worry about her. I just thought if I stayed sometimes it might make her more comfortable."

"You're the best, Nikki." Lilly hurried to her car and drove home.

Laurel got home just a few minutes after Lilly. She was red-faced and out of breath.

"What have you been up to?" Lilly asked with a smile.

"Having a snowball fight. It was fun." Laurel slipped out of her winter coat, hung it up, and went upstairs.

So Bev and Laurel had both enjoyed themselves that evening.

Things were looking up.

Harry was at work the next morning, early as usual.

"How are you feeling this morning?" Lilly asked. They were emptying the vault in the office to place the displays out front.

"Rested and bloated," he replied. "I ate too much because there's so much food in the house, but at least I got some sleep."

"I'm glad to hear it. Someone stayed overnight with you?"

"Yeah. Mary Louise stayed, and tonight I think Mack is going to stay."

"It's nice of them to do that." Lilly turned around when there was a knock on the front door of the shop. The two police officers who had first visited the store stood outside.

She hurried to unlock the door and let them in, then locked it again behind them since it wasn't time to open yet. Harry swallowed hard. "Have you found something?" he asked in a tremulous voice. Lilly could feel her heart beating wildly.

"Not yet," the older officer said. He was the one who had done all the talking the first time.

"Do you need something from me?" Harry asked.

"We've checked with the restaurant and they've confirmed that you were waiting for Miss Davenport on Monday night. We need to know where you were before that."

Harry looked at Lilly. "I was here, at work."

"So you went from work right to the restaurant?"

"No, I went home to change my clothes. I had to put on a suit. I live alone. I went straight home from here, changed my clothes, and went right to the restaurant." Harry's eyes widened. "But there's no one who can prove that."

"Miss Davenport's brother has indicated that you may not have been telling the truth about your whereabouts before you went to the restaurant that evening."

The color drained from Harry's face. Lilly hurried to bring a stool from behind the display case and dragged it over to where he was standing. He dropped into it like he weighed a thousand pounds. The officers watched him, not moving, not saying anything.

"He said that about me?" Harry finally asked. He knit his brows together as if he couldn't understand the implication.

"Yes, sir," the second officer replied.

Harry shook his head slowly. "There's no way for me to prove what I did, but I swear that's all I did." He paused. "How could he say that?"

"Do you have neighbors who might have seen you coming and going?" the first officer asked.

Harry shook his head again. "I doubt it. I don't have any nosy neighbors. I wish I did."

"Can you just put together a timeline of Harry's actions that evening?" Lilly knew she shouldn't butt in, but she couldn't help it. She couldn't stand to see Harry like that. "I can tell you when he left here and I can tell you he wasn't wearing a suit. The manager at Treetops can tell you what time he checked in for his dinner reservation and can maybe even confirm that Harry was wearing a suit. If there is a tight timeline, then he wouldn't have had time to go anywhere else."

"Thank you, Ms. Carlsen," the officer replied in a droll tone. He turned to his partner. "Why didn't we think of that?" The partner smirked and Lilly could feel her face reddening with embarrassment and anger.

"I'm only trying to help." She tried to keep the petulance out of her voice, but one look from the senior officer and she knew she had failed. She figured it might be best for Harry if she kept her mouth shut.

"All right. We'll be back," the officer warned Harry. "Don't go far."

Harry slumped on his stool after they left. "Lilly, I don't know what to do." He raised his hands and let them fall back onto his lap. "How can I prove that I have nothing to do with her disappearance? I *love* her. Why would I do anything like that to her?"

"I'm not sure how you can prove it, but we'll think of something." Lilly hoped her tone was reassuring, but there didn't appear to be much that could reassure Harry. She knew he was beside himself with worry.

The first customers began to dribble in and their conversation had to be put on hold. While Lilly greeted customers, sold jewelry, and paid invoices that day, she formulated a plan. If she couldn't help Harry by proving where he was between the time he left work and the time he arrived at the restaurant on Valentine's Day, she would help him some other way.

When Lilly got home that night, the first thing she did, after checking in with Laurel, was to call Hassan.

"I've missed you," he said when he answered the phone.

"I've missed you, too, but I have an idea for a date," she said.

"What is it?" His voice sounded enthusiastic, and Lilly wondered how long that would last.

"I'd like to go to Lupine…," she began.

"Sounds fun."

"… to visit the strip club where Alice works," she finished.

There was a pause during which it seemed Hassan didn't know what to make of her suggestion.

"Really?" he finally asked. "Huh. I wasn't expecting you to say that."

"I need to help Harry somehow. The police are breathing down his neck and I feel terrible for him. Alice's brother told the police that he thinks Harry's somehow involved in her disappearance."

"I can't believe he would say that. He must not know Harry very well."

"He doesn't. In fact, the family barely knows him at all. Otherwise they'd never accuse him of any wrongdoing, I'm sure."

"So you really want to go on a date at a strip club?" She could hear the smile in his voice.

"We won't be there to sightsee," she said. "We'll be there to ask questions."

He chuckled. "All right, if that's what you want. The things I do for love."

"Very funny. You just keep your eyes off the stage while we're there."

"Yes, ma'am."

"Are you free tomorrow night? We can go then."

"Sure thing," Hassan said. They talked of more pleasant things until Lilly had to hang up. She wanted to call her mom before it got too late.

Nikki answered the phone.

"How's Mom today?" Lilly asked.

"Meh, all right, I suppose. She's had better days," Nikki said.

"Did anything in particular go wrong?"

Nikki lowered her voice. "She seems very agitated that she can't find your father. I've reminded her—gently, of course—that he passed away a long time ago, but she can't seem to shake the idea that he's around here somewhere, hiding from her."

Lilly sighed. It was hard enough for her mom's mental health to be failing, but it was another thing to think that she was upset and lonely because she couldn't find her long-dead husband.

"Do you want me to come over tonight?"

"I'm going to stay tonight, so you don't need to be here," Nikki said, still speaking in a quiet voice. "I just gave her a banana and some chamomile tea and I'm hoping that soothes her and makes her sleepy. I'll see that she goes to bed soon."

"Thanks, Nikki. I'm here, so give a call if you need me."

"Thanks." Nikki hung up. Not for the first time, Lilly was

glad Nikki was looking after her mother. Even if she was dating Beau.

"Mom, can I go out for a little while?" Laurel asked, interrupting Lilly's thoughts.

Lilly cocked an eyebrow at her daughter. "It's a little late to be going out, isn't it? Especially on a school night."

"I'm just going over to Karley's house."

"Can you be back in a half hour?" Lilly asked.

"Probably."

"All right. You can go, but remember. Back here in a half hour."

Laurel rolled her eyes. "Okay."

"And don't roll your eyes at me." Laurel kissed Lilly's cheek and left.

Next Lilly called Noley. "How's the search for Alice going?" Noley asked.

"Not so well." Lilly told Noley about Alice's secret job and of her own plans for the following evening.

"You and Hassan are going to a strip club?" The disbelief in Noley's voice was palpable.

"I know, I know. It's not normally the type of place I would choose to go on a date, but I think maybe we can get some information there."

"Don't tell Bill what you're doing," Noley said. "I don't want him to think that a strip club is a good place to go for a night out."

Lilly laughed. "I'm not going to say anything to Bill, believe me, but not for that reason. I don't want him to know I'm looking for information about Alice."

"I won't say anything to him," Noley said. "He'll be furious if he finds out."

"I know. And thanks."

* * *

Lilly was fuming an hour and a half later. Laurel still wasn't home, despite her promise to be out only thirty minutes. Normally Lilly would have texted her, but since Lilly still had Laurel's phone, it would have been useless. She had no choice but to wait for Laurel.

This was now the second time this had happened. What was going on? Lilly knew she should be worried, but she was more angry than anything else. Then, of course, there was the guilt over being angry instead of worried.

An hour later there was a terse knock at the back door and it opened. Lilly had been in the living room trying to focus long enough to read a book, and when she walked into the kitchen ready to read Laurel the riot act, she stopped short.

Bill, still in his uniform, was standing in the middle of the kitchen with Laurel, who was scowling.

"What's going on?" Lilly felt a twinge of uneasiness prick the nape of her neck.

"You know the vandalism cases I've been working on?" Bill asked.

A cold ball of shock dropped from Lilly's throat into her stomach.

"Yes," she said, hesitating. It couldn't be.

"I found out who's responsible," Bill said in a stern voice. "Tonight's crime spree consisted of putting glue in store locks."

"Don't tell me it was Laurel." Lilly's gaze darted between her brother and her daughter.

"Among others," Bill said. Then he addressed his niece. "Laurel, you can explain everything to your mom."

Laurel stood silent, looking at her feet.

"Laurel?" Lilly asked.

"It wasn't *just* me."

"But you participated?" Lilly's voice was inching toward a full-throttled yell.

Laurel nodded.

"You have got to be kidding me! What's wrong with you?"

"Nothing is wrong with me."

"Don't get smart with me, Laurel."

"I'm not! You asked what's wrong with me!"

Lilly looked at Bill in exasperation, as if he could help.

"Who else has been doing it?" Lilly asked him.

"Two friends of hers," he said, nodding his head toward Laurel. He took a notebook out of his pocket and flipped a few pages. "Their names are Karley and Bella."

I should have seen this coming, Lilly thought. "That's why you've been spending so much time with those girls," Lilly said, addressing Laurel. "And here I am thinking they're nice kids. That's the last time I let anyone in this house without knowing them better."

"They're not bad, Mom." The look Lilly turned on her obviously convinced Laurel to stop talking.

"What about Vanessa?" Lilly asked Bill. "Is she involved in any of this?"

Bill shook his head. "Not to my knowledge. The three girls admitted that they had been pulling off the acts of vandalism lately by themselves."

Lilly turned toward Laurel again. "The places you've been vandalizing belong to people just like me! Small business owners!" she yelled. "How is this going to make me look?"

"*You* didn't do anything," Laurel said in a small voice.

"I raised you!" Lilly shouted. "It makes me look like a jerk and a failure as a parent! How did you even think to put glue in someone's locks? It's despicable!"

Laurel let out a long sigh and Lilly gave her another stink eye.

"Listen," Bill said. "The merchants she vandalized haven't decided whether to file charges. We'll know more once we talk to them again. If I hear anything I'll let you know. In the meantime, I have to get back to work. I've got reports to fill out about this. I told the guys I'd be back after I drove Laurel home."

"Okay, thanks for bringing her home," Lilly said. She opened the back door for him and he turned around before he left.

"Laurel, this is not the end of the world. But you need to stay on the straight and narrow. I wouldn't spend any more time with those girls," he said.

Laurel nodded and Bill left.

CHAPTER 17

The silence hung in the kitchen like a wet shroud. Suddenly Lilly was exhausted. Too tired to be angry, too tired to think up a punishment, she sat down hard at the kitchen table and looked up at Laurel, who was still standing in the same spot.

"Why did you do this?" Lilly asked.

Laurel shrugged. "I don't know."

"How could you not know? Was it your idea? What exactly did you do?"

Laurel remained standing. "I don't know. Karley and Bella were doing it and I was with them." She shrugged again. "They said it was fun and since it was dark, we wouldn't get caught."

"And you just agreed? Like an idiot?"

"I'm not an idiot."

"I beg to differ."

Laurel glowered at her mother. "This is all Nick's fault."

Lilly almost laughed out loud. "*Nick's* fault? How do you figure?"

"If he hadn't dumped me, I wouldn't have wanted to spend

any time with Karley and Bella." The waterworks started, but Lilly had no patience for Laurel's tears this time.

"That's the most ridiculous thing I've ever heard, Laurel. Besides, the vandalism started before you and Nick broke up."

"So?"

"So you can't blame your behavior on Nick. You had complete control over your own actions. This is all on you, Laurel, not Nick. You may wish you could blame this on him, but you can't."

Laurel didn't say anything. She stood still, looking down at the floor, her tears making a puddle at her feet. She gulped and looked up at her mother.

"I want you to go upstairs and go to bed," Lilly told her. "You have school tomorrow."

Laurel gasped. "I can't face people at school!"

"Too bad. Did you really think I would let you stay home from school, unsupervised, while I go to the shop? No way!"

Laurel spun around and went upstairs, still wearing her boots and coat.

Lilly let her chin fall to her chest while she sat there at the kitchen table for a few more minutes, trying to clear her head. How could she not have seen this coming? The previous summer, when the fires were being set in town, she had jumped to the conclusion that Tighe might have had something to do with them. How could she be so blind as to not see the evidence right in front of her?

Laurel had only been going out at night, she had been hanging out with a new group of friends, however small, and now that Lilly really thought about it, Laurel had been out every time an act of vandalism was committed.

I should have known, Lilly thought again. She sighed, pushed herself away from the table with an effort, and let Barney out one last time before bed.

How was she going to deal with this? Obviously Laurel

would have to be grounded for more than just a day or two. She would also have her start doing the housework at Bev's house. But that wasn't enough. Laurel would have to continue life without her phone, at least for another week or so.

Just before finally falling into a fitful sleep, Lilly had an awful thought. She would have to tell Beau about the whole ugly incident. Beau would think she was a terrible mother, too.

And what might a judge do? Surely since this was Laurel's first offense, a judge would go easy on her, right? What was the punishment for a teenager charged with vandalism? Would there be a trial? Would there be a media circus? She shook her head. Probably not. This was all so new and overwhelming. Lilly thought back to all the times she had worried about little things: whether Laurel would ever get out of diapers, whether she would learn to swim, whether she would ever be good at math. Those concerns had ended up being all for naught; what she should have been worrying about were the things she never saw coming.

She almost looked forward to visiting a strip club. At least it would get her away from the chaos at home.

The next day was Saturday, so the store closed early. Lilly drove home, wolfed down a sandwich, and dressed carefully in a sequined dress she had borrowed from Noley. In contrast to the nightlife in Juniper Junction, which was food- and family-oriented, the nightlife in Lupine was geared toward people who preferred to dress up and drink and dance—or drink and watch other people dancing.

Hassan would do the driving to Lupine. She wasn't quite ready when he arrived to pick her up, so he waited for her in the kitchen while she put the finishing touches on her outfit. When she teetered into the room on her stiletto heels, he let out a long whistle.

"Wow! I've never seen you dressed like that."

She turned in a circle in front of him. "Too much?"

"No way. You look great!"

"Thanks." She kissed him and yelled up the stairs. "Laurel, Hassan and I are going out for a while. We'll be a couple hours."

"Okay," came the response.

It was so cold outside. Lilly longed to be wearing thermal underwear and a pair of sweatpants, but it was important to look the part of a club hopper tonight, so she braved the cold that seeped into her toes and up her legs.

Once they had driven to within a few miles of Lupine, Lilly typed the address of Alice's strip club into her phone.

"I expected the place to be right in the heart of town," Lilly mused. "But this is sending us clear to the other side of town."

Hassan listened to Lilly's phone and frowned as the directions took them through Lupine and down a rural route leading out of town.

"Are you sure you typed in the right address?" he asked. "It feels like we've gone too far."

Lilly squinted in the darkness to see what might lie up ahead. "There's a faint glow up there," she said, pointing out the windshield. She looked down at her phone. "It says we're really close."

Another minute later they pulled up to a bar located in the middle of nowhere. The name of the bar, Guy's Place, blazed across a red neon sign on top of a very tall pole out front. The parking lot was full of pickup trucks and giant early model SUVs. The building looked like a bunker, with concrete block walls and a metal front door. In one of the two high windows, a neon sign blinked *Girls Girls Girls*. In the second window, another sign blinked the name of a beer with three blank spaces where letters should have been.

"Classy joint," Lilly said.

"I don't want to jump to any wild conclusions, but I think we might be overdressed," Hassan said. Lilly eyed him, with his long wool overcoat unbuttoned over a pressed Oxford shirt and striped tie, and started to laugh.

"We might as well go inside," she finally said. "We didn't come all this way for nothing."

Hassan came around to Lilly's side of the car and opened the door for her. She gripped his hand, suddenly nervous.

"I've never been to a strip club," she said.

Hassan didn't answer.

"Have you?" she finally asked.

He nodded. "Once, in London. A friend of mine had a party at one." She looked up at him.

"What was it like?"

"Superficial, fake, loud, sleazy. And that was an upscale place."

"I wonder what possessed Alice to work in one. The Alice I know is sweet, quiet, and reserved. Those are all things that Harry loves about her."

"She's probably all those things. But she's a stripper, too. I think they like to be called 'exotic dancers.'"

"Stripper, exotic dancer. It doesn't matter. It just doesn't make sense."

As they made their way through ruts of slush-turned-ice in the parking lot, they could hear the bass thudding through the walls. The noise got louder as they approached the door, and when they walked inside the music assaulted their senses.

Lilly gripped Hassan's hand harder and glanced sideways at him to find that he was glancing sideways at her. They stood in the doorway for a moment, letting their eyes adjust to the dim darkness inside the bar. Then they inched forward into the crowd.

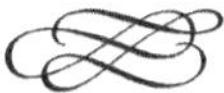

CHAPTER 18

One of the first things Lilly noticed was that she and Hassan were crazily overdressed. The uniform of choice among the men seemed to be jeans, flannel shirts, leather vests, and work boots. The women, and there was a surprising number of women, were almost all dressed in tight jeans, Henley shirts, and tall boots.

The huge room stank of sweat, alcohol, and bad breath. Hassan leaned close to Lilly's ear.

"Do you want to leave?"

Lilly shook her head. "No, we came here for a reason. Let's just get it over with so we can go home."

As they made their way toward the bar, Lilly began to notice people staring at them. She didn't need to wonder why: she and Hassan were strangers, and not dressed like anyone else. They must have looked like a pair of fancy Nancys coming through the door.

She shot Hassan a nervous glance and kept walking. A woman stepped in front of her, blocking her way.

"You sure you're in the right place?" she asked.

"Yes," Lilly said. She hoped her voice sounded stronger to the other woman than it did to her own ears.

"You wanna think about that?" asked a man who sidled up to the small group. He wore a frown under his thick mustache. His eyes glittered hard in the artificial light of the bar and his beard held in its nest several droplets of what Lilly hoped was beer.

"We're just here to get a drink," Hassan said, dropping Lilly's hand and firmly grasping her elbow instead.

"There's other bars in Lupine, ya know," the woman said, lifting her chin slightly.

"All we want is something to drink," Hassan said. "Why don't you step aside so we can get to the bar." It was not a question.

The burly man looked at the woman, who wore heavy, glittery blue makeup and fake eyelashes.

"A Brit, huh?" he asked, jabbing his female counterpart in the ribs. "Check this out," he said. He lifted his pinky finger and pretended to sip tea, saying "time for tea" in a hideous attempt to mimic Hassan's cultured British accent. The woman barked a harsh laugh.

"Y'all don't belong in here." she said, jabbing her pointer finger at Lilly and Hassan. Her nails were about two inches long, painted blue.

By now other people nearby were beginning to take notice of the disturbance. Lilly could feel their eyes on her and Hassan, watching and waiting to see what would happen next, like buzzards waiting to descend on a particularly scrumptious piece of roadkill.

"You a terrorist or somethin'? Where's your turban?" asked Burly Man, looking straight at Hassan.

Lilly let an audible gasp escape her lips. Hassan's grip tightened on her elbow. But something had tripped inside Lilly's brain and she couldn't let such an outrageous question go unanswered. The stupidity of Burly Man emboldened her to finally speak up.

"Of course he's not a terrorist." The scorn dripped from her voice. "Now get out of the way and let us get to the bar."

Blue-Eyeshadow stood in front of them this time, arms akimbo, blocking their way. Lilly's senses were heightened as the moment threatened to become more heated. Images from her peripheral vision flitted across her mind: a pole dancer by the back of the bar, gyrating to the obnoxious music, the bartender popping open a cheap can of domestic beer and pouring it slowly into a glass, a scraggly-looking woman trying to squeeze between two people, two beers held up high in her hands to avoid spilling them.

"We don't allow no terrorists in here," Burly Man said, his voice low. He jerked his head toward the front of the bar. "There's the door."

Lilly opened her mouth to retort, but Hassan spoke first. "All right. We're not here to cause trouble." He steered Lilly toward the door and she pulled her arm away from his grasp.

"What are you doing?" she asked through clenched teeth.

"Not now. We'll talk in the car."

The crowd parted before them as they made their way to the heavy metal front door of the bar. All eyes were on them. It seemed to Lilly as if conversation in the bar had stopped so people could pay attention to her and Hassan, and all she could hear was the pounding of the blood in her own ears. In truth, only a small number of people had seen the hateful exchange between Lilly and Hassan and their tormentors.

When they reached the door someone opened it for them and practically pushed them outside with an obscene hand gesture, slamming the door behind them. Lilly was shivering, but not from the cold.

Hassan let go of her elbow and strode toward the car. She followed as quickly as she could in her high heels.

When she reached the car Hassan was holding the passenger

door open for her. She glanced at him, but his eyes were fixed on something far away, not on her.

He closed her door lightly then came around the front of the car and slid in behind the steering wheel. He sat with his head down and his palms flat on his thighs for several seconds before either of them said anything. Hassan was the first one to break the silence.

"I'm sorry you had to see that."

"I'm sorry for all of it." She touched the back of his hand. "We shouldn't have come."

"I don't often hear the overt hatred like that, but it's hard every time it happens."

Lilly didn't know what to say. She was embarrassed for Hassan, and angry, and somehow guilty because she felt sorry for him. She didn't ask, but she had a feeling he wouldn't want her to feel sorry for him. Her body had stopped shaking once she was safely in the car, but her heart still thumped wildly and she wanted to scream and cry simultaneously.

Instead, she sat staring straight ahead, waiting for Hassan to talk again. But he started the car without saying anything else and headed in the direction of Juniper Junction. She longed to say something that would make him feel better, but she had no idea what that might be.

It was a lonely ride home. Neither spoke and the radio was silent, too. When they pulled up in front of Lilly's house, she asked Hassan if he wanted to come in.

"I really should get home," he said. "I have a conference call early tomorrow morning."

She gave him a sad look. "I'm sorry."

He nodded. "I'll call you tomorrow."

He made no move to get out and open her door for her. She stepped into the snow next to the car and her feet felt an icy sting that took her breath away. She hurried into the house without looking back.

She closed the kitchen door behind her and Barney came racing into the room, skidding to a stop at her feet.

Finally, something to make her smile.

She reached down and tousled Barney's head as she listened for Laurel.

"Mom? Is that you?" Laurel yelled down the stairs.

"Yup. I'm home."

Laurel came downstairs a few minutes later, while Lilly sat in a kitchen chair, still stroking Barney's soft fur.

"What are you so dressed up for?" Laurel asked.

Lilly wasn't about to tell her daughter that she had visited a strip club, and she hadn't thought of a good lie.

"Um, Hassan and I went out in Lupine." It was vague, but hopefully Laurel wouldn't ask any more questions.

"Have you already had dinner?" Laurel asked.

Lilly nodded.

"Is there anything for me to eat?"

"I'm sure there's food in the fridge," Lilly answered. "Take a look." The sandwich she had eaten before leaving for Lupine was still sitting in her stomach like a brick.

Lilly had kept a little of Harry's macaroni and cheese, so Laurel had that for dinner while Lilly sipped a glass of ginger ale.

"Don't you feel good?" Laurel asked, spearing a piece of macaroni with her fork.

Lilly swallowed. "My stomach is a bit upset, that's all."

"I can let Barney out tonight if you just want to go to bed," Laurel said. Lilly recognized the offer as a tentative olive branch, indicating that perhaps Laurel was beginning to accept her punishment for the vandalism.

"That would be great. Thank you." She had kicked off the uncomfortable shoes as soon as she was in the kitchen, and now she reached for them to take them upstairs.

She had some thinking to do.

CHAPTER 19

*L*illy lay on her side under the covers, facing away from the bedroom door. When Laurel let Barney into the room, Lilly pretended to be asleep.

In fact, it took several hours for her to fall asleep and even then, it was fitful and full of bad dreams. Patent bigotry was something she had never experienced and in fact, hadn't really thought about until now: people perceived Hassan, with his Middle Eastern features, differently from the way they viewed her as a white woman. Lilly wondered what others thought when they saw her and Hassan together.

Clearly, the people in the bar had been ignorant. But were they just giving voice to the things that other people thought when they met Hassan? Lilly recalled that her mother, upon meeting him, had asked an inappropriate question, not unlike the man at the bar. She couldn't remember exactly what the question had been, but she remembered clearly that Hassan had taken it in stride and not seemed embarrassed or angered by it at all. Lilly had just taken it for granted that he had shrugged it off as the ramblings of a woman who was losing her filter.

But had he taken it to heart? Had it hurt him? Lilly hadn't

even noticed. Had she been so insensitive that his feelings escaped her completely?

The last thought she had before falling asleep was that she needed to go back to that strip club, but without Hassan. She would ask Noley to go with her.

She was a little surprised when Hassan didn't call on Sunday. She thought maybe he needed some time to digest everything that had happened at Guy's Place, though he did text her once during the day to say he was working. She tried calling him before going to bed that night, but his phone went straight to voicemail.

On Monday morning she was cranky when she got to work, but one look at Harry when he walked into the shop snapped her out of her self-absorption. He looked exhausted and wan, his face devoid of its usual healthy color.

"No news, Harry?" She knew she didn't have to ask. His demeanor told her everything she needed to know.

He shook his head. "It's been a whole week, Lilly. She left her purse and ID and everything behind, so it's looking less and less like she left on her own. She never goes anywhere without her purse." His voice was glum and without inflection.

"They'll find her, Harry, I know they will." Lilly tried to sound buoyant. He nodded, but just barely.

Lilly's fingers itched to phone Hassan that morning, but she wanted to be able to talk to him uninterrupted. Customers coming and going all morning made that impossible. She had just made up her mind to call him that evening after work when he came into the shop. When she heard him talking to Harry, she came out of the office and stood at a discrete distance, waiting until the two men finished talking. Hassan clapped Harry on the back and turned away, toward her. He wore a sheepish look.

"Hi," he said.

"Hi."

"Are you busy for lunch?" he asked.

Lilly shook her head. She was suddenly nervous.

"I thought we could go over to the French bistro."

She nodded. "Okay. I'll get my coat. Harry, can you watch things around here for a bit? If you need to leave in a hurry, put the 'Closed' sign on the door."

"Sure, boss," Harry said. Lilly smiled at him.

She grabbed her coat from the office and joined Hassan out on the sidewalk. Neither spoke again until they had walked a block up Main Street toward the bistro.

"Has the shop been busy today?" Hassan asked. Lilly knew he was trying to make small talk. She would rather he just kept quiet until he was ready to talk about Saturday night.

"Yeah, pretty busy today."

He didn't reach for her hand as he normally would have. Lilly wondered if it was because he was still upset about the incident at Guy's Place or if he was reacting to her standoffishness. She was careful not to brush up against his arm as they walked, keeping about a foot of space between them.

When they got to the bistro he opened the door for her, then followed her inside. Armand, the owner, smiled when he saw them.

They stood in line before the clean white marble counter with the glass-front case of sandwiches and French pastries, waiting their turn to order. Lilly was glad to see the lunchtime crowd inside the bistro—Armand's wife had been murdered the previous summer and Armand hadn't known whether he would continue to operate the small restaurant after her death. But the people of Juniper Junction had rallied around him and convinced him to stay, especially when it was revealed who had killed her.

It wasn't until they had their sandwiches and tea and were sitting across from each other at one of the quaint bistro tables that Hassan started to talk.

"I want to apologize for the way I acted the other night." He paused for several moments. Lilly sensed that he had more to say, so she waited for him to continue.

"That was the first time anyone has made a reference to my skin color since I bought the house in Juniper Junction," he continued, putting his hands, palms-up, on the table in front of him. "And, obviously, the talk about terrorism was a direct insult to the religion that guy assumed I practice. He was right about my religion, of course. But I was angry about it. There are so many Muslims where I live in Minnesota that it just seems natural for one to see them everywhere. But here it's different. And I was finally made to feel different, less-than, on Saturday night."

Lilly opened her mouth to speak, but Hassan went on.

"It makes me wonder what people are thinking and *not* saying about me whenever they see me. I mean, when I walk down Main Street, are people afraid there's a terrorist in their midst? I haven't noticed, but I probably will now."

"I'm so sorry about everything. If I had known what would happen, I would never have asked you to go with me," Lilly said.

"It's not your fault. You couldn't have known that was going to happen. And I'm sorry you had to witness the ugliness."

"I'm glad I was there with you so you didn't have to handle it alone."

"I wish you hadn't seen it at all. It's embarrassing."

"Why should you be embarrassed? Those buffoons at the bar should be the ones who are embarrassed. Every last one of them."

"I doubt they've given it another thought," Hassan said.

Unfortunately, he was probably right.

They ate in silence for a few minutes, each lost in thought, until Armand got a break from the lunch crowds and came over to their table.

"How are things, Armand?" Lilly asked.

He gave an expansive shrug of the shoulders. "As well as can be expected, I suppose," he said. Lilly could have listened to his thick French accent all day long. "It is a good thing that the bistro has been busy. It keeps me—how do you say it—busy in the mind and in the body. I have less time to think."

"Have you been back to France?" Hassan asked.

"*Oui.* I returned to scatter Cerise's ashes in the village where she grew up. It is a beautiful place. Cerise is at rest now."

Lilly smiled sadly at Armand. She had barely known Cerise when the poor woman was murdered, but she had a feeling they could have been friends. And even Noley, who had initially been charged with Cerise's murder, would probably have been good friends with the couple.

That brought her thoughts back to Noley and her plan to ask her best friend to go back to Guy's Place with her to find out more about Alice. She didn't want Hassan to know she was returning to the bar.

Someone called Armand from the kitchen and he left, but not before making Lilly and Hassan promise they would return to visit him at the bistro soon. Once he left, they finished lunch and went back to the jewelry shop. This time Hassan held Lilly's hand and she didn't mind walking close to him.

When they reached Juniper Junction Jewels, Hassan held the door for Lilly, then said, "I'll talk to you later. I'm headed back to the house."

"Wait." Lilly beckoned him into the shop. It was time to show him his Valentine's Day gift.

Hassan tilted his head and squinted slightly. "What's up?"

She grabbed his hand and led him back to the office. Harry looked on, his eyebrows raised.

"There hasn't been a good time to give you your Valentine's Day gift, so I'm doing it now." Hassan smiled and closed his eyes.

Lilly placed a small tray on her desk. The XO template was

on the tray. She covered it with a black cloth and told Hassan to open his eyes.

He opened them and looked at Lilly, then his gaze followed hers to the tray on the desk.

"Is that it?" he asked.

She nodded. "Lift up the black cloth."

He did as she told him to and stood gazing at the XO template in black crystals.

He turned to her with a smile. "What is this?"

"I designed it for you. I mean, not to give you as a piece of jewelry, but in your honor. I tried to design something that exemplifies how I feel about you. I'm going to sell it in onyx, not black glass crystals, and give the proceeds to an Afghan charity."

He stared at her for several seconds, then gathered her into his arms. "This is the best gift I've ever gotten," he said into her hair. He held her away from him and shook his head and shrugged. "I don't even know what else to say. I love you. Thank you."

"I'm glad you like it." She beamed.

hen Lilly got home from work that night, the first thing she did was call Noley.

"What are you doing tomorrow night?" she asked.

"No plans. Bill has to work," Noley replied.

"Care to take a run over to Lupine with me?"

Noley was always up for a road trip, even a short one, so Lilly had known she would say yes.

"Sure. What are you doing in Lupine?"

Lilly would have preferred to spring the reason on Noley once they arrived at Guy's Place, but she figured Noley might appreciate a heads-up.

"I'm going out to Guy's Place. That's where Alice was working."

"You want me to go to the strip joint with you? That's not really my scene, Lil."

"I know, but hear me out. It's not my scene, either, you know that. But I have to do something to help Harry. You should see him in the shop. He's sad all the time, apprehensive, glum. I can't just sit by and do nothing."

"But a strip club? Really? I'm sure the police have already been there asking questions."

"I'm sure they have, but people are suspicious of police asking questions, especially in a place like that. They might speak to us if we go in there like regular patrons."

"Women aren't regular patrons of strip clubs, Lilly."

"You'd be surprised at how many women were there Saturday night."

"Wait. What? You've already been?" Noley asked.

Lilly sighed. "I went there with Hassan Saturday night and it was a complete disaster. I'll fill you in on the way there tomorrow night."

Noley laughed. "Quite a place for a date."

"It was the date from hell."

Noley sobered. "I'm sorry. You'll have to tell me about it."

"I will."

"What time? And what should I wear?" Noley asked. "Did you wear the dress I lent you?"

"Yeah. I was a bit overdressed, to say the least. Just wear jeans and your homeliest flannel shirt. And work boots, if you have any. You'll fit right in."

"And this place is in Lupine?" Noley sounded incredulous. "I don't want to make a fool of myself by going somewhere totally underdressed."

"Don't worry. You won't."

Noley sounded dubious. "All right, if you say so. But maybe I should take a dress with me, just in case."

"Trust me, you won't need it. And if you have any blue eyeshadow, I would recommend wearing that."

"I'm a little concerned about the way tomorrow evening is shaping up," Noley said.

"It'll be fine. I'll pick you up around six. Eat before you go, since I wouldn't trust the food there."

"Now I definitely don't like the way the evening is shaping up."

Lilly could hear the grimace in her voice. Noley didn't like to go to places where the food wasn't good.

"You do this for me and I'll buy you lunch at the bistro," Lilly said.

"Deal."

Lilly hung up and sat back in her chair at the kitchen table, wishing the dinner fairy had visited while she was at work.

"You're going to a *strip club?*" The sound of Laurel's voice made Lilly jump.

Rats, she thought. *Who knew Laurel was eavesdropping? Of all my traits, that's the one she inherits?*

"Yes, but let me explain why," Lilly began.

Laurel held up her hand for silence. "Never mind. I don't think I want to know, Mom. I can never unhear what I just heard."

"You're being a bit dramatic, aren't you?" Lilly asked.

"What would you say if Gran announced that she was going to a strip club?" Laurel asked, her head tilted and her eyes challenging.

I see she also inherited my ability to ask ruthlessly unnerving questions.

"I would say, 'Mom, you are a grown woman and you should spend your free time in any way you see fit,'" Lilly lied. *Honestly, I wouldn't be too surprised to hear Mom announce she was headed to a strip club.*

"You would not. You would react the same way I did." Then Laurel gasped and covered her mouth with her hand. "Does Hassan know about this?"

"Let me explain, will you? Harry's girlfriend Alice works at a strip club in Lupine," she began.

"You're kidding."

"I wish I were. But it's true, and I want to go there to ask the other, um, dancers a few questions about her."

"Does Uncle Bill know you're doing this?"

"No, and he's not going to find out." Lilly pointed at Laurel and gave the girl a burning look.

"Is Hassan going with you?"

"No." Lilly shook her head emphatically. "He went with me the other night and things didn't go well."

"*What?!* You've already been to the strip club? Why would you ever go back?"

"Because Hassan and I were asked to leave."

"Why?" Laurel fixed her mother with a suspicious, confused look.

"It's a long story, but they were harassing Hassan and we thought it would be best if we left. We never made it too much farther than the front door of the place."

"What were they saying to Hassan?"

"That's probably a conversation for another day, honey."

"You can tell me. I'm old enough to take it."

"It's not that, it's just that it was upsetting and I don't really feel like discussing it right now."

"Oh. Okay. So who's going with you tomorrow?"

"Noley."

Laurel shook her head. "My mom and her best friend are clubbing with strippers. This is so embarrassing."

"I'm not clubbing. I'm investigating. There's a world of difference."

"I'm surprised Harry would date a stripper." Laurel looked at Lilly with mischief in her eyes. "How do you think they met?"

"Not at the strip club, that's for sure. He was as surprised as anyone else to learn she's working there."

"Is it safe there?" Laurel asked.

Lilly shrugged. "Safe enough."

"In the movies, murders always take place in strip clubs," Laurel pointed out.

"Well, hopefully there's been no murder at this one. We're hoping to find Alice alive and well. And maybe her co-workers can help."

"Wait 'til I tell Tighe about this," Laurel said. The mischievous look had crept back into her eyes.

"Don't you dare."

"What will you give me?" Laurel asked. Lilly had to hand it to the kid—she was shrewd.

"I won't extend your grounding." Lilly gave Laurel a pointed look.

"We'll see." Laurel turned on her heel and sped toward the stairs. She stopped on the first step. "What's for dinner?"

"Whatever you made."

"Hmm. That would be nothing. Can we order burgers?"

Should she force leftovers on both of them? Nah—burgers sounded good and as long as Laurel was willing to sit and talk to her jailer, it might be worth the schlep in the snow to pick them up.

"Burgers it is. Order them, will you? Make mine medium. I'll go pick them up. After dinner you can go to Gran's with me to do some cleaning."

"Okay."

No argument?

"Who are you and what have you done with my daughter?" Lilly asked with a smile.

Laurel laughed and continued up the stairs.

Having a grounded child in the house wasn't nearly as bad as Lilly had expected.

CHAPTER 21

*L*illy fretted all day Tuesday until it was time to pack up the displays for the evening.

"Are you okay, boss?" Harry asked more than once. It was sweet of him to be concerned for her with all he had on his mind.

"I'm good, Harry. Don't worry about me."

"If you say so."

"Is someone still staying with you at night?" Lilly asked. She felt like chatting, anything to keep her mind off her upcoming field trip.

"Yeah. Mary Louise and Mack are taking turns."

"They're good to you," Lilly mused aloud.

Harry shrugged. "I guess."

Lilly looked up sharply. "What do you mean by that?"

Harry shrugged again. "Mack's okay, but I sort of wish it was just him and not Mary Louise, too."

"Why not?"

Harry blushed to the tips of his ears and down his neck. "She's got kind of a crush on me, I think. At least that's what Mack says."

"Does it make you uncomfortable when she stays at your house?"

"A little. I don't want her to think I'm leading her on."

"Have you told her that?" Lilly asked.

"No, because it's so nice of her to stay with me. I don't want her to think I'm ungrateful."

Lilly could understand his feelings. Especially at such a difficult time, he didn't want to be alienating his friends. But on the other hand, having Mary Louise at his house might be making life harder for both of them.

"Maybe Mack or one of your other friends can say something to her," Lilly suggested.

"Maybe. I'll think about it," Harry said. Lilly was pretty sure that was his way of ending the conversation, so she didn't say anything else about it. But she was a little worried.

"Let me know if you hear anything about Alice," Lilly reminded him as they walked out the door together.

"I will. I promise."

Lilly's mind reeled with preoccupations while she drove home. She didn't want to go back to Guy's Place, but she knew she had to. She was worried that Mary Louise might be taking advantage of a bad situation to ingratiate herself with Harry. And she was still worried about Hassan. She wished he hadn't turned inward when the idiots at Guy's Place had upset him. And she was worried about her mom, as usual.

When she got home she took off her work clothes and slipped into something a little less comfortable: a pair of jeans that had fit her two sizes ago, a long-sleeved tee shirt advertising a local roofer (she had won it in a radio contest years before), an old pair of Tighe's work boots that pinched her feet, and a baseball cap. She gathered her hair into a ponytail and slid it through the opening in the back of the cap. Before doing that, though, she swiped some hideous old makeup on her face.

She was surveying herself in the mirror when Laurel knocked on her bedroom door.

"I just came to see what you were going to wear to your date at the strip club," Laurel said with a laugh.

"Funny girl," Lilly replied.

Laurel looked Lilly up and down. "You look pretty scary." She walked around behind her mother and surveyed her from the back. "Those jeans are a little tight, aren't they?"

"A *little* tight?" Lilly scoffed. "It's going to take three people to get them off me."

"Count me out," Laurel said.

"Thanks."

"How long are you going to be?"

"I don't know. I have to pick up Noley. Then it'll take at least a half hour to drive to the other side of Lupine. We'll just have to see how things go when we get there. We may be able to talk to a few people, we may not."

"Be careful," Laurel said.

"We will. I promise," Lilly assured her.

When she pulled up in front of Noley's house, she had to laugh. Noley was waiting outside for her, dressed in a parka that made her look four times her usual size. She looked like she was ready for an ice-fishing-and-disco overnight. Her jeans were ripped at the knee and she was wearing high-heeled boots. She slid into the passenger seat and turned to look at Lilly.

"I feel ridiculous," she said. "Look at the circus makeup I'm wearing."

She took her hood off and Lilly turned on the inside car lights. She laughed again. Noley's eyelids were caked with bright blue makeup and accented by blue eyelashes. She wore dark rouge and dark red lipstick.

"Is that glitter on your cheeks?" Lilly asked.

Noley nodded with a grimace.

"I wish Bill could see you now," Lilly said, shaking her head and laughing again.

"I would rather die."

"Well, thank you for coming with me." Lilly turned off the lights and started the car. "It would warm Harry's heart if he knew what we were up to."

"Does anyone know what we're up to? I mean, someone should know where we're going, right? Just in case," Noley said.

"Laurel knows where we're going, though I can't remember if I told her the name of the bar."

"Oh, great."

"Think positively. Nothing's going to go wrong. We'll be home and taking off all this makeup before you know it."

They drove in silence for a while. Lilly was thinking about what she wanted to ask Alice's co-workers. She was pretty sure Noley was thinking about what she would order for lunch at the bistro with Lilly footing the bill.

They had passed through the charming town of Lupine and were headed down the rural road that would take them to Guy's Place when Noley spoke.

"Are you going to tell me why your trip to this place with Hassan was so bad?"

"Yes, but let's wait until we're on the way home. I don't want his experience to taint your impressions."

"That sounds bad." Noley paused. "So what's the plan? Are we supposed to be looking for people who know Alice?"

Lilly was happy to change the subject. "Yes. I'd like to find other dancers who know Alice, and if I can talk to her boss, even better. I think you and I should stick together."

"Definitely."

"We just want to know more about Alice—her habits before and after work, if they're friends with her, if she was worried about anything, if she mentioned going away somewhere. Anything that would help us find her."

"You say it like the police aren't looking for her. I'm sure they've been around, asking all the same questions."

"Probably, but maybe the other dancers will be more willing to open up to people who aren't in uniform," Lilly said.

"All right." Noley pointed out the window to the bar looming in the distance, its red neon lights flashing. "Is that the place? I'm afraid to ask."

"Yup."

Noley sighed. "Let's get this over with. You're lucky I'm so nice."

Lilly swung into the parking lot. It was again filled with pickups and old SUVs. Did the same people come here every night? She shuddered at the thought.

Noley left her parka in the car at Lilly's suggestion. Lilly had worn an old denim jacket over her tee shirt, so she didn't bother removing that. Noley looked down at Lilly's legs.

"Pants a little tight?" she asked with a grin.

"They're like compression socks, only much worse."

"Let's go in before I freeze," Noley said, shivering.

Lilly led the way to the heavy front door and opened it. She stood aside to let Noley go in first. Noley walked a few steps and turned around to give Lilly a glare that clearly asked *Where have you brought me??*

Lilly smiled and gave Noley a little nudge as she pushed her way into the crowded bar.

CHAPTER 22

*L*illy needed a couple moments for her eyes to adjust, but when she became accustomed to the gloom, the first person she saw was Burly Man.

"Doesn't that guy ever leave?" she muttered under her breath.

"What?" Noley asked, her voice raised over the din of the bar.

"Nothing. I'll tell you later."

"There's a lot you'll have to tell me later."

Lilly turned toward the bar. She locked eyes for just a second with Burly Man and held her breath. But he looked away almost immediately and showed no sign of recognizing her. She was glad she had worn a baseball cap. Burly Man was talking—rather, shouting—to Blue Eyeshadow, and Lilly noticed that Blue Eyeshadow gave her the once-over, too. Her eyes lingered on Lilly's face for just a moment too long. Lilly looked away, then dared to look back. Blue Eyeshadow had turned away. Perhaps she thought she had recognized Lilly, but decided she didn't. Lilly hoped so.

Lilly and Noley sidled up to the bar as best they could in the crowd. Lilly could feel the music thumping in her lungs. She ordered a beer and Noley did the same. The bartender slid their drinks to them, the beer sloshing over the tops of the glasses. Lilly took a sip and suppressed a grimace. Noley looked closely at the glass, probably making sure it was clean. Lilly couldn't help smiling a little. Noley set the glass down and wrinkled her nose.

They looked toward the back of the giant room, where it was dark, save for the strobe lights that were ripping the dark and revealing several women dancing around floor-to-ceiling poles.

"I guess we need to head over there," Noley said, nodding toward the dancers.

Lilly set her beer down next to Noley's untouched one, took a deep breath, squared her shoulders, and made her way through the crowd. Noley followed closely on her heels.

"Hey, girls, I haven't seen you around. You come here together?" one man asked them as they jostled their way toward the stage. His speech was only slightly slurred. Lilly shot him a withering look and didn't have to turn around to know that Noley was doing the same thing.

Another man tried to grab Lilly's arm, but she shook it off and shuddered for the man's benefit. She could feel Noley close behind her as the man tried the same thing with her. She had an unmistakable sense of danger, so she turned around just in time to see Noley pull her arm back to slug the guy.

"Noley, don't!" she cried. She grabbed her friend's arm and hung on just in time to save the man's face from Noley's wrath.

"Come on, we don't want to get into trouble while we're here," she said in Noley's ear.

"The men here are disgusting." Noley's eyes were hard and narrowed. She was on high alert, that much Lilly could plainly see.

"I know, but hopefully we won't be here long. Let's get the information we need and get the heck out of here."

Noley exhaled loudly and nodded toward the stage. "Keep moving."

When they finally arrived at the stage, having endured a minimum of groping along the way, they found to their surprise that there were several empty tables. Mostly small groups of men sat at the other tables, alternately leering at the dancers and drinking shots.

A waitress, one who had clearly been surgically enhanced, came up to the table where Lilly and Noley sat. She wore a bright pink tank top with "Guy's Place" emblazoned in sparkly rhinestones across her ample front. Her name tag announced her as "Minx." Noley turned to Lilly so the waitress couldn't see her roll her eyes.

"What can I get ya?" Minx asked.

"I'll take a Cosmo." Lilly looked at Noley. "What do you want?"

"A Cosmo's good," she said.

"Two Cosmos," Minx said. "Any food?"

"No," both women said simultaneously. Noley grimaced.

After Minx had left, Noley leaned toward Lilly. "The glasses better be clean this time. And you're buying," she almost growled.

Lilly couldn't help laughing. Noley was really hating this little adventure.

They tried watching everything but the dancers as they waited for their drinks. By the time Minx had brought them to the table, Lilly had decided on a plan of action.

"Excuse me," she began.

Minx leaned down closer to hear better and Lilly was treated to a view she would rather have skipped. "Yeah?"

"We're here to visit a friend of ours, but I don't see her. Do you know Cotton Candy?" It pained her to call Alice by her stage name.

Minx tilted her head and gave Lilly a suspicious look. "You're friends of hers?" she asked.

Lilly and Noley nodded.

"If you're such good friends, why don't *you* tell *me* where she is?" she asked with an icy glare.

Lilly feigned ignorance. "What do you mean?" she asked, furrowing her brow.

"What I mean is, she hasn't shown up for her shift in a week." Minx stood up taller with her hands on her hips. She looked across the bar and raised her hand in the air to signal someone.

Lilly followed her gaze and groaned when she saw Burly Man making his way to their table. She closed her eyes for a moment, then opened them to find Noley staring at her.

"What's wrong?" she mouthed.

Lilly shook her head and pressed her lips together in a thin line.

Burly Man stood next to Minx. "What?" he asked tersely.

She jerked her head toward Lilly and Noley.

"These girls are looking for Candy," she said.

Burly Man gave the waitress a suspicious look. "Why?"

"Ask 'em yourself," Minx said, and sauntered off. Burly Man grabbed a chair from the closest table, not bothering to ask the men seated there if they would miss it, and turned it around so its back faced Lilly and Noley. He straddled the chair and leaned into the back.

"Why are you looking for Candy?" he asked. His eyes were hard as he glared at both of them.

"We're friends of hers and we just stopped in to say hi," Lilly said. She hoped Burly Man couldn't sense her sweating.

"We ain't seen her around here lately. You're such good friends with her, how come you didn't know that?"

"I didn't say we're good friends of hers, I said we're friends. I don't know where she is. Obviously, I thought she was here." Lilly stared back at Burly Man in what she hoped was a convincing manner.

He glanced up as the music changed and new dancers came onto the stage, but he didn't pay attention to them for long. The men at the tables around them hooted and made noisy catcalls. Out of the corner of her eye Lilly could see Noley scowling at the men, her lips curled in disgust.

Burly Man turned his attention back to Lilly and Noley.

"You don't say much," he said, looking at Noley.

"I'm just here for the drink," she said, holding up her Cosmo.

"So are you a friend of Candy, too?" he asked her.

"Yeah, but she knows her better." Noley gestured with her drink toward Lilly.

"You been to Candy's apartment?" he asked Lilly.

"No."

"Maybe she's there. She ain't answering her phone. If you see her, tell her Guy wants to talk to her."

"Can I speak to him?" Lilly asked.

"You're talkin' to him now." Burly Man puffed out his chest ever so slightly.

"You're Mister Guy?" Lilly asked.

"No. I'm just Guy."

"When was the last time you saw Candy?" Lilly asked. If she had Alice's boss right in front of her, she was going to take advantage of the opportunity to ask questions, regardless of how odious he might be.

"Monday afternoon a week ago. She came in here to get her schedule. I remember because it was Valentine's Day and she had asked for the night off. She's a good worker, so that's why I gave her the night off. Probably cost me a bundle not to have her here."

"I'll bet." Lilly assumed Guy wouldn't notice her droll tone.

He didn't.

"Did she have plans for Valentine's Day?"

He shrugged. "It's none of my business. I don't care or want to know what my girls do in their spare time."

Lilly and Noley exchanged enraged glances. *His girls?* Between Guy's treatment of Hassan and his crystal-clear opinion of women, Lilly wanted nothing more than to give him a good, swift kick in the shins. But, with a little effort, she refrained. Instead, she swallowed her anger with a swig of her Cosmo.

"Does she have any friends here?" she asked.

"I s'pose. Hey, you're a friend of hers. Don't you know?"

"We haven't talked to her in a while. That's why we thought we'd surprise her by coming in tonight."

Guy was momentarily distracted by a shout from Minx, who slapped a patron across the face just as Guy, Lilly, and Noley looked up. Then he returned his attention to the topic of Alice.

"Don't you want to go over there and see what the problem is?" Noley asked him, nodding toward Minx.

"Nah. Minx is a tough cookie. She'll take care of the guy. He probably touched the merchandise."

"Merchandise?" Noley asked. "These women are for sale?"

CHAPTER 23

"*D*on't be stupid. Don't you know a figure of speech when you hear one? You know what? I don't need two strange broads asking me a lot of nosy questions. Either shut up and order another drink or get out." He pushed himself away from the table and stalked away, leaving a few patrons staring after him. He caught Minx's eye and gestured toward the table where Lilly and Noley sat.

Lilly was the first one to speak.

"I can't believe what a jerk he is. Can you imagine working for him?"

Noley shook her head. "I feel so sorry for Alice."

Minx was at their table just a moment later.

"What did you say to piss Guy off?" she asked.

I see subtlety is not her bailiwick, Lilly thought to herself.

"He mentioned something about his 'girls' being for sale," Noley said with a disapproving frown.

"We're not, trust me," she said.

"Are you a dancer, too?" Lilly asked.

"Of course I am," Minx said with an unattractive scowl. "God knows my boyfriend spent enough on this body." Lilly swallowed to tamp down her gag reflex.

"Are you a friend of Alice?" Noley asked. Then she realized her mistake. She gritted her teeth. "I mean, Candy?"

Minx fixed the women with a shrewd stare. "So you really do know her," she said.

"I told you we did," Lilly said.

"Listen. I'm going on break in about twenty minutes, then afterward I have to change and get on the stage. Come meet me at the dressing room door in fifteen." She pointed to a dark area toward the rear of the stage.

Lilly nodded and glanced at Noley, who gave her a look that said, *We have to stay longer?*

A few minutes later Minx brought over two more Cosmos, though Lilly and Noley hadn't ordered any. They accepted the drinks and thanked Minx.

The women said little for the next fifteen minutes, looking around the bar and observing the other guests. Lilly didn't worry that anyone would be offended by their staring, as they were all otherwise occupied with the show on the stage.

Fifteen minutes passed slowly, and when the time came, Lilly and Noley threw money down on the table and went in search of the dressing room door.

They found it in a dark recess behind and to the left of the stage.

Lilly wrinkled her nose. "It smells rank back here."

Noley pointed down a dimly lit hallway. "The restrooms are probably down there."

They waited for several minutes before Minx showed up. She nodded toward a door that was marked "Private" and they followed her inside.

They found themselves in a dressing room of sorts. The concrete floor was cold, even through the bottoms of their boots, and several women in various stages of undress were walking around. They must have been freezing. There was a bathroom off to one side and several mirrors lined the concrete block walls. Privacy was at a premium.

Minx flopped down on the closest chair and took off her sensible black shoes. She rubbed her feet as Lilly and Noley looked on. Lilly wondered if she did that before her waitress shift, too. She said a silent prayer that Minx hadn't made the Cosmos.

"So, Minx," Noley began.

"I hate that name. My name is Suzanne, so call me that."

"Thanks, Suzanne," Lilly said.

"So, Suzanne, are you friends with Alice?" Noley asked.

"I guess you could say that. I mean, we work together."

"Did she say what her plans were for Valentine's Day?" Lilly asked.

"She just said she was going out to dinner with her boyfriend," Suzanne said. "I don't know him."

"Was that last Monday?" Lilly asked.

Suzanne thought for a moment. "Yeah. She just came in to get her check, then she left again."

"Does she have other friends here?" Noley asked.

"Everybody likes her. To tell you the truth, though, she doesn't really belong here," Suzanne said.

Lilly had known *that* the minute she found out where Alice worked, but she didn't say anything.

"She's just, you know, too sweet to work here. She hasn't developed that hard shell that the rest of us have."

"What do you mean?" Lilly asked.

"Look. No one *wants* to be a stripper. We all do it for the money. Alice is pretty, but she doesn't have that go-to-hell atti-tude that the rest of us have. You saw me earlier: if a guy touches me, I let him have it. Alice is afraid to do that."

"So Alice just lets men touch her?" Lilly was incredulous.

"If one of us sees it, we help her out. A couple weeks ago one of the other girls smacked a guy who was bothering Alice. Alice just gets this scared look and we know she needs help."

"Doesn't Guy mind?" Noley asked. "He seems like the type who can smell weakness and wouldn't tolerate it."

Suzanne shrugged. "He is. But the rest of the girls kind of keep an eye on Alice. Like I said, everyone likes her. We protect her."

Not well enough, apparently.

"Hey, girl." A young woman in jeans and a sweater walked by and was speaking to Suzanne.

"Hi, Trace. Wait a sec," Suzanne replied. Trace stopped walking and turned to face Suzanne.

"What's up?"

Suzanne indicated Lilly and Noley with a sweep of her hand. "These two women are friends of Alice. They came in to see her and I told them she hasn't been around since Valentine's Day. Did Alice say anything to you about where she might be going?"

Trace gave Lilly and Noley a suspicious look.

"They're okay," Suzanne told her. "Lilly, Noley, this is Tracy. She's a dancer, but on stage she goes by Fluff." Lilly and Noley shook hands with Tracy.

"She didn't say anything to me about where she was going," Tracy said. She thought for a minute, then pointed a long, manicured finger at Suzanne. "Did you work Sunday night before Valentine's Day?" she asked.

Suzanne nodded.

"There was this guy who was bothering Alice while she was waiting tables. Kept calling her over and asking her out," Tracy said. "She told him no every time." She looked at Suzanne. "Did you happen to see him?"

"You know, now that you mention it, I do remember that," Suzanne said. She squinted. "But I didn't know the guy. And since Alice seemed to be handling it herself, I didn't interfere."

"Do you know who the guy was?" Lilly asked Tracy.

"No, but she seemed to recognize him. He'd probably been in here before when she was working. She waved it off as not a big deal, but I know it bothered her."

"Have you ever seen him in here before? Or since then?" Lilly asked.

Tracy thought again, her head tilted to the side. "Maybe," she said. "I can't really remember for sure. We get a lot of guys in here, as you can imagine."

"I don't know, either," Suzanne said.

"Would you recognize him if you saw him again?" Noley asked.

"I might," Tracy said, nodding slowly. Suzanne nodded her agreement.

"Would you call me if you see him in here again?" Lilly asked. She whipped out her cell phone. "Oh, and I assume you've all talked to the police about Alice. Did you tell them about this guy?"

"I'll definitely call you," Tracy said. "I didn't tell the police about the guy because I just remembered it now. I can call them after my shift."

"Same here," Suzanne here.

"Thanks," Lilly said. She exchanged cell phone numbers with Tracy and Suzanne and Tracy went further back into the cold room to change out of her regular clothes and into something far less modest.

While the four women were talking, Suzanne changed out of her waitress garb and into her dance clothes, if they could be called that. She wore a royal blue satin corset, fishnet thigh-high stockings, tiny shiny panties, a bra-like contraption with tassels, and black stilettos. Whereas she had worn her hair up in a ponytail while she served food and drinks, she let it hang down her back for her dance performance. The transformation was astounding.

Lilly didn't know what to say. Should she compliment her

new friend? Should she tell her to break a leg? She knew that's what to say to an actor going onto a stage, but a stripper?

She decided to say nothing except to thank Suzanne for her time.

"I appreciate you talking to us, Suzanne. And thanks for the Cosmos," she said. Noley, who was standing behind Lilly, nodded.

"No problem, girls. Let me know if there's anything I can do to help." She seemed sincere. "I gotta go." She spit out the gum she had been chewing and headed for the stage door, striding confidently in her teetering heels.

"Should we stick around to talk to anyone else? Any of the other dancers?" Noley asked.

"Let's just go home for now. I've had about enough of Guy's Place for one night."

"I thought we'd never leave." Noley grinned.

When they left the so-called dressing room, the bar seemed even louder than before. At least the noise had dulled a bit while they were talking to Suzanne and Tracy. They made their way through the crowd, which was thick around the bar as the dancers' shifts changed, and toward the front door. Lilly caught Guy's eye as she approached the door.

He scowled, but didn't say anything. He watched them leave.

When they got in the car Noley leaned back against the headrest and Lilly put both hands on the wheel without starting the car.

"I feel like I need a shower," Noley said.

"Me, too."

"We learned a couple of interesting things." Noley began counting on her fingers. "First, Alice is not a natural-born stripper, according to Suzanne/Minx. Second, she needs help from the other women when someone hits on her. And third, there's one person who hit on her whom she didn't seem to need help with."

"That's the one that's most interesting to me," Lilly said. "I could have told you that Alice isn't a stripper by nature. But if she didn't need help fending off someone's advances, it suggests that, possibly, she knew the person."

"We also know that she went into work on Monday afternoon before she was supposed to meet Harry for their Valentine's Day dinner," Noley pointed out.

"Also interesting," Lilly said. "I don't know if the police have a timeline of when she disappeared, but it must have been within a few hours of meeting Harry."

"I almost hate to ask this, but you trust Harry, don't you?" Noley asked. Her voice held a note of hesitation.

"Absolutely," Lilly said firmly. "I trust him absolutely."

"Just checking," Noley said. "Have the police cleared him yet?"

"I don't know. They might have cleared him by now. All they had to do was gather some security camera footage to know he was where he said he was on Monday night."

"Okay, so let's assume Harry's in the clear. Where does that leave us?" Noley asked.

"Maybe I should talk to Bill to see if the police have looked at any security camera footage from Guy's Place."

"Remember not to let on that you've been there," Noley warned.

"I won't. But I may have to say something. Unless I go back to talk to some of the other dancers. Maybe they know that guy."

Noley groaned. "We have to go back?"

"*You* don't. Now that I know Suzanne and Tracy, I can handle it on my own," Lilly said.

"You're not going back there by yourself. Hey, that reminds me. Why did things go so badly when you and Hassan were here?"

"First of all, you saw how everyone was dressed in there. Like they got dressed in the dark. So when Hassan and I showed up dressed to the nines, people looked at us as if we had three heads. Each."

"So people stared at you. It's only because you were both so devastating."

"That wasn't the really awful part. The worst part was when they started insinuating that Hassan was a terrorist."

Noley's mouth dropped open. "You're kidding."

Lilly shook her head ruefully. "I was really afraid. I don't know that I've ever been in such a threatening situation before."

"What did Hassan do?"

"He steered me out of there fast. We haven't really talked about it too much, so I don't know if he's ever been in a situation like that before. He certainly hasn't since he bought the house in Juniper Junction, at least that I know of. But I mean before that, maybe in Minneapolis or somewhere else."

"Was he upset?" Noley asked.

"Yes. Very upset. He didn't want to talk about it on the way home and to tell you the truth, I didn't know if he was mad at me or mad at the situation or what."

"He had no reason to be mad at you."

Lilly shrugged. "I know, but I think he was embarrassed. You know how when you're embarrassed sometimes you get mad at the people who are there to witness it? I think maybe he felt some anger over that."

"I'm sure he's over it by now," Noley said.

"We went out to lunch together yesterday and talked about the situation a little bit. I think it's just taking him some time to deal with it in his own way."

"I can understand why he wouldn't want you going back there. Are you going to tell him you and I went?"

"Not if I don't have to. You know what really makes me mad? Guy, the *owner* of the place, instigated the whole thing. You'd think he would want all the business he could get in that dump, but he's too busy turning away people who don't look like everyone else in there." Lilly could feel her cheeks getting hot and she gripped the steering wheel tighter.

"Listen. You're getting all worked up over this. Just be glad you were able to get out of there before anything *really* bad happened." Noley made a scoffing noise. "I knew Guy was a bad apple the minute I laid eyes on him."

"He's no good, that's for sure."

"Let's talk about something different. Let's talk about what I'm going to order for lunch when you take me to the bistro as a thank you for coming along on this awful adventure. I think I'll have one of everything," Noley said. Lilly laughed out loud, grateful that her friend had changed the subject.

"You are entitled to everything you want for going with me tonight," Lilly said with a grin.

Noley changed the subject again. "So you're not going to mention this, um, outing to Bill?"

Lilly thought for a moment. "I think I'll wait and see if Tracy and Suzanne remember to tell the police about that man who was pestering Alice. If they don't say something, I will."

"How will you know if they've told the police anything?"

"I'll go back and talk to them in person. I would rather see them face-to-face than talk on the phone."

"Then you're really thinking of going back?" Noley groaned. "I hoped you were kidding earlier."

"I wasn't kidding. I do think I need to go back. But like I said, you don't have to go with me."

"I don't think you should go by yourself."

"Don't worry. I won't be in there for long and I think I can count on Suzanne and Tracy to help me."

"If you insist. Just make sure someone knows where you're going and when. Preferably me or, better yet, Bill."

Despite Lilly's insistence that she return to the bar alone, she was a little surprised that Noley was so willing to let her go back to Guy's Place by herself. Noley knew better than to suggest that Lilly alert Bill to her activities.

When she dropped Noley off at her house, Lilly thanked her again for going and providing moral support.

"You'd do it for me." Noley gave her friend a hug. "I just want you to be careful."

Lilly smiled and drove off, already planning her next trip to Guy's Place.

When she got home, an anxious Laurel was waiting for her. "Mom, I was worried about you at that strip club."

"Why? I was perfectly safe."

To her shock, Laurel started to cry.

"Laurel, what's wrong?" Lilly asked.

"It's just that between worrying about you doing God-knows-what, and Gran, the whole thing with Karley and Bella, and Nick dumping me, I feel like I'm losing my mind." Laurel sat down at the kitchen table and put her head on her arms.

Lilly pulled out the chair next to her and put her arm around Laurel's shoulders and stroked her hair.

"Listen to me, Laurel. You don't have to worry about me, ever. I would not do anything to jeopardize my own safety. As for Gran, we just have to wait and see what happens. But in the meantime, I think we should enjoy the time we spend with her and cherish the lucid moments she has. Nikki is a competent and caring woman and she is there to help her. I trust her completely to take good care of Gran."

She was at a loss for words when it came to Nick.

"Do you think I'll ever get over feeling this sad about Nick?" Laurel asked with a loud sniffle.

"Of course you will. It will take some time, but eventually you'll be able to look back on this time without hurting. Maybe you and Nick can even be friends someday."

Laurel scowled. "Don't count on it."

CHAPTER 25

"Tell you what," Lilly said. "Let's plan to do something fun tomorrow night, just us. How does that sound?" It came out of her mouth before she even had a chance to think about it, and suddenly she found herself a little nervous that Laurel might say no, that she might not want to do something with just her mom.

Laurel's face brightened a bit. "That sounds good. Maybe we can go see a movie."

Lilly beamed. "You pick the movie and tell me when to be ready. We can grab some dinner beforehand."

"Okay. Thanks, Mom."

Laurel went upstairs and Lilly sat at the kitchen table for a while longer, stroking Barney's ears. He had come to join the group when Laurel was crying. Poor dog. He probably didn't know who needed his furry love more—Laurel or Lilly.

Lilly sighed and let him out one last time, then headed upstairs to get ready for bed. Before snuggling in for the night, she called Hassan.

"Sorry I couldn't come into the store today," he said. "I was trying to talk to one of my suppliers in Afghanistan and it took half the day just to find him and get connected."

"That's okay. Are you feeling any better about everything?" Lilly asked quietly. She figured he knew what she was talking about.

She could practically see him shrugging. "I guess. I need to get a little distance from it, I think."

"You mean physical distance? Are you going back to Minnesota?"

"No. I mean time. I can't stay upset forever, so as time goes on I won't be as down about it."

"Anything I can do to help?"

"Just be yourself," he said. She could hear the smile in his voice. "Are you busy tomorrow night?"

"Actually, yes," she said. She lowered her voice, though she knew Laurel couldn't hear her from her own bedroom.

"Laurel had kind of a meltdown tonight and I promised her I would take her to dinner and a movie tomorrow night, just us girls."

"What caused the meltdown?" Hassan asked.

"She was upset because I—" Lilly stopped. She had almost spilled the beans about where she went earlier in the evening.

"Because you what?" Hassan asked.

Lilly had to think quickly for something that was technically true, even if it was a tiny bit misleading. "Because I've been wrapped up in trying to help Harry." Then she hurried on to list the other reasons for Laurel's funk, hoping Hassan would accept her explanation without comment. "Plus she's worried about my mother and, of course, the whole thing with Nick."

"She's got a lot on her mind, poor kid," Hassan said. "You're doing the right thing to spend some quality time with her. I'm just sorry I won't see you tomorrow night."

"We can do something together one of these days."

"Call me when you get home tomorrow night," Hassan said.

"I will probably spend most of tomorrow trying to get a hold of my guy in Afghanistan again. He's got some lapis lazuli he wants me to see. I may actually need to plan another trip over there one of these days."

Great. Alice is missing, my mother is failing, my daughter is distraught, and my boyfriend wants to wander off to a war zone. What else could possibly go wrong?

"You still there?" Hassan asked.

"Yes. Just thinking. Is it safe for you to go over there?"

"I have a team of people I trust to get me in and out of tight spaces if need be," he assured her. "And it's not a definite that I'm going. If I can get a good look at the lapis without leaving American soil, I won't go."

"Okay." Lilly yawned.

"I can hear how tired you are. Get some sleep and I'll talk to you tomorrow night. I love you, Lilly."

"I love you, too."

Lilly hung up and tried to sleep, but sleep wouldn't come.

All this worrying is wearing me out.

* * *

Lilly was on her way to work early the next morning when her cell phone rang.

"Hello?"

"Lilly, it's Nikki."

Lilly felt her chest tighten. "What's wrong?" She pulled the car over to the side of the street so she could talk to Nikki and focus.

"Your mom's gone."

The cold chill that gripped Lilly's throat caused her to gasp for breath.

"Lilly, you all right?" Nikki asked.

Lilly nodded tightly as if Nikki could see her. "I'm okay. Where are you?"

"At your mom's house. I just got here. She likes to make coffee herself first thing in the morning. It gives her a sense of independence."

The story was taking too long. *Get to the point, Nikki!* Lilly wanted to scream. But she kept her mouth shut and let Nikki talk.

"Anyway, when I got here all the lights were off and I didn't smell coffee, so I figured she had slept in. I went upstairs to her bedroom to wake her and she wasn't there."

"Had the bed been slept in?" Lilly asked. She realized she was holding the phone in a vise grip and tried to relax her fingers.

"Yes. She was sound asleep when I left her last night."

"Do you know how she got out?"

"I think so. The front door was unlocked when I came in, so somehow she must have found the key and let herself out."

"The alarm wasn't on?" Lilly asked. She hadn't meant for her tone to sound accusatory, but that's how it came out.

"No. It malfunctioned yesterday and someone from the alarm company is coming today to take a look at it. When it went off yesterday, it scared your mother so much she started to cry. I've never seen her so upset. I decided it would be best not to turn it on last night in case it went off in the middle of the night. And here we were worrying that it might scare her into leaving. It more likely would have scared her into staying."

"I would have done the same thing," Lilly said, as much as she hated to admit it. "Okay. Next step. Have you called Bill yet?"

"No. I called you first."

"I'm on my way to the house right now. I'll call Bill on the way and have him meet us. Are there any footprints in the snow out front?"

"No. If she left footprints behind, the wind has blown new snow over them by now," Nikki said.

"I'll keep an eye out for her on my way over. There's no telling how long she's been gone."

Lilly did a U-turn in the street and sped toward her mother's house. On the way she called Bill, told him what had happened, and asked him to meet her at Bev's house. Then she called Harry and asked him to open the store for her and keep an eye on things until she could get there.

She drove slowly, scanning the sidewalks, yards, and porches for any sign of her mother. Surely if anyone had seen her wandering around, they would have called the police. That gave her cause for more alarm. Where could she be if no one had seen her?

She slowed the car even more as she approached her mom's block, hoping she would catch a glimpse of Bev. But by the time she made it to Bev's house, she hadn't seen a single soul outside. It was still early in the morning, and people were probably getting ready for work, not paying attention to an old lady who might be walking the streets by herself. And who knew what she was wearing? Lilly hoped she had been thinking clearly enough to put on a coat and gloves.

She pulled up to the curb in front of Bev's house and ran up the front steps. Nikki had obviously been watching for her and she opened the door to let her in as soon as Lilly reached the top step.

"Any word?" Lilly asked. Nikki shook her head.

"Bill's on his way. I didn't see any sign her on the way over here." Lilly pulled off her coat and paced the living room. "Nikki, can you think of anything she may have said yesterday about wanting to go somewhere?"

Nikki thought for a moment. "Not that I recall."

"Do you remember anything you talked about yesterday? I'm just thinking maybe something jogged her memory."

Nikki snapped her fingers. "Your mom wanted to look through old photo albums again yesterday. Maybe she saw a place she remembers and went there."

"That's a good place to start," Lilly said grimly.

The front door opened and Bill, in full uniform, stood in the doorway.

"Fill me in," he ordered.

*L*illy told him about the alarm malfunction and explained that Nikki had gone to look for the photo albums she and their mother had perused the day before.

"I've got every patrol cop looking for her," Bill said. "Between them and us, we ought to be able to find her."

"I just hope she's dressed warmly," Lilly said. "Nikki," she called. "Did you happen to notice if Mom's winter coat is missing?"

Nikki came into the living room bearing an armload of photo albums. Lilly recognized some of them from her own childhood, so she knew they were decades old. "No, I didn't think to do that. I'll do it now." She placed the albums on the coffee table and hurried to the front hall closet, where Bev kept her outerwear.

"The coat's missing," she called from the hall.

"Thank God," Lilly breathed. "Are her gloves gone, too?"

"Yes," Nikki said, coming back into the living room. "So that's one good thing. She's warm."

"Let's see what you two looked at yesterday," Bill said. He sat down on the sofa in front of the coffee table and Lilly sat down next to him. Nikki pulled a chair over to the opposite side of the table and ran her fingers down the spines of the albums.

"I think we started with this one." She checked the first page of photos. "Yes, because we went in chronological order." The album began with photos taken of Bev and a handsome young man with dimples and dark brown hair. It was Bill and Lilly's father, Daniel.

As much as Lilly would have loved to take her time browsing through the photos, she needed to concentrate on the backgrounds—not the people smiling for the camera. They were looking for places nearby—places Bev might have suddenly decided she wanted to visit.

The first several pages of photos had been taken in Mountain Vista, the town where Bev and Daniel had both grown up. It wasn't that far away, but it wasn't exactly right up the road, either. It was about thirty miles away. Lilly grabbed a pen and paper and began scribbling down the names of the places they could identify in the photos' backgrounds. By the end of the first album they had found the first wedding photos of Bev and Daniel and they had a short list of places to check. Most of the places were in Mountain Vista.

They put the first album aside and began going through the second one.

Bill looked at his watch. "We have to move this along. She must be frozen out there, even with a coat and gloves."

Bill flipped through the pages and Lilly scribbled faster. As soon as they got to the photos taken after Bev and Daniel had moved to Juniper Junction, Bill told Lilly to hold on. He took out his phone and dialed a number. As they turned pages and noted different places around town where Bev and Daniel had been, Bill barked names into the phone.

"What are you doing?" Lilly asked in a whisper.

"Dispatch is taking down the names I give them so they can send officers to specific places to look for Mom."

Not for the first time, Lilly was thankful her brother was on the police force.

Before long they came to the pages showing Bill as a newborn. Lilly smiled when she saw his scrunched-up, screaming face, thinking how much Noley would love to see these photos.

But that would have to wait. They hurried through those photos and soon came to the ones of Lilly as an infant, looking remarkably like her big brother.

In the fourth album, they came to a stretch of several pages of photos of the small family taken at a park in Juniper Junction.

"Remember that park?" Lilly asked, pointing to a photo of her and Bill on a swing set. A long, shiny metal slide gleamed in the background. "I haven't been there since Laurel was a baby."

Bill nodded. "That playground is still there. The play equipment has changed, though."

"Oh, my gosh!" Nikki exclaimed. Bill and Lilly stared at her.

"What?" they asked in unison.

"Your mom talked about that park while we were looking at these pictures. She said you kids had always loved it there. She said she wondered what it looked like now."

Lilly looked at Bill. "I'll bet that's where she went."

Bill had put Dispatch on hold while they looked through more photos, but he spoke into the phone again, tersely stating the name of the park.

"Should we go over there?" Lilly asked him.

Bill ended his call and thought for a minute. "Dispatch said they had someone in the vicinity of the park, so it won't be long before we know something. Let's keep making the list of places in case we're wrong."

They continued looking through the albums and Lilly wrote

down the names of places they recognized. She knew, though, that the best chance of finding Bev was in that small park.

And she was right. About ten minutes after Bill had talked to Dispatch, his phone squawked with the five most wonderful words Lilly had ever heard.

"We've got her. She's okay."

CHAPTER 27

*L*illy let out a breath as though she had been holding it for the last hour. She slumped back into the sofa as Bill did the same thing. Nikki closed her eyes and her lips moved ever so slightly.

"That was a close one," Bill said.

"We can't let this happen again," Lilly said.

Nikki piped up. "Well, the person from the alarm company should be here sometime soon. Once the alarm is fixed, I'll go back to arming it every night."

Lilly glanced at Bill. "Do you think the alarm should be on all the time? Even when they're home and it's daylight?"

Bill took a moment before answering. "Probably. What if Nikki just has to run to the bathroom or something? We can't risk Mom taking that opportunity to run off."

"She wouldn't be able to get very far," Nikki pointed out.

"That's true. But we also don't want her to feel like she's a prisoner in her own house," Lilly said.

"Why don't you ask your mom and see what she has to say about it?" Nikki suggested.

Lilly looked at Bill, her eyebrows raised.

"Okay, we can ask her," he said. Lilly nodded her agreement.

The small group chatted for several minutes until they heard a heavy step outside the front door. Bill sprang to his feet. "There she is." He opened the door.

Next to the towering police officer, Bev looked tiny. She bustled into the house and turned to invite her rescuer inside.

"Thank you, ma'am, but I should be on my way," he said. Bill stepped onto the front porch while Bev hung up her coat and peeled off her gloves.

"I'm chilly," she said, rubbing her hands together. She looked from Lilly to Nikki and back again. "What's wrong?" She went through the living room and into the kitchen, where she plugged in the coffee maker. Lilly and Nikki followed her.

"Mom, what happened to you?"

"What do you mean?" Bev asked. Her eyes were wide and innocent.

Lilly tried to keep the exasperation out of her voice. "I mean, why did you leave? Where did you go? How come you didn't tell Nikki where you were going?"

"What are you talking about?" Bev asked. "I told your father I was going to the park. You should have just asked him." She shook her head as if Lilly were simple.

Lilly lifted up her hands and let them drop down at her sides again as she shrugged and gave Nikki a frustrated glance. *What do I say to that kind of logic?* she wondered.

Nikki went to the refrigerator and opened the door, scanning the contents. She took a container of yogurt and set it on the table. "Bev, why don't you come over here and have a yogurt? I'll pour the coffee when it's ready."

"All right, dear." Bev sat down obediently and took the spoon Nikki offered her. Lilly sat down across from her mother.

"Mom, you need to tell Nikki when you want to go somewhere."

"Why? Your father is perfectly capable of giving her a message."

Lilly had to think quickly to come up with a response. "To be honest," she said in a conspiratorial tone, "Dad doesn't always have the greatest memory. When you left, no one could find you and no one knew where you had gone."

"I'll have to have a talk with your father. He should have written it down when I said where I was going."

"Mom, Bill and I worry about you when you're outdoors alone."

"You're a silly Lilly and Billy," her mother said with a tinkling laugh. Lilly fought the urge to retch. "Of course nothing's going to happen to me outside."

"I'm sure you're right, but would you do us a favor? Please? Will you tell Nikki when you want to go somewhere?" Lilly asked.

"That way, if Lilly or Bill calls or stops by and wants to know where you are, I can tell them," Nikki added. She turned and winked at Lilly. Lilly caught the meaning—of course Nikki had no intention of letting Bev go wandering around outside by herself.

Just then Bill walked into the warm kitchen. "Mom," he began. "The officer who brought you home—"

"He was a very sweet young man," Bev said with a benign smile. "It was kind of him to offer me a ride home."

"Mom, do you remember leaving the house earlier?" Bill asked. His voice sounded stern.

"Billy, don't use that tone of voice with me." Bev pointed at him. "I am your mother."

"I'm sorry," he said in a softer tone. "Do you remember what time it was that you left?"

"Of course I do. It was two-thirty."

"Two-thirty in the morning." Bill repeated the time.

"No, dear, it was afternoon."

"No, Mom, it was two-thirty in the morning."

"It was?" Bev's face wore a worried look for the first time since coming home. "Why did your father let me go out at that hour?"

*B*ill looked to Lilly for an explanation.

"She told Dad," Lilly said with a shrug.

Bill sighed. "Mom, you can't do that again." He gestured toward Lilly. "Lilly and I think that once the alarm is repaired, it should be on all the time to make sure you don't leave without telling Nikki. What do you think? Does that sound all right to you?"

Bev looked from her son to her daughter to Nikki. "I told your father I was leaving," she said in a quiet voice.

"I know, Mom, but it's Nikki who needs to know where you are all the time," Bill said. "She doesn't want to get in trouble for not knowing where you are."

Bev looked at Nikki with concern. "Oh, Nikki dear, I'm so sorry. I hope you didn't get in trouble because of me."

Nikki reached out and patted Bev's hand. "Don't worry, Bev. It turned out okay this time. But you do need to remember to tell me if you want to go somewhere. It's my job to know or to go with you."

"Okay." Bev sat staring at her yogurt like a chastised child. "I just wanted to go to the park. I have such happy memories of that place." One fat tear rolled down her cheek and Lilly had to turn away so Bev couldn't see the tears forming in her own eyes. In her peripheral vision she noticed Bill swallowing hard.

Only Nikki seemed composed, and Lilly was grateful for her steady response to Bev.

"That's great, Bev. Isn't it nice to have such happy memories? Next time you go I'd love to go with you. I wouldn't bother you. I'd just sit while you enjoy yourself. But, remember, it's my job to make sure you're safe."

Bev wiped her cheek and looked around at her small audience. "All right. You can come with me. Do you want to go this afternoon?"

"I would love that, Bev. Let's get you warmed up. I think you might want to rest before we go anywhere, too. You didn't get much sleep last night."

"I am rather tired," Bev admitted.

"What about the alarm?" Lilly asked with a cringe. She hated to bring up the subject again, but it hadn't been settled.

Nikki looked at Bev. "What do you think?" she asked. "I know *I* would feel better with the alarm on. Would you?"

"I think so, yes," Bev said.

"Good. Once the alarm is repaired today, we'll leave it on all the time."

Lilly and Bill stood up to leave. As Lilly was pulling her coat on, she turned to Nikki, who had accompanied them into the foyer. "Thanks for everything, Nikki. Crisis averted. I don't know what we'd do without you."

Bill nodded. "We appreciate all you do for Mom."

"This isn't my first rodeo," she said. "I've had experience with this. I just want to keep your mom safe."

Lilly and Bill left with a promise to visit the following day.

The morning was half over by the time Lilly got to work, and she was glad to see Harry waiting on customers in his characteristic folksy manner. He smiled, told stories, and almost always made a sale. And better still, waiting on people gave him something to think about besides Alice.

When the customers left with their purchases, Harry leaned over the glass counter. "I'm exhausted," he said. "It's hard to act happy when I'm not."

"It's good for you, though," Lilly said. "You worked your magic with those people." She smiled at him.

"Lilly, do you think they'll ever find her?" Clearly, Alice was never far from his mind, no matter what else he was doing.

Lilly walked over to him and put her hands on his shoulders. She looked straight into his eyes. "Listen to me. Alice is going to turn up, I just know it. I feel it. Do you hear me?"

Harry nodded and gave her a wan smile. "I wish I had your confidence."

"I have enough for both of us."

Lilly insisted that Harry wait on the rest of the customers who came in that day. She knew he was tired, but she also knew he needed to stay busy or he would lose his mind.

Lilly sped home after work that night so she would have time to change her clothes before she and Laurel went out. Laurel was waiting for her when she arrived.

"Hurry, Mom, the movie starts in an hour."

Lilly changed into jeans and a sweatshirt, then she and Laurel headed to a diner just outside town. It wasn't far from the movie theater. They ordered quickly, wolfed down dinner, and got to the theater just before the lights dimmed.

A small crowd sat in the theater, and they scanned the seats quickly to decide on the best place to sit. They chose two seats about a third of the way back in the theater. Luckily the row was empty, so they didn't have to push by people to get to the middle. Lilly held the popcorn while Laurel got comfortable, then she handed it off so she could sit. As she did, she noticed a couple sitting three rows ahead of them. The woman had her head on the man's shoulder, but it was the man who caught Lilly's attention. She studied him for a moment from the back, then he turned his face just a little. She could see his profile.

It was Harry.

Lilly inhaled sharply.

"Mom, what's wrong?" Laurel asked in a loud whisper.

Lilly glanced around quickly to see if anyone else had heard her gasp. She shook her head at Laurel and put a finger over her lips. Laurel just stared at her.

When the theater was in darkness and the previews started, Lilly leaned over toward Laurel, who also leaned closer. Lilly whispered, "That's Harry up there with a woman, but I don't know who the woman is."

Laurel's eyes widened and she craned her neck to see who could be down there. Even if she could have seen the woman in the darkness, it didn't matter. Laurel barely knew Harry—she wasn't likely to know the woman sitting with him.

Lilly didn't pay much attention to the movie. Her thoughts were consumed with wondering who the woman was and why Harry was out with her. It couldn't be a female relative; no female relative would act like that.

Then she began to wonder how she could leave the theater gracefully. Should she stay to see who the woman was, then pretend she hadn't realized Harry was there? Should she try to make her escape before they stood up to leave?

As much as she wanted to know the identity of the woman, Lilly decided to leave as quickly as possible once the movie ended. Something told her that she should give this some thought before letting Harry know she had seen him with a woman who clearly wasn't Alice.

Lilly couldn't wait for the movie to end. She would have to rent it sometime and watch it again since she missed most of it. She fidgeted and fretted until she knew the denouement was imminent, then she started gathering her purse and coat.

"What are you doing?" Laurel whispered. "The movie's not over."

"It's almost over," Lilly said. "I want to get out of here fast, so be ready the second the credits start to roll."

"But I love to watch the credits," Laurel whined in a low voice. "Sometimes the producer puts something cool at the very end."

"Not this time, Laurel. I don't want Harry to see me."

"You're acting like a teenager," Laurel hissed.

Lilly shot Laurel a glare that Laurel probably couldn't see in the darkened theater, but Laurel seemed to sense Lilly's anxiety.

"You can go. I'll stay," she told Lilly.

"Fine." Lilly was ready to bolt.

The moment the screen went dark and the music changed, Lilly knew it was time for the credits to start rolling. She grabbed her belongings and stepped over Laurel's knees, tripping in the process and falling face-first into the seat next to Laurel. A woman two rows behind them gasped and asked loudly, "Are you all right?"

Immediately every eye in the theater turned to watch Lilly hoist herself up to a standing position next to Laurel. By this time the lights were coming up so people could make their way out of the theater if they didn't want to stay for the credits. Laurel looked up at her mother and rolled her eyes.

"Mom, this is so embarrassing."

"All you had to do was move your knees and I wouldn't have tripped," Lilly snarled back.

"Lilly?"

It was Harry. Lilly groaned and turned around. He was pulling on his coat, and Mary Louise stood next to him, a slight grin on her face.

"Hi, Harry," Lilly said.

"I didn't know you were here."

"Yes, well...." She hadn't thought of what she might say to

him if he saw her—all her attention had been focused on getting out of the theater first.

"What did you think of the movie?" he asked.

"It was good," Lilly answered blandly. She looked pointedly at Mary Louise.

"Oh, you remember Mary Louise," Harry said, giving a half-smile and gesturing toward his companion. She looked up at him with a smile that made Lilly's insides churn. *Those brown doe-eyes are really too much*, Lilly thought.

"Of course. Hello, Mary Louise." Lilly turned her attention back to Harry. "Blowing off some steam from the stress of looking for Alice?"

CHAPTER 29

*L*aurel tugged at the back of Lilly's coat, clearly wanting the conversation to head in a different direction.

Harry laughed nervously. "Yeah. You know, it's just been so stressful. We thought it might be a good idea to get out for a while and take our minds off the situation."

"I see. Seems like that would be hard to do," Lilly replied, raising her eyebrows just a touch. Mary Louise smirked.

"It is, believe me." Harry fidgeted with the zipper on his coat, and his eyes darted from Lilly to the exit and back again.

"Well, come on, Laurel," she said. "Time to head out."

"Can't I just watch the rest of the credits?" Laurel pleaded.

"Sometimes there are cool things at the end of the credits," Harry pointed out.

"I know," Laurel said. She craned her neck to see around Lilly.

What was the use of leaving now? Lilly figured she might as well wait for Laurel to watch the credits. She hadn't escaped the theater unnoticed, so there wasn't much point in trying to run out now. Besides, Harry and Mary Louise were making their way down their row of seats and toward the exit, and Lilly wanted to avoid any further conversation with them. Harry lifted his hand in a half-hearted wave and Lilly just glared at him.

"Just wait until I talk to him in the morning," she said through clenched teeth.

Laurel didn't say anything until the credits had ended and nothing funny or interesting happened. "We stayed for nothing," she grumbled. *Oh, not for nothing,* Lilly thought. *I made a fool of myself tripping over you and Harry found out I was here.*

"Are you mad at Harry?" Laurel asked as they walked to the car.

"Yes."

"What was he doing that was so wrong?" Laurel asked.

Lilly thought that Laurel, of all people, should have known why she was mad—not only was Harry at the movies while Alice was still missing, but he was there with another woman. After what Laurel was going through with Nick, Lilly thought she would understand.

"I don't think he should have taken Mary Louise to the movies. He's practically engaged to someone else. Someone who happens to be missing. Not only is it just plain wrong, but it looks bad to anyone who might see them out."

"But it could be totally innocent," Laurel said. "Like two friends just going to the movies."

"Maybe so, but what if one of the police officers investigating Alice's disappearance happened to be here tonight? It might not look so innocent."

Laurel nodded slowly. "I guess you're right. In that case, Harry needs to be more careful."

"He's going to have some explaining to do tomorrow morning," Lilly said aloud to herself.

"What?"

"Nothing. I'm sorry. I didn't mean to let this ruin our girls' night out."

"It's not ruined," Laurel said. "I had fun. Didn't you?"

Lilly glanced over at her daughter, who suddenly looked very young. Her heart did a flip-flop as images of Laurel as a little girl flitted through her memory like still photos on an old movie projector.

"I did have fun," she said with a wistful smile. "We should do this more often."

When they got home Laurel thanked her mom for taking her out and hugged her. Lilly couldn't hold back the tears.

"Mom, what's wrong?" Laurel's brows furrowed.

"It's just been a long day, that's all," Lilly said. "A girls' night out was exactly what I needed. Thank you." Laurel hugged her again and went upstairs. Lilly sniffled for a little longer, then called Hassan.

"How was your day?" she asked.

He sighed. "Long."

"So was mine. What happened?"

"I finally got in touch with my lapis supplier in Afghanistan and he thinks I should start planning a trip."

A cold feeling snaked its way through Lilly's stomach and chest. He had told her about other trips to Afghanistan he had taken. It was a dangerous place, made more so if the wrong people figured out what he was there for and that he carried a lot of money with him on such trips.

"So are you going?" she asked in a hesitant voice.

"I don't think I have a choice."

She groaned. "That is not the news I wanted to hear tonight."

"Believe me, it's not the news I wanted to share tonight. But I've given it a lot of thought and I think he's right. I do need to go over there to see the mines for myself and talk to the men in person."

"It's so dangerous, though."

"I won't go right away. It's still winter over there and it's almost impossible to travel around in the mountainous areas where I need to go. I'll have to wait until spring."

"Doesn't the fighting always break out in spring?" Lilly asked.

"Usually, yes." He was drawing out his words, as if he was trying to figure out what to say without alarming her. "But I know people who will help me stay away from it. They've got ears on the ground and in the high levels of government. I can trust what they tell me. I've been working with them for a long time."

"So you'll be leaving in the spring?" She was having a hard time keeping the disappointment out of her voice. She wanted to be excited for him, but at the moment all she could think about was how much she would worry and how much she would miss him. It wouldn't be like the times he returned to Minnesota.

"To Afghanistan, yes, probably. But I'll be going to Washington sooner than that. In a couple days, in fact. There are people there I need to speak to before I can start planning the trip to Afghanistan."

"What people?"

"People at the Afghanistan and Pakistan embassies. I'll also meet with officials in the US State Department to talk about heading overseas to look for gems. I've done all of this before, so it's no big deal."

"Well, I wish you were staying in Juniper Junction where I know you'll be safe, but I know you can't always be here." It was the best she could do. Her mind was reeling with the thought of losing Hassan to tribal fighting on the other side of the globe.

"I'll come back, don't worry. And I'll only be in Washington for a few days. We'll have lots of time together before I go overseas," he assured her.

She told him about seeing Harry and Mary Louise at the movie theater. He was concerned for the same reasons she had been: first, it seemed disloyal to Alice; and second, how would it look to the authorities if they saw Harry and Mary Louise out together?

"You can be sure I'll be talking to Harry about that first thing in the morning," Lilly said.

Hassan chuckled. "Poor Harry."

Lilly finally smiled. Poor Harry, indeed.

She didn't have the energy to tell Hassan about the episode with her mother. Had it only happened that morning? When he told her he wanted to take her out to lunch the next day, she knew she would be in a better frame of mind to discuss her mom then.

They said goodnight and Lilly was asleep almost before her head hit the pillow. It had been a long day.

The next morning she awoke refreshed and with a single-minded purpose: to get Harry to explain what the heck he had been thinking the night before. She got ready for work with ruthless efficiency, planning to arrive before Harry so she could put him on his back foot before he even knew what was happening.

She realized when she got to work that she had white-knuckled the drive over, and she forced herself to relax. She took several deep breaths and wiggled her fingers to get the blood flowing again. She made the trip from the vault to the display cases several times, readying for her confrontation with Harry.

She was so focused on rehearsing her speech to him that she didn't even notice him standing at the back of the store as she made another trip to the display cases out front. When she whirled around to get the next batch of gems from the vault, she gasped and put a hand to her chest.

"Harry, you startled me!"

"Boss, before you start in on me, I want to explain last night." Harry held up his hands in a gesture of supplication. His eyes carried heavy gray bags and he looked like he had spent the night in someone's car.

Lilly stopped in her tracks. She hadn't expected him to make the first move and it took away some of the exhilaration she had looked forward to when she gave him her scolding.

"So explain."

CHAPTER 30

"*You* know Mary Louise has been taking turns with Mack, and sometimes Wayne, staying over at my house to keep me from losing my mind."

"Yes." Lilly crossed her arms in front of her chest.

"And you know that I think Mary Louise has a crush on me."

"You told me that, yes."

"It was her turn to stay last night and she started in on me as soon as I got home from work. She kept saying, 'Let's go to the movies.' 'I'm bored. Can't we go see a movie?' Eventually I couldn't take her nagging any longer and I agreed."

"Interesting," Lilly commented. "I clearly saw her head on your shoulder last night. That's not something platonic friends do at the movies."

Harry's shoulders slumped. "I know, believe me. I was trying to inch away from her, but there was only so far I could go in that theater seat."

"Did it occur to you to ask her to stop?" Lilly asked. She set her lips in a thin line.

Harry nodded. "Yeah, but I didn't want to have a scene in the middle of the theater. I figured I would talk to her about it on the way back to my house."

"And did you?" Lilly asked.

"Yeah. It was ugly, Lilly. She cried and carried on long after we got to my house. She was mad, too. She said she knows things about Alice that are even worse than being a stripper in secret and that she is going to wait for the right moment to tell me. Then she stormed out and went to stay at her own house."

"It sounds like that's not such a bad thing."

"It's not. I have no idea what to do in a situation like that. She was just so *forward*. Alice would never do anything like that."

"Harry, just out of curiosity, how well does Mary Louise know Alice?"

"I would say they're acquaintances. They know each other through me, even though they both go to the community college. I have been friends with Mary Louise for a long time, and I introduced them after Alice and I started dating last year."

Lilly grimaced. "I'm a little reluctant to mention this, Harry, but do you think it's possible that Mary Louise knows something about Alice's disappearance?"

Harry shook his head. "I really don't think so. Mary Louise can be annoying, but I don't think she's evil."

"I'm not saying she's responsible for Alice's disappearance. I'm just wondering if maybe she knows where Alice went and she's not telling."

"The police have talked to her and she swears she doesn't know anything."

"She wouldn't be the first person to lie to the police."

Harry rubbed his chin, his eyes worried. "Do you think it's possible?"

"I don't know. I'm just throwing it out there. I don't know whom to trust, and after seeing the way Mary Louise fawns over you, I'm not sure she can be trusted. I have to wonder about her, especially after hearing how upset she was when you talked to her in the car last night. She's got it pretty bad for you."

Harry blushed. It didn't take much to embarrass the man.

"What should we do?" he asked.

"There's not much we can do, but I think we—you—need to keep an eye on her. Do you think she'll come back to your house to stay overnight?"

"I don't know. She was pretty mad."

"Do any of your other friends know about this?" Lilly asked. "How about Mack or Stu?"

"Stu knows Mary Louise has a crush on me, but he doesn't know Mary Louise as well as I do. They only know each other from school. I haven't told him about last night. Mack met her for the first time the night you were at my house."

"And what was the other guy's name? William?"

"Wayne. He's known Mary Louise for a long time, too, and he doesn't like her."

I think I can see why, Lilly thought.

"To tell you the truth, it was nice to be alone in the house after Mary Louise left," Harry said.

"You haven't had much time alone since Alice disappeared, have you?" Lilly asked. "Why don't you tell everyone that you're ready to stay by yourself?"

"I could do that. But I don't want them to feel like I don't appreciate what they're doing."

"Harry, you need to stop worrying about other people's feelings and start thinking about *you* for once. You and Alice should be your only priorities right now."

He sighed. "I know. I'll talk to them."

Lilly smiled. She had known Harry would have difficulty asking his friends to stop spending the night at his house. Not because he didn't want to be alone, but because he wanted them to know how much he appreciated them.

Alice was a lucky woman to snag Harry.

* * *

Hassan came into the store a few hours later and Lilly left Harry in charge so she could go out for lunch with Hassan.

"You're spoiling me," she said as they sat down in a small restaurant near the town square.

"You deserve it," he said with a smile, covering her hand with his.

"Anything new this morning?" she asked.

"I've made some phone calls and I'm waiting to hear back from several people to make appointments to see them. As soon as I start getting appointments, I'll make my travel plans."

"What's the timeline?" Lilly asked.

"I'll go to Washington as soon as possible."

Lilly sighed. "I wish I could go with you."

"Do you think there's any way you can?" he asked, his eyes lighting up. "We could spend an extra night and see some of the sights."

Lilly shook her head. "I've got too much going on here. Between my mother trying to escape from her house and Alice's disappearance, I don't think I should go anywhere right now."

"What happened to your mother?"

Lilly remembered she hadn't told Hassan about her mother's excursion to the park by herself in the middle of the night. She explained the situation while Hassan's face grew more concerned.

"Are you and Bill going to hire someone to stay overnight with her?" he asked.

"Not yet. We're not ready to deprive her of all her privacy and independence. Nikki is going to keep the alarm on all the time, even when they're in the house, so she knows if Mom tries to leave. We're hoping that solution works."

"I hope so, too. And there's been no word on Alice?"

"No." Lilly toyed with her napkin, her thoughts grim. "I wish I could do more to help find her."

"You're letting the police deal with Alice's disappearance, right?" Hassan asked. He gave her a suspicious look.

"Of course." She knew he would assume she was leaving the *entire* investigation to the police, and she didn't say otherwise. "I just want to be in Juniper Junction in case Harry needs help. And this is not a good time to leave him in charge of the store. Plus—" She stopped. She had almost mentioned her planned solo excursion to Guy's Place, and she figured that would not go over well with Hassan.

"Plus what?" he asked.

She thought fast. "Plus I want to make sure Laurel is following my orders and not going anywhere."

He nodded. "I can understand that."

The server came by to take their orders and Lilly sat back with an inward sigh of relief. She was ready to change the subject.

"Why do you need to meet with people from the embassies before you go to Afghanistan?"

"When I visit a country to collect gems, I always take along letters from that country's ambassador to the United States that explain why I'm there. That way, if there are any questions, I can just whip out the letter instead of waiting for several days for someone to get in touch with the embassy to make sure I am who I say I am."

"Are there people who don't believe what you tell them?"

"Plenty of people. And when I'm in the Middle East or Southeast Asia, where there is almost always fighting, it helps to have the letter because it explains that I'm not there to take sides. I just want to buy my gems and get back home. Not everyone who looks at the letters can read, but there's almost always someone around who can read it to them."

"And what about all the money you'll be carrying?" This

issue worried Lilly, since she knew banditry was common in the mountainous regions of Southeast Asia.

"I keep the money in a bank in the capital city of wherever I go, then I transfer it to accounts of the gem miners and sellers whenever I'm in the capital. They trust me, so that arrangement works. I don't carry much on me. That's not how it used to be, though. While I was working to earn the trust of the people I deal with, I had to carry huge sums of cash with me to pay for the gems on the spot. It's easier and less dangerous now."

Lilly smiled. "I still worry."

"I know. So does my family, even though my father spent decades doing the very same thing. It's natural. I worry sometimes, too."

"Let's talk about something else before I'm too worried to eat lunch." Lilly tried to smile, but it turned into more of a smirk.

Hassan laughed. "All right. I don't want you to worry."

Their meals arrived and Lilly told him all about talking to Harry about Mary Louise.

"He talked to her about putting her head on his shoulder in the theater. She was apparently pretty upset when he asked her to stop. What do you make of it?" she asked.

"I definitely think Mary Louise is taking advantage of a terrible situation, but I don't know if there's any more to it than that."

"I don't either," Lilly agreed. "But I don't think it should be overlooked. There's always a possibility that she knows more than she's saying. I just think Harry needs to be careful around her."

"If nothing else, he needs to rethink his friendship with a woman who would connive like that to get closer to him."

Lilly was liking Mary Louise less and less.

$\mathcal{L}$illy avoided lecturing Harry again that afternoon, choosing instead to focus on telling him a little about Hassan's upcoming trip. Since Harry's Uncle Robert, Lilly's mentor, had taught Harry all about the jewelry business, he was interested in learning more about the supply end of the business and where the gems came from.

"It would be so cool to go on a trip like that," he enthused.

"I'm not so sure. Afghanistan can be a dangerous place," Lilly said. That got her thinking all over again of how worried she would be while Hassan was gone and she regretted her choice of conversation topics.

"Let's talk about something else," she suggested. But there seemed to be no safe topic, so they fell silent as the afternoon wore on.

Few customers came in that day, so they were able to lock the front door right at closing time and get the displays put into the vault quickly. Lilly was grateful for it, since she wanted to stop at her mother's house to check on things before going home for the night.

When she arrived, she knocked on the door and Nikki

peered through the curtain on the front door to see who it was. Seeing Lilly standing on the porch, she disarmed the security system and opened the door.

"How is everything today?" Lilly asked.

"Great," Nikki said. Then she lowered her voice. "She's been spending more and more time in her past, in her memories, but they're happy memories, so that's not a bad thing."

Lilly nodded, not quite sure what to expect when she saw Bev. And when she walked into the living room, she was shocked to see Bev wearing a 1960s-style A-line dress in a hideous tangerine hue and low-heeled patent leather loafers, sitting in her armchair and watching television.

"Hi, Mom. I love your dress!"

"This old thing?" Bev asked with a smile, making a dismissive gesture with her hand. "I've had it for years."

Lilly gave Nikki a questioning look. "She found it in an old trunk," Nikki explained. "She asked me to go up in the attic and bring it down. It's full of old clothes. It's like playing dress-up," she added with a smile.

"How fun!"

"Your father should be home from work any minute," Bev said. "Then we'll have dinner."

"Sounds good, Mom," Lilly said. She glanced at Nikki, who smiled at her and nodded.

Lilly sat down and watched television with her mom and Nikki for a little while. Bev smoothed the skirt of her dress several times and looked down at her feet, rotating her ankles so she could see her shoes from different angles. It was simultaneously heartwarming and heartbreaking.

Lilly looked down at her lap. She missed the old Bev, the bustling mother who was organized, keen-minded, and always ready for anything. This new Bev, the one with the slightly vacant look in her eyes, the one who was dressed up in old clothes, patiently waiting for her long-dead husband to get home from work, scared Lilly a little bit.

She knew she needed to concentrate on something else or she would be overcome with sadness and fear of the future.

"Mom, I thought I'd bring Laurel over tomorrow evening to visit. How would that be?" she asked.

"I would love to see Laurel. Tighe called just—oh, Nikki, when did Tighe call?"

"Yesterday."

Bev continued. "Oh, yes. Tighe called yesterday and he is studying hard. I'm so proud of him."

"When he comes home for spring break, I know he'll be happy to see you," Lilly said.

Bev smiled. "I'll be very happy to see him, too." She sighed deeply. "Nikki, I think I would like to go to bed now."

"Now?" Nikki asked. "You haven't even had dinner yet."

"I know, dear, but I'm not hungry." The vacant look was still there in Bev's eyes. Lilly wondered what was going through her mind.

"All right, you can go to bed anytime you'd like," Nikki said. Bev pushed herself out of her armchair. Lilly noticed Nikki sitting forward on the sofa, her hands ready to assist Bev if needed. Nikki was watching Bev with concern.

When Bev had left the room, Lilly turned to Nikki. "Is she all right? I noticed the way you were watching her."

Nikki held up a finger to Lilly, indicating that she would be right back. She stood at the bottom of the stairs, watching Bev make her way upstairs to her bedroom.

Nikki returned and sat down next to Lilly. "I didn't want to say anything while Bev could hear me, but I've noticed in the past day or two that she's been a little unsteady on her feet."

"Has she fallen?"

"No, she hasn't. But she's been wobbling a little bit." Nikki sat back against the sofa cushions. "Unfortunately, it's all part of the progression of her illness."

"So we should expect it to get worse?" Lilly fretted.

Nikki nodded as she looked at Lilly sympathetically. "Hopefully it will be a slow progression. I've seen it happen slowly and I've seen it happen quickly. When it happens slowly, the person has more mobility for longer, but it's hard watching them decline like that."

"There's nothing good about this, is there?" Lilly asked with a sigh.

"It depends on how you look at it," Nikki said. "If you think of all the happiness she has spending time in her own memories, which seem very vivid, then it's not as bad as it could be. And despite the mobility issues we're starting to see, she's still able to get around the house. I'm thankful for the alarm system, because without it I would worry constantly not only about her leaving the house without telling me, but also about falling once she's outside."

Lilly sighed again. Her life seemed to consist of nothing but worry lately.

Once Nikki had gone upstairs to check on Bev and confirmed that she was already asleep, Lilly went home. She and Laurel ate dinner together, but Laurel didn't seem to want to talk and Lilly didn't feel like discussing her day. Or Hassan, or Harry, or her mother.

Laurel didn't seem to notice. She was preoccupied with something else.

"Everything okay?" Lilly asked as they were washing the dishes together.

Laurel shrugged. "I dunno."

"Want to tell me about it?"

"I think Nick is going out with some other girl. I saw them in the hallway at school today, holding hands."

Lilly glanced sideways at Laurel and saw that she was wiping a tear from the corner of her eye.

She put down the dishrag and turned to Laurel, putting her hands on her daughter's thin shoulders. "Laurel, this is Nick's loss. You remember that. You're sweet and thoughtful and pretty and confident and you don't need some dumb boy to know how important you are."

Laurel's tears fell faster.

"The right person will come along, but before that happens you'll have to kiss a lot of frogs. Think of Nick as one of the frogs."

The corners of Laurel's mouth turned up just a little bit.

"Ribbit," Lilly said quietly.

Laurel laughed in spite of herself.

"See how easy that is?" Lilly asked, putting her arm around Laurel's shoulders. "Nick may be the right person for someone, but it isn't you. You're destined for someone better."

"Ribbit," Laurel replied with a smile. She wiped her cheek with her hand and then ran her sleeve across her runny nose.

"Put that shirt in the laundry," Lilly advised.

Laurel laughed again.

"I went over to see Gran today," Lilly said as they were finishing up the dishes. "I offered to take you over there to see her tomorrow night. She thought that sounded nice."

"Okay," Laurel said. Then she rolled her eyes and looked at Lilly. "It's not like I'm going anywhere."

Lilly smiled. "You're getting very good at being grounded."

Laurel smiled back at her. "It isn't as bad as I thought it would be."

Lilly was glad to be taking Laurel over to Bev's the following evening. She had other plans, and it would be best if Laurel was occupied.

The next day went quickly. There were more customers than the day before and Lilly made sure she kept Harry busy all day. She knew he was growing increasingly depressed over the lack of leads on Alice's whereabouts, and if his sunken eyes and stooped shoulders were any indication, the burdens of worry and concern were weighing on him more and more every day.

But she was going to do something about that.

As soon as she and Laurel had finished dinner that evening, she drove Laurel over to Bev's house. She went inside to say hello to her mom and Nikki, made sure Bev had had a good day, and told everyone she had work to do.

She knew they would assume she was headed to the jewelry shop, and that was fine with her. She let them believe it.

She drove home and changed into her Guy's Place "uniform" of tight jeans, flannel shirt, long-sleeved white tee to wear underneath the flannel, and boots. She grabbed her phone and dialed Noley, who answered on the first ring.

"I was afraid you weren't talking to me anymore," Noley said in a teasing voice.

"Of course not! I've just been busy the last couple days. I haven't had time to talk. And actually, I don't have time right now. I'm headed over to Guy's Place."

"Okay, be careful. I'm glad you told me, so now at least someone knows where you'll be."

"I'll let you know how everything goes." Lilly hung up and slid behind the wheel of her car.

She drove through the quiet streets of Juniper Junction to the main highway connecting the town to Lupine. There she sped up, eager to get to Guy's Place, talk to Suzanne and Tracy, and get home before it was time to pick up Laurel from Bev's house. She would have to hurry.

After driving for a little while once she was out of Lupine, she saw the lights of Guy's Place brightening the night sky in front of her. The butterflies started to amass in her stomach, and she again wished Noley had offered to come along. It hurt a little that she hadn't.

She parked as close as she could to the front of the hulking concrete building, since the thought of walking through the semi-dark parking lot by herself was unappealing, to say the least.

She found a spot two rows from the entrance and got out of the car. There didn't seem to be anyone hanging around outside the bar. She hurried to the front door and swung it open slowly.

Everything inside looked the same—the dim light, the blinking neon beer signs over the bar, the thumping music coming from the back, the strobe lights accompanying the music. She allowed herself to stand still for just a moment to let her eyes adjust, and then she moved toward the bar.

"Yeah?" the bartender greeted her when she set her hand on the sticky surface of the bar.

"Got any wine?" she asked. In response, the bartender pointed to a corner of the bar, where several boxes of wine stood at the ready.

"Gimme a white wine," Lilly said. The bartender shoved a beer glass under the tap of the box of white wine and let the light liquid flow.

"How much?" Lilly asked.

"Six."

Lilly handed him a ten dollar bill and told him to keep the change. She figured it couldn't hurt to be on the good side of the bartender if anything went wrong tonight. The bartender nodded at her and smiled.

She held the wine over her head so it wouldn't get jostled and spill before she found a place to sit by the dancers. As she had the last time, she chose a seat near the stage but concentrated on not looking at the dancers performing.

A waitress, clad in a sparkly tank top like all the others, came up to her and smiled.

"What can I getcha?"

"Actually, I'm looking for Suzanne. Um, Minx. Is she here tonight?" Lilly knew Suzanne was around because this was one of her nights to work.

"Yeah, she's getting ready to perform," the woman said with a smile. "If you wanna stick around, she gets a break when she's done. These girls just started," she added, jerking her head toward the stage.

"Okay, thanks." Lilly took out her phone and started scrolling through emails while she waited for Minx to perform. *What kind of woman comes into a bar like this and sits alone with a glass of wine?* Lilly thought. *I must look like a loser.*

And, indeed, she was drawing attention to herself. She noticed several men looking at her from nearby tables. Many of them wore suits and wedding rings. She wondered if their wives knew where they were—and whether they cared. When they weren't looking at her, probably wondering what kind of a sorry social life she had, their eyes were glued to the stage. Lilly wrinkled her nose reflexively and said a silent prayer of thanks that Hassan wasn't the type who enjoyed hanging out at strip clubs.

As the music continued to blast, Lilly's head started to hurt. She looked at her watch about a thousand times, wondering when Suzanne would come on stage. After fifteen agonizing minutes of waiting, the lights over the stage dimmed and the music changed. The dancers left the stage and a new group of three women came out, dressed in practically nothing.

Suzanne was among them. Lilly breathed a sigh of relief that she would only have to wait another twenty minutes or so until she could go backstage and talk to her.

The waitress came by one more time and Lilly ordered another glass of wine. She continued scrolling through her phone, not watching the goings-on around her, until the music changed again, signaling the arrival of a fresh batch of dancers. She finished her wine, located her waitress and paid her bill and the tip, and went backstage.

The dimly lit hallway leading to the dressing room still smelled bad. Lilly tried breathing through her mouth.

When she knocked on the dressing room door, she didn't wait to be admitted; she just opened it slowly and walked in. Suzanne was at the table closest to the door, unfastening the ankle straps of her stilettos.

"Hi, Lilly," she said, her face breaking into a smile. "What's new?"

"I was hoping you could tell me." Lilly pulled out a chair and sat down across from Suzanne.

"I haven't heard or seen anything," Suzanne said, shaking her head. "In fact, Tracy and I were talking about it on the phone earlier. She's off tonight. She knows about as much as I do."

"Have any of the other employees mentioned Alice?" Lilly asked.

Suzanne thought while pulling her work tank top over her head. "I've heard people talking about her, you know, but it's always stuff like 'I wonder what happened to Alice' or 'I hope Alice is okay.' Nothing that would make me think they knew anything about her disappearance."

"What about Guy?" Lilly suggested. She managed not to sneer while she spoke. She could barely hide her dislike for Guy and part of her almost hoped he knew something about Alice that he wasn't sharing. She would love to see him busted by the police for impeding an investigation. But, she had to remind herself, the most important thing was to find Alice, so if Guy had information, she wanted him to share it. That gave her a thought—maybe she should come out to the bar during the day when Guy wasn't as busy. Maybe he could talk to her about Alice then.

She turned her attention back to Suzanne. "Well, thanks for keeping your eyes open." She sighed. "I hope Alice turns up soon and that she's okay."

"I should give you my phone number," Suzanne said. "That way you don't have to come all the way out here just to talk." She scribbled her number on a piece of paper and handed it to Lilly.

"Thanks. I'll be in touch. You'll let me know if you hear anything, right?"

"You bet," Suzanne said. "Wait a sec and I'll walk out with you. I'm on my break now, so I'm going to put in an order for food." Lilly waited while Suzanne put on her comfy shoes for waiting tables and they left the dressing room together.

Back in the foul-smelling hallway, Lilly could see two men waiting for the restroom, though their features were hidden in shadow. She could see, though, that one of them turned in time to see her and Suzanne leave the dressing room. He looked away quickly.

Lilly and Suzanne pushed their way through the crowd—Suzanne to the bar and Lilly to the front door. Lilly was reaching for the door handle when someone grabbed her arm.

She whirled around and was shocked to see Suzanne standing there.

"What is it?" Lilly asked in alarm.

Suzanne leaned in close to Lilly's ear. "That guy. You know, the one who was bothering Alice? He's here," she said, her eyes wide. She tipped her head toward the stage.

Lilly jerked her head toward the stage. "Which one is he?" There were so many men around, and it seemed that most of them were standing directly in her line of vision.

Suzanne stood on tiptoes to get a better look. She turned her head left and right, scanning the area around the stage.

"I don't see him anymore," she finally said.

Lilly glanced at her watch. It was getting late and she didn't want to delay getting back to her mother's any longer or Laurel and Bev would start asking questions.

"I've got to go pick up my daughter," Lilly said. "If you see him, can you chat him up? I mean, see if you can get his name, where he lives, stuff like that. I'll call you later tonight to see what you can get out of him. But be careful and don't walk to your car alone. Make sure Guy or the bartender or someone goes with you."

"Got it." Suzanne turned around and headed back into the crowd.

Lilly opened the door again and stood outside the bar for just a moment, letting the frigid air cool her skin and scanning the parking lot quickly to make sure there was no one around. Her ears rang from the silence after the ear-splitting music indoors.

She shivered as the cold air came into contact with the sweat on her body and gave her goosebumps. She pulled her car keys out of her back pocket and headed toward her car.

She never heard the person coming up behind her. She felt a blinding pain on the back of her head and a moment later she was unconscious on the gravel parking lot.

CHAPTER 33

When Lilly came to, Noley was crying and kneeling next to her on the cold ground. She tried lifting her head up, but the pain was almost unbearable. She blinked several times very slowly.

"What's going on?" she asked. Her lips felt thick and useless.

"Someone hit you from behind." Noley grasped Lilly's hand.

"Where am I?" Lilly asked. "It's cold."

"You're outside Guy's Place, in the parking lot."

"My head is killing me."

"I know. I've already called for an ambulance and it's on the way." Noley wiped a wisp of hair from Lilly's forehead.

"I don't need an ambulance," Lilly protested. "Where's Laurel?"

"I don't know, but she's not here. She's probably at home." That didn't sound right to Lilly.

A small crowd had started to gather around them. Lilly closed her eyes when she heard someone shout, "Has anyone called the police?"

"I called nine-one-one," Noley answered. "They're sending police and an ambulance."

Lilly opened her eyes. She couldn't remember why, but she knew she didn't want the police to come.

"No police," she murmured.

"They've already been called," Noley said quietly. "The person who did this can't get away with it. Are you warm enough?"

Lilly tried to nod, but it hurt too much. She closed her eyes again and tried to shut out the murmurings of the people around her, but she was unsuccessful. Before long a gruff voice joined the others.

"I recognize her. What happened?"

Lilly opened one eye. Guy was standing at the front of the crowd. From where Lilly lay on the ground, his bulk was even more intimidating than usual.

"Get Suzanne out here," he growled. "I saw them two talking together." He jerked his head toward Lilly. "This one's a troublemaker."

Lilly tried to scowl, but it fizzled out as the effort was too tiring.

Lilly thought she could hear a siren not far off. The sound was excruciating. She tried to put her hands over her ears, but she was too weak to lift her arms. She could see the red and blue and white lights from the ambulance blinking and rotating off the cars parked nearby, so she knew help was very close. Noley tightened the grip on her hand and looked up at the ambulance, which parked near the crowd of onlookers. The paramedics hadn't even gotten to Lilly before the police arrived. Two officers jumped out of the cruiser and began clearing the crowd away from the paramedics so they could have some space. They approached Noley as the medics worked on Lilly. Lilly could see them talking, but then Noley pointed to her and the officers nodded and walked away, heading toward Guy.

Just a moment later someone called out, "Oh, my God! Lilly! What happened?" Lilly recognized Suzanne's voice right away.

She tried lifting her head again to see Suzanne, but one of the paramedics gently put his hand over her forehead so she would remain still.

"Hi, Suzanne. Remember me? I'm Lilly's friend, Noley." Lilly breathed a sigh of relief that Noley was handling everything now. She strained her ears to hear what they were saying, but the two women had moved away from the noise around the ambulance to talk.

She was beginning to remember a little more. Those first few minutes after she was whacked on the head were a blur of confusion, but the fog was starting to lift just a bit and she could recall talking to Suzanne in the bar before coming out to the parking lot. She couldn't remember what they were talking about. She also remembered that she was supposed to pick Laurel up from her mother's house. A wave of anxiety washed over her as she wondered how long she had been lying on the ground. Was she late? Were Laurel and Bev worried about her? She became agitated, breathing more quickly and making fidgety gestures with her hands.

"What is it, Lilly?" asked one of the paramedics.

"I need Noley," Lilly whispered.

"Noley? Is there a Noley?" the paramedic called into the crowd.

Noley was at Lilly's side in an instant.

"Are you all right?" she asked.

Lilly swallowed. "Laurel and Mom. They're going to wonder where I am."

"I'll call them and tell them. A few minutes ago you couldn't remember where Laurel was. You think she's at your mom's house?"

"Yes. I was supposed to pick her up. What time is it? Am I late?"

"Don't worry about anything," Noley said. Lilly, even in her fog, noticed that Noley didn't answer her questions. "I'll call over there and I'll pick up Laurel later. Maybe she can spend the night at your mom's."

"Don't tell them what happened," Lilly said. She closed her eyes again.

Noley looked at her and pressed her lips into a thin line. She dialed the phone and stood near Lilly so Lilly could hear at least half of the conversation.

"Hi, Nikki. It's Noley. Are you spending the night at Bev's?"

...

"There's been a slight change of plans."

...

"Do you think Laurel could spend the night at Bev's house, too?"

...

"Thank you. I'll pick her up and take her home tomorrow morning."

...

"Lilly got a bump on the head and she probably won't be able to come over."

...

"She's okay, but she doesn't want anyone to worry, so maybe tell Laurel and Bev as little as possible? Lilly just doesn't want to upset them."

...

"Of course. I'll give her the message. Thanks, Nikki."

Noley hung up and turned to Lilly. "She realizes there's more wrong than just a bump on the head, but she's going to spare Bev and Laurel any details. She actually doesn't know any details, so that should be easy."

"Thank you," Lilly murmured.

One of the paramedics came over and motioned Noley toward him. She was gone for just a minute, then she returned and spoke to Lilly.

"I'm going to follow you to the hospital in my car. We'll pick up your car another time."

"I don't want to go to the hospital," Lilly protested.

"You're going," Noley said. Behind her Lilly could see the paramedic grin. She rolled her eyes, but it hurt.

The paramedics hefted the stretcher into the back of the ambulance and the driver went up to the front. One remained with Lilly in the back. Noley squeezed her hand one more time and walked away.

It wasn't long before they arrived at the hospital. Lilly had been there before, most recently when her neighbor, Mrs. Laforge, had been struck by a car and Lilly went to visit her. She was taken into a different entrance this time, and pretty soon Noley came back into the Emergency Department. She had gone through the front. She smiled when she saw Lilly, but the smile didn't reach all the way to her eyes. Her eyes were worried.

"How do you feel?" she asked.

"Lousy, but I remember more than I did earlier. What did Suzanne tell you?"

"She told me that the guy who was bothering Alice was in the bar tonight. She lost him, though. Lilly, I'll bet that's who hit you from behind."

"Did you see him?" Lilly asked.

"No." Noley said, shook her head.

Lilly squinted at her friend. "What were you doing at Guy's Place?"

"What do you think I was doing? Trying to keep an eye on you, that's what. I didn't do a very good job, I'm afraid. I was getting concerned about you being in the bar for so long, so I got in my car and was calling your cell when I saw you come out. Then someone ran up and hit you from behind. It happened so fast I couldn't react in time to stop it. I ran over to where you were, but you were on the ground and the person had already taken off."

"But I don't understand how you were at the bar at the same time as me."

"You didn't really think I'd let you go to a place like that by yourself, did you? I just didn't want to talk to the dancers because I wasn't much help the last time. I figured they'd be more willing to talk if it was just you."

"You could have just told me that," Lilly grumbled. "Besides, it's not true. You were a big help."

"If I had told you that, you would have insisted on me coming in with you."

"I might not." Lilly lifted her chin a tiny bit in an attempt to challenge her friend.

Noley raised one eyebrow. "I know you better than that, Lil."

"Okay. I suppose you're right."

"Of course I'm right." Noley pointed to Lilly's head. "Now, we need to talk about what you're going to tell people about this, uh, injury."

Lilly let out a shallow sigh and fixed her eyes on the wall behind Noley. "I'll just tell people I bumped my head on the car door."

"And the ambulance happened to be driving by and took you in?" Noley raised an eyebrow again. "That doesn't exactly have the ring of truth."

"I'll tell them that you were there when it happened and you panicked because I lost consciousness and you called nine-one-one."

"That sounds a little better. Do you want to know what I think? I think you should just tell the truth."

"The truth?" Lilly choked out with as much indignation as she could muster. "If I tell the truth, everyone will be mad at me. Bill, Laurel, Hassan, Harry. Maybe even my mother, since she's bound to find out somehow."

"Would that really be the worst thing?" Noley asked. "Everyone just wants you to be safe."

"I know. I'll be safe from now on."

The doctor diagnosed Lilly with a severe concussion, bruising around her eyes, and lacerations to her face and neck. There was even a bruise on her back where her unknown assailant had hit her when he—or she—pushed Lilly down.

Noley helped her into the house at about three thirty in the morning. Lilly was exhausted. They had made her stay awake at the hospital in case there was further head injury, but they eventually determined that the concussion was the extent of her serious injuries.

But that was serious enough. The doctor had given her a long list of taboo activities: stay off the computer, no television, no reading, only light work at the jewelry store and nothing involving the cash register or filling out paperwork, and cell phone only in emergencies. He even told her not to think too hard about anything.

"Why don't you just kill right me now and put me out of my misery?" Lilly had suggested to the doctor.

"Because in time, you'll heal from this. Then you'll thank me for not killing you," he joked. Lilly supposed he was right, but it was going to be rough.

"I'm staying here tonight," Noley said. "I'll go pick up Laurel later this morning, so I'll just sleep on the sofa. I'm going to get you into bed and I want you to sleep as long as you can. I'll check on you every few hours to make sure you're all right."

"Thanks. I'm sorry to put you through this."

"Don't be silly. I'm happy to do it. You know that." Noley waited in the hallway upstairs while Lilly got ready for bed, then she came in to shut off the light and make sure Lilly didn't need anything. "I'll check on you before I pick up Laurel," she said.

Lilly nodded sleepily and Noley left her in darkness. Sleep came quickly.

The next morning Lilly stirred when she heard the soft creak of her bedroom door, followed by a gasp. She peered through her swollen eyelids.

Laurel was standing there, looking at her in horror.

Lilly opened her eyes as wide as she could. "What's wrong?" she asked in alarm.

"What happened to you?" Laurel asked, rushing to the side of the bed. Her eyes widened when she saw Lilly up close.

Lilly's mind was still fuzzy, so it took several seconds for her to remember what she and Noley had agreed to tell people.

"I banged my head on the car door."

"And your whole face is swollen from it?" Laurel asked. She eyed her mother suspiciously.

Rats. I forgot about my face. We should have thought of something else!

"Yes," Lilly lied. "It knocked me right to the ground."

"I think you're lying," Laurel said, putting her hands on her hips. "Are you okay? You look like you were hit by a car." She gasped again and covered her mouth with both hands. "*Were you hit by a car?*"

"No, of course not. I'd tell you if I had been hit by a car. I just banged my head on the car door, that's all. I must have hit my face harder than I thought."

Could that be any lamer? Lilly thought.

"Noley told me you have a concussion."

"That's what they tell me."

"Can I do anything?" Laurel asked.

"No, but thank you. I'm just going to sleep today."

Just then Noley knocked on the open bedroom door. "I'll stick around today to keep you company," she told Laurel.

"Okay," Laurel said. "I'll go take a shower."

Laurel turned and left the room and Noley went downstairs to make breakfast. A few minutes later Laurel was back. "Mom, where's your car?"

Shoot, I forgot about that, too, Lilly thought with an inward groan.

"What?" she asked, stalling for time to think of a good answer.

"It's at the jewelry store," Noley answered, coming to stand behind Laurel in the doorway. Lilly breathed a sigh of relief.

"Why is it there?" Laurel asked. Her face was working as though she was trying to figure out what was going on and coming up blank.

"That's where your mom hit her head," Noley said. "When she fainted, I panicked and called nine-one-one, then she went to the hospital by ambulance and I followed in my car. We'll pick her car up as soon as she can drive."

"So you were at the shop when it happened?" Laurel asked Noley.

Noley glanced quickly at Lilly. "Yes."

Laurel gave her a skeptical look. "So Harry's taking care of the store today?"

Lilly nodded. *Rats.* She had forgotten to call Harry. She

suspected this concussion was going to cause no end of problems.

"Yes. I spoke to him this morning and he'll take care of everything until your mom is ready to go back to work," Noley said.

Thank God for Noley.

"Whatever you say. I'm taking my shower now." Laurel left again.

"Thank you," Lilly said. Noley had moved closer to the bed and stood staring down at her.

"Don't you think it's time to start telling the truth?" she asked.

"No way." Lilly tried shaking her head on the pillow, but it hurt. "I'm not about to tell Laurel that I was attacked. It would scare her to death."

"I don't mean tell Laurel everything that happened, but maybe tell her you banged your head while you were trying to find out where Alice is. That's the truth, even if it's not the *whole* truth."

"I promise I'll tell everyone the truth when the time comes."

"And when will the time come?" Noley asked.

"When Alice is safe and sound."

"I had a feeling you'd say that." Noley sighed. "So what are you going to tell Harry? You can't tell him your car is at the store because it obviously isn't."

"What did you tell him?" Lilly asked.

"That you banged your head and can't come to work. He didn't ask for details—I think he's a little preoccupied."

"Of course he is. And now I've gone and made his life harder. Bah," she said through gritted teeth. "I definitely don't want him to know the truth. He'd be so upset if he found out this happened because I was trying to help him."

"I'm going to bring breakfast up. Let's stop worrying about

this right now because you're thinking too hard already. That's against the doctor's orders."

Barney came crashing up the stairs and into Lilly's room. He watched her from the side of the bed, his tail wagging furiously. Noley hadn't let him sleep with Lilly after she got home from the hospital, so he was thrilled to see her.

She patted the covers. "Come on up, Barn," she said. He jumped onto the bed and commenced licking her face as soon as he had all fours on the mattress, and Lilly laughed despite the pain.

Noley had just returned to Lilly's room with a breakfast tray when the doorbell rang. Barney launched himself off the bed in a furry haze of frenzied barking and dashed down the stairs. Though she knew it was unreasonable, Lilly started to tremble.

"What if the person who hit me followed us?" she asked in a scared whisper.

Noley put her hands on her hips. "That's impossible. That person took off as soon as you hit the ground." She turned around to follow Barney, but Lilly noticed her footsteps hesitated at the top of the staircase.

"Don't answer it," Lilly called.

"I'll just see who it is," Noley replied. Lilly heard her go down the stairs.

Just a few seconds later Barney had stopped barking and Lilly could hear low voices. She waited, not saying anything, knowing Noley would tell her who was at the door.

She strained her ears to listen and it wasn't long before she heard a heavy tread on the stairs.

"You've got a visitor," Noley called out.

A moment later Bill was standing in the doorway.

"Lilly! Oh, my God! What happened?"

CHAPTER 35

$\mathcal{L}$illy groaned. Now she would have to spill the whole story. Bill had a way of sniffing out the truth no matter how hard she tried to conceal it from him. Noley gave her a pointed look and Lilly grimaced at her. Noley knew lying to Bill would be in vain.

"I banged my head," Lilly said. She prayed he wouldn't ask any more questions, but she knew him better than that.

"How? Where?"

Lilly didn't answer, weighing the options in her foggy mind.

"Lilly?" Bill pressed.

She looked at Noley, who nodded solemnly. It was time to come clean.

"Someone pushed me down," Lilly said.

"She has a concussion, so it might be better to talk about this later," Noley suggested. *Why couldn't she have said that ten seconds ago?* Lilly thought.

"I won't make her talk much," Bill said. "I just want to know what happened. Where were you pushed down?"

"In Lupine," Lilly said. If he was going to be nosy, she wasn't going to make it easy for him.

"Where in Lupine?"

"At a bar."

"What bar?"

"Just a dive bar." He closed his eyes and she could see his lips moving. He was counting to ten.

"Lilly, what is the name of the bar?" The jig was up.

"Guy's Place."

"You went to Guy's Place? Where I specifically told you not to go?" His voice was rising and his face was getting red.

"You are not the boss of me. I don't have to do what you say." Her kids used to say the same thing—when they were four. Out of the corner of her eye, she could see Noley smiling.

"If you went there for the reason I think you went there, then I *am* the boss of you. You are interfering with a police investigation. I've told you not to do that!"

Finally Noley stepped in to stop a spat that was clearly about to escalate.

"Okay, you two. Bill, you should probably wait to get mad at her. She's got a severe concussion and she's not supposed to be doing much of anything. That includes arguing. And Lilly, try to remember that Bill is a professional and doesn't want to lose his job because his sister is meddling in police business."

Lilly scowled at her.

"Whoever pushed me would have pushed him, too, so I did him a favor," she said.

"Wanna bet?" Bill asked.

Noley held up her hands and stepped between Bill and the bed where Lilly lay fuming. "Enough. Lilly, you are to finish your breakfast and then rest. Bill, come downstairs with me and I'll make you breakfast, too." She took him by the hand and led him into the hallway. She peeked behind her to wink at Lilly before closing the door.

Lilly finished the food on her tray and reached for the book on the nightstand. She let it fall when she remembered she wasn't supposed to be reading. This was going to be so boring.

She tried sleeping, but found that she was too restless to sleep. What could she do that wouldn't hurt, make Noley's job harder, or annoy anyone?

Nothing, that's what. And exactly how was she supposed to stop thinking? It was impossible.

Sighing, Lilly withdrew a pad of paper and a pencil from the drawer of her nightstand. She shouldn't be writing anything down, but a few words wouldn't be a big deal. She wanted to make a list of the people who were most likely to know something or have something to do with Alice's disappearance.

Mary Louise: acquainted with Alice, has crush on Harry, stays with Harry at night, demanded that Harry take her to the movies, says she knows things about Alice that she isn't sharing.

Guy: Alice's boss, mean, doesn't want Suzanne or Tracy talking to me, distrustful, misogynist.

Man from Guy's Place: probably pushed me down after I talked to Suzanne, bothered Alice at work.

David: Alice's brother, doesn't get along with her, accused Harry of having something to do with Alice's disappearance.

Writing the short list made Lilly's head hurt. She put the pad and pencil aside, closed her eyes, and lay back against her pillow.

It wasn't going to be easy to figure out who was responsible for Alice's disappearance if she couldn't keep her eyes open for more than a few minutes at a time.

Noley came upstairs a while later. Lilly had fallen into a light sleep and woke up as soon as Noley came into her bedroom.

"Where's Bill?" Lilly asked. She reached for her phone to look at the time.

"Uh-uh," Noley scolded, holding out her hand for the phone. "He left about an hour ago."

"Is he still mad?"

Noley shrugged. "You know Bill. He's concerned about you and he thinks you take unnecessary risks to solve problems that are best left to the professionals."

"But I might be able to get information that people aren't willing to share with the police."

"Lil, you don't need to explain it to me. I understand and I even agree with you sometimes. I'm just telling you how it looks from Bill's point of view."

"Why did he come over here, anyway?" Lilly asked.

Noley looked down at her feet for a second and Lilly knew something was up. "It's your mom. I guess she woke up this morning upset about something and Nikki can't get her to calm down. Bill said she can't stop crying. He went to the jewelry store to ask you to go over and talk to her, but Harry told him he'd find you here."

"Poor Mom," Lilly said. "I don't think I can go over there right now—"

"You're darned right. You're not going anywhere."

"What I was saying was," Lilly began with a pointed glance at Noley, "I can call Mom and see how she's doing. I wonder if she'll tell me what's upsetting her."

"Good idea," Noley said. "I'll give you your cell phone if you promise not to do anything on it except call your mom." She grinned. "It stinks, I know."

"I promise. But you can't keep me in here forever, you know. I have to go to work at some point."

"Well, since tomorrow is Sunday, you'll have a forced day off. Maybe you can go back on Monday. With limited responsibilities, obviously. I'll call Harry and make sure he's okay with that arrangement."

"All right, Doctor Appleton." Lilly held out her hand for the phone. She dialed her mom while Noley slipped from the room.

Nikki answered the phone. "What's going on over there?" Lilly asked. "Is Mom all right?"

"Lilly, I've never seen her like this. Laurel left before she woke up, and I think that upset her. But I can't get her to explain."

"Can I talk to her? I can't come over right now because of my concussion, but I can try to figure out what's wrong."

"Sure. I'll put her on. I hope you're following the doctor's orders," Nikki warned. "Concussions are serious."

"I'm following the ER doc's advice as well as Doctor Noley's advice."

She could hear the smile in Nikki's voice. "Good. Now here's your mom."

"Lilly?" Bev asked in a tremulous voice.

"Hi, Mom."

"Oh, Lilly...." Bev began to cry, speaking garbled words that Lilly couldn't understand.

"Mom, listen. I can't understand what you're saying while you cry. Take a few deep breaths if you can and try to calm down a bit. I want to help you, but I can't when I can't understand you."

There was a pause while Bev took a few jagged breaths. She came back on the line and her voice was a little bit clearer.

"It's hard to get old, Lilly."

"I know, Mom. But you're doing so well."

"I miss your father." The tears started again, and this time there were tears on both ends of the call.

There was silence for several moments as both women sniffled and swallowed. "I know you do, Mom. I miss him, too."

All those times Bev had talked about her late husband, all those times she insisted that he was still living in the same house with her, all those times Lilly had reluctantly decided against reminding her that he wasn't around anymore—they all came rushing back to Lilly and she wondered how she ever could have wanted to remind her mother of the cruel truth.

It was far better to let her mother live in her memories. At least there she was still happy.

"**C**an you and Billy come to see me tonight?" Bev asked, sniffling. "I miss you both."

Lilly swallowed around the lump in her throat. "I'll ask him, Mom." There was no way she was going to let Noley keep her in the house tonight when her mother needed her. And she was going to make sure Bill went over, too. No work excuses, no nothing.

She called Bill as soon as she hung up with her mother. "Bill, Mom wants us to go over there tonight."

"Did you find out why she's so upset?"

"Yeah. She misses Dad." Bill didn't answer, but Lilly knew what was going through his mind—the same things that went through her mind when she talked to her mom.

"I'll be there," he said. His voice held just a hint of huskiness. "You're not going, are you?"

"I can't *not* go," she said. "I'm not using this concussion as an excuse when Mom needs us both."

"All right. I'll pick you up and drop you off afterward," he offered.

"See you later."

She put the phone next to her on the bed and tried going back to sleep, but she was still restless. She got out of bed and made her way downstairs, where she found Noley in the kitchen talking on her own cell phone. She hung up when she saw Lilly.

"What are you doing out of bed?" she cried.

"I have to move around or I'll atrophy," Lilly said. "What's going on down here? You didn't have to hang up, you know."

"I know. But I need to talk to you about something."

"What?" Lilly was immediately on alert, as much as she could be with her brain fog.

"That was Harry. He said the police came into the store to talk to him again. They found something of Alice's and they wanted to know if he knew anything about it."

"What did they find?" Lilly asked. Her heart did a little flip-flop, but not in a good way.

"A shoe."

"Where did they find it?"

"Outside Guy's Place in some bushes."

Lilly stood still for a moment as Noley's words sank in. "Why would anyone leave a shoe in the bushes?"

"They wouldn't."

"Then that's definitive proof that she was taken against her will. This is the second clue that she didn't go away on her own." Lilly shivered.

"I think we've always known that," Noley said.

"Of course, but now the police have more to go on. Maybe there are fingerprints on the shoe."

Noley looked doubtful.

"How is Harry taking it?" Lilly asked.

Noley shook her head. "Not well. He sounded pretty distraught when he called me."

"I really should go over there," Lilly said. "Do you think it would be okay if I went over for just a little while?"

"No, I don't. As Harry said, there's really nothing he can do right now except worry, and when he's in charge of the shop he has less time to worry."

"I could at least be there for moral support," Lilly said. "I'm no use to anyone here."

"That's not true," Noley countered. "Don't forget that it's for your own good that you're staying home. You're no use to anyone if this concussion gets worse and you end up bedridden."

"All right. I'll stay here," Lilly mumbled.

"You're not the most patient patient," Noley said with a grin.

"I'm bored. I hate not being able to do anything."

"You are doing something—you're healing. Now go back upstairs and quit your whining." Noley made a *shoo* motion with her hands and Lilly headed back upstairs.

Now she had one more thing to worry about on top of everything else: there could no longer be any doubt that Alice had been taken against her will.

Where was she? And was she okay?

* * *

That evening Bill picked Lilly up in his cruiser after dinner. They said little on the ride to Bev's house, each lost in thought.

When Bill pulled up to the house, Lilly turned to him. "I'm worried about Mom."

"Me, too."

"How long do you think she'll be able to stay at home, with Nikki taking care of her?"

"I've heard of people who go on for years like that," Bill said.

Lilly sighed. "I think it's almost better when she's in a fog. At least she's not lonely and she just carries on as if it were years ago."

"I think it's better, too. She seems to be pretty happy on the days she's confused."

"All right. Let's go in," Lilly said. She couldn't procrastinate any longer.

They knocked on the front door and waited while Nikki disarmed the security system. She opened the door with a smile on her face. "Come on in. She's doing much better tonight."

Lilly exhaled in relief. Bill led the way into the living room, where Bev was in her favorite chair with a fuzzy blanket wrapped around her legs. "Lilly! Billy! What are you doing here? Is everything all right?" Bev asked, her face crumpling in concern. Then she gasped. "Lilly, what happened to your face?"

Lilly spoke immediately, not wanting to break the spell. "Everything is fine, Mom. I fell, that's all."

"You should be more careful, Lilly," Bev said, wagging her finger.

"I will, I promise. Bill and I just thought we'd come by and say hello."

"Well, wasn't that sweet of you both. Billy, you work so hard. You should be relaxing with your lovely wife, not worrying about me." Lilly rolled her eyes. Yes, her mother was definitely back to her old self. She caught Nikki's eye and Nikki laughed silently, shaking her head. Even Bill couldn't keep from smirking. He didn't bother reminding Bev that he and Noley weren't married.

The small group chatted for a while before Bev announced that she was getting tired and would like to go to bed. Lilly and Bill left while Nikki helped Bev get upstairs for the evening.

"Billy, you work so hard," Lilly squeaked in a mocking voice once they were in the car.

Bill laughed. "Can I help it if Mom is impressed that I spend my days defending Juniper Junction from ne'er-do-wells and the criminal element?" he asked with a grin.

"Humph."

"Don't be jealous. And don't be fooled. You're the one she turns to every time there's a problem," Bill reminded her. "She knows you're more capable than I am when it comes to taking care of other people. You're the one who makes her feel better."

Lilly opened her mouth to say something and then closed it. He was right. Their mom *did* call her when she was feeling blue or scared. Suddenly she felt a little lighter.

"Did you hear me?" Bill asked, breaking into her thoughts.

"About Mom?"

"No. About Alice. I told you they found one of her shoes."

"Oh. Harry talked to Noley this morning and he told her about it."

"That doesn't bode well for Alice," Bill said.

"I know." They were silent for the rest of the trip back to Lilly's house.

Lilly opened the door to get out of the car and turned to Bill. "Will you keep me posted? About Alice, I mean?"

"I'll try. Her family, obviously, will be the first ones to know if we find anything, then Harry. But I'll try to keep you in the loop."

"Has anyone been back out to Guy's Place to look at security camera footage or any other evidence that the guy who pushed me may have left behind?"

"Yes. Unfortunately, the camera footage was too grainy and the guy seemed to know exactly when and where to keep his head down so he wouldn't be recognized on the tape. We've asked the dancers and the other employees at the bar and they know who we're talking about, but he doesn't come in too often and no one knows his name. Incidentally, the officers have also gone back to look at security camera footage from the bar the day Alice disappeared. The cameras weren't even turned on that day."

"Of course not." Lilly's voice was heavy with frustration.

"Can any of Alice's co-workers describe the guy who pushed me?"

"Yes, but their descriptions match about a hundred thousand people. It's not enough to go on."

Lilly pushed the door open further. "All right. I'll let you know if I think of anything that would help."

"Good. Tell Noley I'll call her later," Bill said.

Lilly went inside and Noley, who had been nervous about her visiting her mother's house, made her go straight to bed. As much as she hated to admit it, her head hurt and she was a little dizzy and nauseous from her visit at Bev's. Maybe it was a good thing tomorrow was Sunday.

CHAPTER 37

 illy rested all day Sunday, so when Noley allowed her to go to work on Monday morning, Lilly felt a little better.

When she walked in through the front door of Juniper Junction Jewels, she was shocked to see Mary Louise leaning against one of the glass counters, talking to Harry. To his credit, he had the grace to look uncomfortable when he saw Lilly.

"Good morning, Lilly," he said, coming around from behind the counter. "How are you feeling? Are you sure you should be here?"

Mary Louise turned around to look at Lilly with raised eyebrows, but she didn't say anything.

"I wasn't going to stay long, but now that I'm here, maybe I'll stick around for a while," Lilly answered with a pointed look at Mary Louise.

Harry cleared his throat and looked from Lilly to Mary Louise and back again. There were several long moments of complete silence until Mary Louise finally spoke. "I should get going. I have class in a half hour."

She slung her purse over her shoulder and left after telling

Harry goodbye and ignoring Lilly. When the last tinkling notes of the bells over the door died out, Lilly gave Harry a look that she hoped bored right into his soul.

"What was she doing here?" she asked, trying to keep her voice light.

"I know it looks bad, Lilly. I tried telling her to leave, honest. But she won't take 'no' for an answer."

"Have you told her you're ready to stay by yourself at home?"

Harry nodded. "Yeah."

"And has she been staying away?"

He nodded again. "I think that's why she came in today and on Saturday." Suddenly he stopped, but it was too late. Lilly had heard him.

"She was here Saturday, too?"

Harry took a deep breath. "Yes, but only for a few minutes. She had to get to campus."

"Look, Harry. You know I don't care if you get a visitor in the store, but I don't think it's a good idea for that particular visitor to be here. Would it make things easier for you if I said you're not allowed to have visitors while you're working?"

His features relaxed. "Yes, that would be great."

"Then here's my new rule, effective immediately and until I say otherwise: no visitors at work." She smiled. "Now if she gives you a problem, let her deal with me."

"Thanks, Lilly. That gives me an excuse to force her to leave."

"I'm not going to be able to work as many hours as I usually do for a little while, at least until this concussion is better. So I'll just have to trust that you're sending her away when I'm not around."

"You got it, boss. I'll just tell her she has to go or I'll get fired. That ought to work."

"I hope so. Now, tell me more about the shoe the police found."

"It was a sparkly high-heeled shoe. They knew it was hers because her fingerprints were on it. I wouldn't have believed it was hers because I've never seen her in shoes like that, but knowing now that she's a stripper in secret, I believe it's hers."

"And they're sure there was nothing else in the bushes outside the bar?"

"Yeah. They told me they did a thorough search outside the building and the only thing they found was the shoe."

"Did they say anything else about it?"

"No."

"Have you heard anything else from Alice's family?"

"No. Like I told you, they're a little weird. David called me, though. He was shouting and wanted to know why I didn't tell the family about Alice's job. The family is furious that she was working as a stripper. David didn't believe me when I told him I had had no idea Alice was doing that. She had always told me she worked at a grocery store in Lupine, and I never visited her at work. Besides, even if I had known, I wouldn't have told them. If they had known, they would have been even angrier."

"They must be hurting," Lilly said.

Harry shrugged. "I guess. You can see there's not much love lost between me and them. And I can't stand David."

Suddenly a thought struck Lilly. "Wait. Did Mary Louise say she was going to class? Where does she go to school?"

"The community college."

"The same one as Alice?" Lilly asked.

"Yes. I told you that."

"I guess I forgot."

A look of confusion crossed Harry's face. "Why do you ask?"

Lilly asked another question rather than answering Harry's. "Are they in any classes together?"

"I don't think so. Alice never mentioned it and Mary Louise hasn't mentioned it."

"What about the police? Did they check?"

Harry shook his head. "I don't know."

"I'm going to find out," Lilly said.

Lilly strode to her office, picked up the phone, and dialed Bill.

"Bill, did anyone check to see if Alice Davenport and Harry's friend Mary Louise are in any classes together at the community college?"

"I don't know. Let me see if there's someone around I can ask." Bill put Lilly on hold and she waited several minutes for him to return. While she waited she tried to complete some of the paperwork that was piling up on her desk, but it made her eyes ache to look at the rows of numbers. She closed her eyes and leaned her head back while she waited.

When Bill came back on the line, his voice startled Lilly. "Someone checked with administration. Alice and Mary Louise aren't enrolled in any of the same classes."

"Thanks for checking," Lilly said in a disappointed tone.

"Why do you ask?"

"I forgot they both went to the community college," Lilly said. "I thought maybe there was a connection through the school that someone had missed."

"Nope. Lilly, we know how to do our jobs," Bill said dryly.

"I know that, but I can think about it, too, can't I?" She was trying to keep the testiness out of her voice.

"Sure you can. But don't think too hard. And stay out of it. Your concussion proves that this isn't work for an untrained civilian."

Lilly scowled and wished Bill could see her.

"All right, all right. You've made your point."

"You know those two friends of Laurel's who were vandalizing places around town?" Bill asked, changing the subject to one Lilly couldn't resist.

"You mean Bella and Karley?"

"Yes."

"What about them?" Lilly had a funny feeling in her stomach.

"They've been at it again. They got caught yesterday. Good thing Laurel is grounded. I'd ground her for longer if I were you," Bill said.

Lilly's shoulders sank. She hated to hear that Laurel's friends were in trouble again. They obviously hadn't learned their lesson the first time. "That's too bad."

"They're getting bolder, too. The last couple instances were in the daytime," Bill continued.

"I'm sorry to hear it. I know from experience that the older kids get, the more trouble they can get into," Lilly said. Though her first instinct was to say Bella and Karley were bad kids, she was trying hard not to be judgmental. More than once the previous summer, Tighe had come close to being in serious trouble with the law, and he wasn't a bad kid. Sometimes good kids just made bad choices.

Sometimes adults did, too.... That thought brought Lilly back to the present and the missing Alice Davenport.

"Bill, what could that shoe in the bushes mean?" Lilly asked. She was almost afraid to hear the answer.

"It could mean several things. Maybe it fell off during a struggle, maybe she threw it there as a clue so the police would know something was amiss, maybe she dropped it out of a backpack and an animal dragged it under the bushes. We really don't know yet. We have to look at it in the context of other leads and clues."

"Are there a lot of other leads or clues?"

Bill paused. "Unfortunately, no. There are still a few leads the detectives are working on, but no new leads have come in since the night you were attacked at Guy's Place."

"It's been two weeks since she went missing," Lilly said.

"I know," came the grim rely. "Listen, I've got to get going. I'll talk to you later."

Lilly returned to the front of the shop, where Harry gave her an expectant look. Lilly gave him a tight shake of her head, which made it hurt. "Bill said someone checked with the administration and Alice and Mary Louise aren't enrolled in any classes together."

"I wish she'd come back," Harry said glumly.

"So do I, Harry."

CHAPTER 38

It wasn't long before the ache in Lilly's head got worse and she decided, against her own wishes, that it was time to head home for the day. Hassan had said he would visit her for lunch, so she wanted to rest and take something for the headache before he got there. Noley had gone to her house to take a shower and get a change of clothes, so Lilly called her to ask for a ride home.

Noley fretted in the car on the drive to Lilly's house. "You shouldn't have gone to work today, I knew it."

"Well, one good thing came of it," Lilly said. "When I got to the shop Mary Louise was there talking to Harry."

"She has no shame."

"I know that. But I think just having me there made her uncomfortable enough to leave after a minute or two. I am the boss, after all. So I told Harry, sort of with a wink and a nod, that he's not allowed to have visitors at the store anymore. That way he won't be lying to Mary Louise when he tells her that she can't come in to see him while he's working. As annoying as she is, I think he doesn't like the idea of being dishonest with her. The new rule gives him a legitimate excuse to get rid of her."

"And what about his other friend?" Noley asked. "Is he still staying with Harry at night?"

"Mack? I don't think so. Harry said that he's ready to be alone, so he was going to talk to Mack and tell him to stay home."

"I hope the police find Alice soon. *The police*," Noley repeated, giving Lilly a hard look.

"You sound more like Bill every day," Lilly said with a grimace.

Just then Lilly's phone rang.

"You're not supposed to be on your phone," Noley cautioned.

"I can talk. I just can't stare at it." Lilly hit the *talk* button. "Hello? Oh, hi, Suzanne. Anything new?" She listened for a moment.

"You're kidding," she said.

"What? What's up?" Noley asked in a whisper. Lilly held up her hand.

"Okay. I'll be out there later today." Lilly hung up. "That was Suzanne."

"I know. And what do you mean telling her that you'll be out there later today? You'll do no such thing."

"Just listen. She said that the man who was bothering Alice was back at Guy's Place again last night."

"So? He's probably also the guy that hit you. You're not going back there to look for him."

"He wouldn't be there. Suzanne said she thinks Tracy got a picture of him."

"So have Tracy text you the photo. I refuse to take you out there. I shouldn't even have taken you in to work. If your doctor knew, he'd be furious with me."

"I won't tell him, I promise. You really won't take me out there?" Lilly pleaded.

"No. There's no need to go to Lupine when a cell phone will do."

"I'm not supposed to be looking at my cell phone, remember?"

"Nice try. If the choice is a cell phone or a car ride to Lupine, a cell phone is preferable."

Lilly sat back in the seat and tried not to look out the window. It made her dizzy.

"What time is Hassan coming over?" Noley asked.

"About noon. He was surprised that I was home today."

"He actually thought you'd go in to work with a concussion?" Noley asked.

"He doesn't know about the concussion," Lilly said.

"*What*? You're kidding. Why didn't you tell him?"

"He's got so much on his mind. I only talked to him for a couple minutes yesterday and I didn't want to tell him because he was so preoccupied. He's trying to get ready for a trip to Washington, not to mention a trip to Afghanistan. He's been busy making the travel arrangements and trying to set up meetings with all the people he needs to see in Washington."

"You should have told him."

* * *

Noley went home to work on a couple recipes after she dropped Lilly off at her house.

"I'll be back later this afternoon," she said when Lilly got out of the car. "I want to give you two some privacy. Enjoy your lunch and please lie down and rest once Hassan leaves."

"I will." Lilly hurried into the house. The first thing she did was take something for her headache, which was becoming more intense with every passing minute, then she rested on the sofa while she waited for Hassan. He was bringing lunch from Armand's bistro.

She hadn't gotten much rest when Hassan arrived.

"Why didn't you go in to work today?" he asked as he took off his coat. Then he turned to look at Lilly's face.

"My God, Lilly! What happened?"

"I got a concussion."

"You got more than that. You're covered with bruises. What happened? Why didn't you tell me?"

Lilly had given her response to the inevitable questions a lot of thought over the past day, even though she wasn't supposed to be thinking very hard. She had decided to tell him what she told Laurel.

"I banged my head on the car door."

He tilted his head and looked at her, his brow wrinkled. "Why didn't you tell me?"

"Because I didn't want you to worry."

"Are you all right? Shouldn't you be lying down?"

"I will, right after lunch."

"If you say so," he said. Lilly pulled out a chair at the kitchen table and sat down. There was a secret part of her that wished Hassan would fuss over her with murmurs of concern and offers to bring lunch to her on a tray while she bundled up in the living room on the sofa, but if he wasn't going to do that, she would have to buck up and stop feeling sorry for herself.

Hassan unpacked the paper bag he had brought from the bistro. There were two *jambon-beurre* sandwiches and a small container of French carrot salad.

"Why don't you get us something to drink and I'll put these sandwiches on plates," Hassan suggested. Lilly got up from the table, opened the fridge, and took out a pitcher of iced tea. Hassan brought two glasses to the table and Lilly filled them both. She had looked forward to being waited on just a little bit, but he obviously wasn't going to do that, either.

When they were seated, Hassan took a bite of his sandwich before asking Lilly for the details of her concussion.

"You banged your head on the car door?" he asked.

Lilly was chewing, so she nodded.

"Where did this happen?" he asked.

She swallowed and took a sip of her tea. "The shop," she said. She didn't meet his eyes.

"Is that why your car isn't in the driveway?"

She nodded again.

"I can go pick up Harry and have him drive it here, then take him back to the shop," Hassan offered.

"Don't bother," Lilly said. "Noley is planning to do that."

"Any news about Alice?" Hassan asked.

"Not much, except the police found one of her shoes in the bushes outside Guy's Place."

"I wonder what that means," he mused aloud.

"Bill said it could mean any number of things." Suddenly she couldn't stand this stilted conversation any longer. "Hassan, is something wrong? You don't seem like yourself today."

Hassan wiped the corners of his mouth with a napkin. "Lilly, I ran into Bill at the bistro. He told me what happened. At the bar." His face, normally soft and warm, looked hard and cold to Lilly.

She looked down at her food. She knew she wouldn't finish her sandwich. In fact, the few bites she had taken were turning to stone in her stomach, making her feel sick.

"I'm sorry," she said quietly. "I shouldn't have lied."

"You didn't just lie once, either. You concocted a whole elaborate story. Why didn't you just tell me the truth?"

"Because I didn't want you to get mad at me for going back to Guy's Place by myself." Lilly looked up, but she still couldn't meet his eyes.

"I would have gone with you, you know."

"But it was terrible for you the last time," Lilly said, finally looking him in the eyes.

"You know what's more terrible? That you've lied to me. I'm relieved that a concussion was the most serious injury you sustained, but what would have happened if Noley hadn't been there? You could have been killed." he said.

Lilly couldn't say anything.

"If you and I are going to be together, I have to be able to trust you, Lilly." He folded his napkin carefully and placed it on the table next to his plate. He pushed his chair back. "I need some time to think about everything. I don't think we should see each other right now. I'm sorry."

He gathered his coat and gloves and left.

CHAPTER 39

*L*illy had stopped crying by the time Laurel got home from school, and she pretended to be asleep on the sofa so Laurel wouldn't see her bloodshot eyes and wonder what had happened.

I am so stupid. I shouldn't have lied. I shouldn't have gone to Guy's Place by myself. I shouldn't have gotten so involved with Alice's disappearance. I should have let the police take care of it instead of putting myself and other people at risk. The thoughts went around and around in her head until the pain was terrible behind her eyes and she felt like she was going to throw up.

There was a knock on the back door and for one glorious moment Lilly thought that perhaps Hassan had come back, ready to forgive her.

But it was Noley. She let herself in with the key Lilly had given her and walked straight to the living room.

"Lilly?" she asked quietly. Lilly didn't move. Maybe Noley would go away if she continued to pretend to be asleep.

"Lilly, if you're awake, listen to me. I spoke to Hassan."

Lilly swallowed and turned over so she was facing Noley.

She couldn't look at her friend, though. "He dumped me," she said.

"He didn't dump you," Noley said.

"Humph."

"He's upset that you lied to him. He'll get over it, I'm sure. He just thinks you two should take a break. He called me so I would come over and check on you. That's not the behavior of someone who doesn't care about you," Noley said. Her tone was soothing, but Lilly felt anything but soothed.

"He may still care about me, but the trust is gone," she said with a choked sob. "There's nothing there to build our relationship up again."

Noley sat down next to Lilly and put her arms around Lilly's shoulders. "Don't cry, honey. I don't think you made a fatal mistake. You're just going to have to give him some time."

"Time," Lilly scoffed. "Time can't build trust again."

"By itself, time can't build trust again. But once Hassan cools down he'll understand that you lied to protect him. That'll count for a lot," Noley said. She gave Lilly's shoulders a squeeze. "Want to go for a walk? It's cold out, so it'll be nice and brisk. Then I'm going to make a super-duper dinner for you and Laurel and me."

"I can't eat," Lilly said.

"You don't know how good it's going to be," Noley said with a smile. "You won't be able to resist it. Come on, we're going outside."

With an effort, Lilly pushed herself up from the sofa and got her coat out of the front closet. She called upstairs to Laurel to let her know she would be back soon, then she and Noley stepped outside, where the snow was falling gently.

Noley took a deep breath. "I know a lot of people get sick of the snow, but I love it. I think I could be happy living at the North Pole."

Lilly smiled for the first time in hours. "I love it, too, but I bet you'd get sick of it eventually."

"Would not." Noley picked up a handful of snow and shaped it as they walked. She hung back a bit when they passed through the wrought iron gate leading to a small neighborhood park, then tossed her snowball at Lilly.

Lilly whipped around, blinking. Noley lobbed another snowball at her shoulder. Lilly grinned in spite of herself and bent down to gather a handful of snow.

Whack! Noley got her again. Lilly straightened up, drew her arm back, and let her snowball fly. It hit its mark, right in the middle of Noley's chest. Noley let out a shriek and fired again. Lilly began shaping snowballs as fast as she could, stockpiling them for quick use, now and then pelting Noley with one. Noley was doing the same and after about twenty minutes the two friends were laughing so hard they couldn't keep making ammunition. They both flopped down onto a snowy bench, exhausted.

"That was fun," Lilly panted.

Noley laughed. "I got my exercise for the day." Then she paused. "We probably shouldn't have done that. How's your head?"

"It's killing me, but I don't care. I needed that."

"You hungry?" asked Noley.

"I think so."

Noley grinned and they walked back to Lilly's house.

"What happened to you two?" Laurel asked when Lilly and Noley tromped into the kitchen. They were both still covered with snow.

"We had a snowball fight," Lilly said with a laugh.

Laurel smiled. "What's for dinner?" she asked Lilly.

Noley answered. "It's a surprise. Now go upstairs, finish your homework, and let me get cooking. Lilly, you go lie down on the sofa."

Laurel and Lilly did as they had been told and pretty soon the aromas wafting from the kitchen were making Lilly's mouth water. She was trying to rest without thinking about Hassan, but it wasn't easy. Tears sprang to her eyes more than once, but she was determined not to cry and not to let Laurel see that she was upset.

"Dinner," Noley said, peeking around the corner into the living room. "I'll call Laurel down." She called upstairs for Laurel while Lilly padded into the kitchen in her sock feet.

Noley had outdone herself. In the middle of the table sat a plate with three pork chops. They had some kind of sauce on them. A bowl of mashed potatoes sat next to the chops, and there was a green salad that didn't look like it was made of lettuce. A sweet scent permeated the air in the kitchen.

"Wow!" Laurel exclaimed. "This looks good. What is it?"

"Apple cider-glazed pork chops, garlic mashed potatoes, and shredded Brussels sprouts salad with pomegranate arils. It's the ultimate comfort food dinner. There's dessert, too, but you have to clean your plate." She winked at Laurel.

"Thanks, Nol," Lilly said with a sad smile. She was thinking about Hassan again.

"Sit down," Noley told her briskly. "You need to eat after playing in the snow." She poured beverages for all three of them and then joined Lilly and Laurel at the table. Over dinner Noley kept the conversation going at a swift clip, not letting silence fill any of the time. She asked about Laurel's homework, her teachers, the classes she was most looking forward to taking in college, and her wardrobe. They talked about Noley's favorite classes in high school and college, the towns and cities where she worked before moving to Juniper Junction, and her favorite-ever meals.

If Lilly wasn't completely exhausted from the snowball fight, the conversation at dinner finished the job. It wasn't boring—just fast-paced. By the time Noley brought homemade butterscotch pudding with whipped cream from the refrigerator, Lilly was having a hard time keeping her eyes open.

"Laurel and I are going to do the dishes," Noley announced after dinner. "Lilly, you're going to bed. You've had an extremely long day."

"I want to go to the shop in the morning," Lilly said. She was so tired her lips felt too thick to talk.

"We'll see. It depends on how you feel when you wake up," Noley said. "Now, shoo. Off to bed."

Lilly hugged Noley and gave Laurel a goodnight kiss. "Thanks, Noley. I needed that."

"Needed what?"

"Everything."

Lilly was so tired she didn't even have time to dwell on Hassan before falling into a deep sleep.

But he was the first thing on her mind when she woke up the next morning. Noley had slept on the sofa again, so she was already making coffee when Lilly went downstairs.

"How do you feel this morning?" Noley asked.

Lilly swallowed. "Okay, I guess." Her bottom lip started to quiver.

"None of that this morning," Noley scolded. "Do you think you feel well enough to go into the shop for a little while?"

Lilly nodded, pouring herself a mug of coffee. She added creamer to it and stirred it thoughtfully. "Maybe I'll stay all day."

"Why don't you just go in and see how things go? Maybe you'll want to come home and rest this afternoon. I'll drop you off and then whenever you want to come home, just call my cell and I'll come pick you up."

Lilly nodded.

"Lil, Hassan will be back. That's the way he is. You need to stop worrying."

"Did he tell you he'd be back?" Lilly asked, hope surging in her chest.

"Well, no," Noley admitted. "But I just know he will."

Lilly's spirit sank again. "I doubt it. But I can't sit around here all day or I'll go nuts. I'll be better off at work."

After Laurel had left for school, Noley drove Lilly to the jewelry shop. Harry wasn't there yet, so Lilly unlocked the back door, opened the vault, and set about putting all the pieces of jewelry in their display cases in the front of the store. It would be another hour before the shop was open for the day. She had promised Noley she wouldn't do any paperwork, so although the paperwork was practically screaming for attention, Lilly forced herself to ignore it.

She was in the front of the store, arranging a necklace against its burgundy velvet background, when the office door opened.

"Morning, Harry," Lilly said, then looked up with a smile.

But it wasn't Harry standing there. It was Mary Louise.

CHAPTER 40

"What are you doing here?" Lilly asked. She eyed Mary Louise warily.

"I just wanted to have a little talk before Harry gets to work." Mary Louise kept her tone light, but her eyes glittered with malevolence.

"A talk about what?"

"Your new rule," she said, putting air quotes around the word 'rule.'

Lilly moved slightly farther behind the display case. "It's not a new rule, Mary Louise. It's an old rule that I've begun enforcing."

Mary Louise took a step forward. "I don't appreciate you interfering with my relationship with Harry."

"I'm not trying to interfere with anything, but I do think you're trying to take advantage of Alice's disappearance to finagle your way into a romance with Harry. As far as I'm concerned, that's despicable. But it's Harry's business, not mine."

"So why enforce your stupid rule?" Mary Louise asked with a sneer.

"Because visits from people were causing a lot of stress for

Harry and I can't have an employee who's not focused on his work." Lilly didn't add that it was visits from a certain someone who were causing stress, and that the stress wasn't just Harry's —it was hers, too.

"If you're referring to me, I can assure you that *my* visits aren't causing Harry any stress," Mary Louise said quietly.

It was the tone of her voice that set off alarm bells in Lilly's head, which was starting to ache. Mary Louise took one step closer to Lilly. And when Lilly glanced toward the window facing Main Street, that's when Mary Louise acted.

With a sudden burst of movement, Mary Louise ran around the end of the display case where Lilly was standing. Lilly backed up to the wall behind her, but couldn't go any further. Everything happened so quickly. She put her arms up over her face to protect herself as Mary Louise came at her with fists flying.

"Mary Louise! Stop!" Lilly cried. "What's the matter with you?" Since Mary Louise had her backed into a corner, there wasn't much Lilly could do in the face of the onslaught, but she did manage to kick Mary Louise in the shin. Hard.

"Ow!" Mary Louise howled. Lilly kept kicking, grateful to discover that, despite her concussion, she had the ability to fight back. Mary Louise was trying to reach for Lilly's neck when Lilly landed a kick right in the center of her knee. Her leg buckled and she dropped to the floor, clutching her knee.

Lilly acted quickly. She jumped over Mary Louise and ran for the office door. The front door was closer, but it was still locked and she was afraid Mary Louise would get up and grab her if she took the time to grapple with the key to unlock the door.

She flung open the office door, slammed it behind her, and ran straight into Harry.

"Harry!" She collapsed into him with a flood of relief.

"Lilly! What happened?" he asked.

"It's Mary Louise," Lilly said, taking a ragged breath. "She's out there. She attacked me." She waved a limp hand toward the front of the shop.

"Are you all right? Can I leave you in here for a minute?" Harry asked quickly. Lilly nodded and waved toward the front of the store again.

Harry wheeled around and was just reaching for the office door when they heard a terrific crash coming from the front.

He turned back and looked at Lilly with wide eyes. "Don't tell me...." He yanked the office door open. Lilly stood up on shaky legs and followed him.

They both gasped in dismay at the millions of shards of glass on the floor of the shop and the gaping hole left in the front window. Mary Louise was gone. A metal stool lay on the sidewalk. Cold air had already permeated the store and Lilly shivered. She closed her eyes. "I don't believe it."

"I'll call the police." Harry grabbed his cell phone from his back pocket and hit nine-one-one. He spoke into the phone briefly, then turned to Lilly. "They'll be here in just a minute."

Head pounding and heart racing, Lilly could do nothing but stand there, frozen in shock.

It was Bill who answered the call to Lilly's shop. Lilly watched as he pulled his cruiser to an abrupt stop out front, then spoke into the walkie-talkie on his shoulder as he strode toward the store. Lilly picked her way carefully to the door, glass crunching beneath her feet. She unlocked the door and opened it to admit Bill. It seemed foolish to unlock the door in view of the huge hole in the window.

"What happened?" he asked, looking around.

"A woman came in and tried to attack me. I got away and ran into the office. She must have smashed the window with that stool and run off when she heard Harry's voice," Lilly explained. She had managed to calm down and think more clearly while she waited for police to arrive, but her explanation was hurried and breathless.

"Are you hurt?" Bill asked. Lilly shook her head. "Do you want me to call for an ambulance, just to be on the safe side?"

"No. I'm fine. My head hurts, but that's from the concussion." Bill turned away and spoke into his walkie-talkie again.

They only had to wait a few minutes for other officers to arrive on the scene. Like a well-oiled machine, they began processing the scene and asking questions of Lilly and Harry.

Lilly told the officer who was questioning her that Mary Louise had been the culprit. The officer issued a bulletin for the rest of the department to be watching for her and asked that two officers be dispatched to her home and to the community college.

Only a couple minutes later, an ambulance drew up in front of the police cars lining Main Street. Two paramedics came into the store. Lilly recognized the one who had treated her at Guy's Place. He looked at her in surprise.

"You again?" he asked.

Bill walked over to the paramedic and explained briefly that he wanted Lilly checked out because of the concussion.

"Bill, I told you not to call an ambulance," Lilly said between clenched teeth.

"You're not the boss of me," he said with a grin. Lilly had to smile. The paramedic gave Bill and Lilly a look of confusion.

"She's my sister," Bill explained. The paramedic nodded.

"My sister's not the boss of me, either," he said. "At least sometimes."

"Exactly," Bill said.

"Okay, everyone. Can we get this show on the road?" Lilly asked in exasperation. She looked at the paramedic. "I'm fine, really. I know you're going to tell me I need to lie down or do something equally useless to treat the concussion, but I can't leave here now. I have to contact the insurance company and call around to get the window replaced."

"Let me check you over. Then we'll go from there, okay?" the paramedic suggested. Lilly submitted to his tests and ministrations while police buzzed around her. Proprietors from neighboring shops came over and stood on the sidewalk talking to Harry, calling out to Lilly with their good wishes. She could only nod as the paramedic worked. Finally he finished his examination.

"You're right, you should go home and rest," he said. "It's not a good idea to stay in a place that's so hectic. So I'm going to advise you to go home—obviously, whether you take that advice is up to you. But I will need you to sign off on something that says I told you to go home."

"I'll sign anything," Lilly said. "I just want to get started cleaning up this place. So much for shatterproof glass."

Before long the paramedics and the ambulance pulled away and only one police officer was left in the store. Bill had been one of the last officers to leave, telling Lilly he would stop by after his shift so he could help clean up. The officer who was left approached Lilly. "Do you plan to press charges against Mary Louise Morrison?" he asked. Lilly exchanged glances with Harry.

"Do I have to decide that right now?" she asked.

"No, but we're still going to bring her in for questioning," the officer answered. "The district attorney may bring charges against her regardless of what you decide, so be aware of that."

"I will, thanks," Lilly said. The officer left, telling her he'd be in touch after someone questioned Mary Louise.

Lilly and Harry set about cleaning up the shop. Several of the Main Street merchants sent employees to help with the task, and by lunchtime all the glass had been swept up. Harry had put away all the jewelry displays once the police had allowed it, and someone from the hardware store had brought wood and tools to board up the front window until the glass could be replaced.

When Lilly had thanked all the helpers who had given their time to clean up, she and Harry were left alone in the shop. Lilly sat down on the stool Mary Louise had thrown through the window.

"Are you going to press charges?" Harry asked, leaning on the glass display counter beside her.

She sighed. "I don't know yet. Part of me says I should and part of me is afraid of what she might do the next time she gets a chance."

CHAPTER 41

"She's unstable, Harry," Lilly said.

"I know. I should have seen this coming. I blame myself for this whole thing, Lilly. If I had been more straightforward with her, this might not have happened."

"It's not your fault, Harry. You didn't force her to attack me or to break the window."

"Hmm...."

The events of the day were beginning to take their toll on Lilly. She had managed to keep Hassan out of her thoughts until that moment, but the memory of the look he had given her when he caught her in the lie suddenly loomed large. She closed her eyes and willed herself to stay calm. She had looked forward to the days he would come into the shop and eat lunch with her, but today she would be eating alone. It wasn't being alone that she minded—it was the reason. She took a deep breath and was relieved when a representative of her insurance company phoned just a moment later to begin discussing the damage to the store window. The agent promised to hurry over to inspect the damage before the glazier got there, so Lilly's mind would be kept away from thoughts of Hassan, at least for a little while.

The insurance agent arrived, took the necessary measurements, statements, and photos, and left. She was followed shortly by the glazier, who took more measurements and photos. As much as Lilly wanted to stay in the shop, she had to admit that a nap sounded good.

"Harry, let's close up for the rest of the day. Go home and try to relax. That's what I'm going to do, too."

"Easier said than done, boss," he said.

"I know. But there's no use in staying open this afternoon. You're welcome to hang out at my house if you want, but I'm afraid it'll be pretty boring."

"That's okay. I'll head home."

Harry left and Lilly called Noley for a ride. When she explained what had transpired at the jewelry store that morning, Noley was horrified.

"Have you talked to Bill?" she asked in alarm.

"Yes. He called an ambulance after I told him not to."

"Good for him," Noley said. "You are never going to heal from this concussion, I swear. I'm taking you home and making sure you don't do another thing today. I'll be there in ten minutes."

Lilly pushed the *End Call* button, then, without thinking, dialed Hassan's number to tell him what had happened.

"Hello? Lilly?"

She gasped in horror. "Oh, I'm sorry. Um, I called you by mistake. I'm sorry about that." She hung up, her cheeks burning with embarrassment.

Not five seconds later, her phone rang. Of course it was Hassan. Should she answer it? She decided to let it ring. If he wanted to, he could leave a voicemail. She was too ashamed to answer his call. Telling him everything was just automatic—she would have to be more careful about that in the future.

And sure enough, Hassan left a voicemail. "Hi, Lilly. I'm just calling to make sure everything is okay. Give me a call if you need anything." To Lilly, though his words sounded sincere, the tone of Hassan's voice radiated distance and coolness. They definitely didn't have the timbre of someone in love.

Lilly was miserable.

She was so miserable that she went right to bed once Noley took her home, but not before throwing away the remainder of the gourmet chocolate Hassan had given her. Just looking at them twisted her stomach into knots—she certainly wasn't about to eat any more of them.

She woke up several hours later and padded downstairs quietly. Noley and Laurel were in the kitchen talking. She listened to their conversation from her place on the stairs.

"It was definitely a rough day for your mom," Noley was saying.

"Why would someone break the window like that?" Laurel asked.

"It all started over a man," Noley replied. "There are three reasons I think Mary Louise did it. First, she was very angry. Second, she's not playing with a full deck. And third, she probably knew she shouldn't have approached your mom and was embarrassed to see Harry right then. As she saw it, the only way to deal with the situation was to get out of there as quickly as she could."

After several moments of silence, Laurel spoke.

"I'm sure you know I'm grounded because I was with a couple girls when they put glue in the locks of a few stores on Main Street."

"Yeah," Noley said in a quiet voice.

"Do you think this happened to Mom because of what I did?"

"You mean like some kind of karma?" Noley asked. It was clear from her tone that Laurel's question had confused her.

"Yeah, I guess like karma."

"I don't believe in karma," Noley said. "I don't think what

you did had anything to do with what Mary Louise did at the jewelry shop."

"Well, I feel really bad about it. I wish I had never done it, and not just because I'm grounded over it," Laurel said.

Lilly had to smile to herself. Laurel was engaging in introspection. Maybe there was a silver lining in the day's events, after all.

That night as Lilly, Laurel, and Noley sat down to dinner, Laurel remarked, "Hey, why hasn't Hassan been over for dinner?"

Lilly and Noley exchanged glances.

"What? What's the matter? Is he okay?" Laurel asked.

"Hassan has been busy," Noley said. Lilly knew she was trying to help, but she had learned her lesson about lying—at least for the moment.

"Hassan and I aren't seeing each other right now," she said gently.

Laurel's mouth dropped open and she put her fork down. "What happened?" she asked in bewilderment.

"He's angry at me," Lilly said. She may have learned her lesson about lying, but she had already lied to Laurel about the origin of her concussion, so why tell the truth now and risk having her *and* Hassan mad at her?

"Why is he mad?" Laurel asked.

"I lied to him about something," Lilly admitted. "It was stupid and I won't do it again. But he found out and he, rightly, doesn't want to see me right now because I broke his trust." She put her own fork down, suddenly not hungry anymore.

"I thought you would marry him," Laurel said quietly.

Lilly had to swallow around a sob that threatened to burst from her throat.

"I think we shouldn't jump to any conclusions about Hassan," Noley broke in. "I'm sure things will work out, but we just have to give him some time. You two aren't going to let this delicious dinner get cold, are you?"

Lilly and Laurel both sighed and picked up their forks again.

"Honestly, it's a good thing I'm here," Noley said. "You ladies wouldn't eat anything!" Her remark elicited smiles from Lilly and Laurel, and conversation after that was a little more upbeat.

Lilly's cell phone rang right after dinner. It was Bill.

"I just wanted to let you know that we brought Mary Louise into the station for questioning."

"And what did she say?" Lilly asked.

Bill hesitated. "Well, she more or less corroborated the story you gave the police."

"More or less? What does that mean?"

"I can't really discuss her statement, but don't be surprised if you are questioned again. She kind of implied that you might have attacked her first."

"What?!" Lilly exclaimed. "Of course I didn't attack her first!"

"Easy does it," Bill said. "No one thinks you attacked her first, but the officers in charge of the file can't let that allegation go without investigating it. They can tell from talking to Mary Louise that she has a screw loose."

"Did anyone ask her again about Alice? I can't help thinking she has something to do with Alice's disappearance. And if she didn't actually do it, she must know more than she's saying about it."

"They did ask her again, and she swears she knows nothing."

"You just said yourself that they think she has a screw loose."

"No doubt she does, but without any proof that she did anything, there's not much anyone can do. There are no leads that point to her," Bill said.

Lilly sighed. "Attacking the boss of a missing woman's boyfriend isn't enough?"

"I'm afraid that's a bit of a stretch," Bill replied.

Then I'll just have to find a lead myself, Lilly thought.

"How are you feeling?" Bill asked.

"Well, aside from the pounding in my head and the stress that comes along with property damage and the business I lose from having to close for a day, really well." Lilly smirked even though Bill couldn't see her.

"Get some rest and I'll talk to you tomorrow," Bill said. "I talked to Nikki earlier. She said Mom had a good day."

Lilly could feel the shame creeping into her cheeks. "I haven't even called over there," she said. "I'll go see Mom tomorrow."

It was late when Lilly got ready for bed that night, since she had taken such a long nap during the afternoon. Noley had decided, at Lilly's insistence, that she would stay at her own house that night. She told her she would be over early in the morning to check on things.

Lilly was climbing into bed when her cell phone rang. For an instant she hoped Hassan was calling, but when she looked at her phone she didn't immediately recognize the number.

"Hello?" she asked.

A sob erupted on the other end.

"Who is this?" Lilly demanded.

"It's Tracy. You know, from Guy's Place."

"Tracy? What's wrong?" Lilly asked.

"Suzanne is gone."

CHAPTER 42

"*W*hat do you mean *gone?*" Lilly asked. "Where did she go?"

"She's missing." Tracy sniffled loudly. "She didn't show up for her shift tonight and there was no answer on her cell or at her apartment. Guy asked me to go pick her up and she's not there."

"Have you called the police?" Lilly asked.

"Yes. I called them and then I called you right away. Do you think this has anything to do with Alice's disappearance?"

"I don't know," Lilly said. "But it's a pretty weird coincidence if they're unrelated. Is there anything I can do?"

"I don't think so." Tracy let out a short sob. "It's just that Suzanne is my best friend and I'm really worried about her."

"I am, too. My brother is on the force in Juniper Junction. I'll ask him what the police in Lupine are saying about it. He won't know anything tonight, but by tomorrow I ought to be able to get some information from him."

"Would you do that? That would be great. Do you want me to call you in the morning?" Tracy asked. The pleading tone in her voice was heartbreaking to hear.

"I'll call you as soon as I talk to Bill," Lilly promised. "Are you at Guy's Place now?"

"Yeah. Guy's beside himself. Two dancers missing less than three weeks apart isn't good for business."

"There's a lot more at stake here than Guy's bottom line," Lilly said wryly. "The lives of two women are much more important."

"You know that and I know that, but try telling Guy."

"Hang in there, Tracy. I'm sure the police will find both women," Lilly said before she hung up.

She hoped she was right.

She was afraid she wouldn't be able to sleep that night, knowing that there was someone out there preying on dancers, and she turned out to be right. When Noley dropped by early the next morning, she let out a cry of dismay when she saw Lilly in the kitchen making coffee.

"What happened to you? You look terrible."

"Suzanne went missing last night," Lilly said in a monotone.

Noley gasped. "Have the police found her yet?"

Lilly gave a dejected shrug. "I doubt it. Tracy probably would have called if they found Suzanne. She's the one who called me last night to let me know."

"I wonder if Alice and Suzanne are together somewhere," Noley said.

"As much as I hate that Suzanne is also missing, I do hope they're together," Lilly said. "Their chances of escaping or even surviving are better with two of them, I would think."

"I agree," Noley said. "Have you talked to Bill?"

"Not yet. The case is with the Lupine police, so Bill probably won't know anything about it yet. But I'll give him a call in a couple hours to see if he's heard anything."

"Can I do anything around here?" Noley asked.

"There's nothing to do," Lilly said. "That is, unless you want to give me a ride to work. I have a doctor's appointment this afternoon to see if she'll clear me to drive. Then, if you don't mind, maybe you and I could drive out to Guy's Place so I can get my car."

"That's fine," Noley said. "Are you sure you're ready to go back into the shop today?"

"Yes. The glass company is supposed to replace the window first thing this morning, so I have to be there for that. Then I want to get things back to normal as soon as possible."

"I can understand that. Just don't overdo. I know you, and I know you'll be tempted," Noley said with a mocking frown.

Lilly smiled. "You won't know what to do with yourself when my concussion has healed and Laurel and I are ready to be on our own again."

"Oh, I'll think of something." Noley chuckled. "Maybe I'll reacquaint myself with Bill. I haven't seen him too much lately."

The mention of Bill brought Hassan straight to the forefront of Lilly's mind and Noley seemed to sense that. She said briskly, "Now, let's have some breakfast and you need to get ready for work. I brought muffins. Is that coffee ready?"

Lilly nodded, grateful for Noley's attempt to redirect her thoughts.

As soon as everyone had eaten and Laurel was on her way to school, Noley drove Lilly over to the jewelry shop.

"Do you need a ride to the doctor?" asked Noley.

"No, she's just up Main Street. I'll call you if she's ready to let me drive again." Lilly crossed her fingers and held them up.

As soon as she was in the shop, she called Bill. She explained that one of Alice's co-workers had gone missing and asked if he could find out anything about it. He promised to make some inquiries and get back to her.

It wasn't long before Harry arrived, followed almost immediately by the people to install the new window. It took a while, but the result was worth the wait. The man in charge of the installation confirmed that the glass was shatterproof this time, then the crew were on their way. Lilly and Harry bustled around the shop, readying the display cases for the day, and soon the customers started to come in.

While Harry was talking to a couple who had come in to buy a birthday present for their daughter, Lilly's cell phone rang. It was Bill. She went into the back so she could talk where it was quieter and more private.

He didn't waste any time getting to the point. "I've got bad news, Lilly."

Lilly froze. "What is it?" she asked, terse and quiet.

"They found Suzanne's body this morning."

"Oh, no," Lilly breathed. She sat down hard at her desk. "I can't believe it."

"I'm sorry to have to be the one to tell you," Bill said.

"Who found her?"

"The owner of Guy's Place."

"Guy found her? Where was she?"

"In the woods behind her apartment building. He says he went there himself to look for her."

"How did he know to look in the woods?" Lilly asked.

"Apparently he noticed some trampled brush and he went to investigate it," Bill replied.

"Is he a suspect?" Lilly asked. She hoped he was. There was something about that man—besides his overt racism—that she didn't like.

"I don't know about that. The Lupine police are working the case. I don't have all the details."

"Thanks for letting me know." Lilly hesitated. She wasn't sure she wanted to know the answer to the question she had to ask. "Bill, what do you think this means for Alice?"

"I wish I knew. There isn't enough information yet about Suzanne's death. We'll know more when the police finish their initial investigation."

"Should I tell Harry?" Lilly asked.

"He's going to find out sooner or later that the body of a stripper from Guy's Place was found. The police may not release her name, and you don't want Harry to panic. You might want to soften the blow and tell him before he finds out on the news."

Lilly took a deep breath. "All right. I'll tell him. Keep me in the loop, will you?"

"I'll tell you what I can. Since the Juniper Junction police aren't really involved in this one, it may take some time for me to get information on it. But I've got some buddies on the force in Lupine, so they'll let me know what they find."

"Thanks." Lilly hung up. She closed her eyes, wishing she didn't have to call Tracy. But when Tracy answered the phone, she told Lilly she had already heard the news. She was too distraught to talk about it just then. Lilly hung up and sat at her desk, staring into space for what seemed like a long time, until there was a knock on the office door.

"Boss," Harry called, "Hassan's here to see you."

I can't deal with him right now, Lilly thought. But she knew she should go out and talk to him. The flutter that seemed to take shape every time the phone rang, every time she hoped Hassan was calling to forgive her, wasn't there. In its place was the dread of having to tell Harry what she had just learned. For once, Hassan wasn't on the top of her list of priorities.

She stood up, squaring her shoulders, and walked into the front of the shop. Hassan stood by the door, as handsome as always in a long wool coat and leather gloves.

"Hi," Lilly said. Suddenly she felt shy.

"Hi. I just came in to let you know I'm leaving for Washington this afternoon."

She had focused so intently on his face that she hadn't seen the suitcase on the floor behind him.

She nodded. "Okay. Have a safe trip."

He gave her an unreadable look. "Are you okay?"

She nodded, but remained silent. She had no right to discuss Suzanne's death with anyone before she talked to Harry.

"Do you think we could talk when I get back?" he asked.

"Yeah. Just give me a call," she said. Her gaze drifted briefly toward Harry, who was conspicuously staying away from them. She focused again on Hassan.

Hassan reached for the handle of his suitcase and turned toward the door, but he looked back over his shoulder. It looked like he was opening his mouth to say something, but Lilly stopped him by speaking first.

"Have a safe trip," she repeated.

"Okay," he said with a nod. He walked out onto Main Street and didn't look in her direction again.

Every emotion with the exception of happiness was running through Lilly's head. She didn't know if she wanted to cry or scream. With an effort, she turned away from watching Hassan head up Main Street and spoke to Harry.

"Harry, we need to have a talk."

CHAPTER 43

*H*arry gave her a confused look. "Am I in trouble? I hope I'm not in trouble. I couldn't handle it."

"Of course you're not in trouble. But I have something to tell you," she said, echoing Bill's words.

"Is it about Alice?" His breathing was quicker, his eyes wide.

"No, it's not about Alice. But there is another dancer, Suzanne, who works with Alice, who went missing last night. They found her body this morning. I just wanted to tell you—"

Harry sank to the floor, his head in his hands.

"Oh, no." Harry shook his head back and forth vigorously. "What do you think that means?"

He looked up at Lilly, his face contorted with grief and fear.

"It doesn't mean anything just yet, except that there will be people trying to find Alice around the clock if there aren't already. I suspect there already are."

"What happened to Suzanne?"

"I don't know. I just got the information from Bill. And Suzanne's best friend, Tracy, called me last night to let me know that Suzanne was missing."

"So you don't know how Suzanne died?"

Lilly shook her head.

"I don't think I want to know, anyway," Harry said. "Do they think the person who killed her is the one who took Alice?"

"I don't know, Harry, but let's not lose hope. Suzanne could have surprised a burglar, she could have been the victim of a random attack—we just don't know. Bill's going to let me know once he hears something."

"I can't stand the waiting. That's the worst part, Lilly. I wish there was something I could do to help find Alice." His unspoken words hung in the air between them: *or Alice's body*.

"The best way for you to help would be if you were able to think of something the police don't already know—something that would provide them with a lead."

"I know. Believe me, I know. All I do is try to think of something we've missed."

"Would you like to go home?" Lilly asked.

Harry stood up from the floor, closing his eyes and taking a deep breath. "I think I'd better stay here. I appreciate the offer, but if I go home I'll go nuts."

"Okay. But if you want to leave, just let me know. I have to go to a doctor's appointment this afternoon, but I can close the store if you don't want to be here."

"No, no. You go to the appointment. I'll take charge here for a little while."

It was a busy day in the shop, for which Lilly was grateful. When the time came for Lilly to slip out to her appointment, Harry was busy with a customer and there was another one waiting to talk to him. Lilly gave him a quick wave and left.

The doctor's office was a short walk, so Lilly was back at work in no time, complete with the doctor's permission to drive again and her blessing to get some paperwork done. The first thing Lilly had done after leaving the doctor's office was to call

Noley to tell her the good news about driving and the bad news about Suzanne. Noley was shocked that Suzanne's body had been found.

"I hardly knew her, but she seemed really nice," Noley said.

"She was," Lilly said. "She gave me the impression that she could take care of herself, so I think the person who attacked her must have surprised her."

"Meaning it was someone she didn't know?"

"Maybe. Or maybe it was someone she did know who came out of nowhere and attacked her."

"Are you sure you want to go out to Guy's Place to get your car so soon?" Noley asked. "I'm not sure we should be going out there with everything that's gone on. I don't mind driving you around, so don't think you need to do it for me."

"I know. I just want my car back," Lilly said. "I like having it because I know I can go somewhere in a hurry if I have to, without calling you or waking you or disturbing you."

"If you say so," Noley said. "I can pick you up after the shop closes and we can go from there if you want."

"Sounds good. See you then. And thanks."

"I hope you know what you're doing," Noley said with a sigh.

"Of course I know what I'm doing," Lilly said.

"Famous last words."

* * *

Lilly didn't hear from Bill for the rest of the day and she hesitated to call him because she didn't want to bother him any more than necessary.

When she and Harry had put away the displays and locked up for the night, Harry went home and Lilly stood on the sidewalk waiting for Noley to show up. She was worried about Harry. He had kept up a brave front for the customers who had come into the store that day, but it seemed to have exhausted him. When he left he looked worn out and haggard. Lilly had made him promise to get a good night's sleep and come in to work late the next day if he was able to sleep in.

Noley pulled up to the curb and Lilly slid into the passenger seat.

"Are you sure about this?" Noley asked.

"More than sure."

"I can't believe Suzanne is dead," Noley murmured.

"I know. I'll call Tracy again tonight and see how she's doing. She was too upset to talk earlier. She and the other dancers must be afraid."

"I wonder if the two cases are related," Noley mused.

"I wouldn't be surprised. What are the chances that two dancers from the same bar go missing in the same month and the two cases are unrelated? Pretty slim, I would say."

"You're probably right. All the more reason to get in your car and get the heck away from Guy's Place as soon as we can," Noley said.

"I keep wondering about Guy. I just don't like him."

"That doesn't mean he's a killer," Noley pointed out.

"I know. I'm just thinking out loud. He was just so rude the night Hassan and I tried to get some information from the dancers." She expected Hassan's name to send a wave of self-pity over her, but it didn't. "He came into the shop today," she said.

"Guy?" Noley exclaimed.

"No, Hassan," Lilly said with a little laugh.

"Really? What did he want?"

"Just to say that he was headed to Washington and that he'd like to talk when he gets back. With everything else that's been happening, I've been thinking about him a little less. I suppose that's a good thing."

Noley shrugged. "I guess. He didn't say anything else?"

"Actually, I think he was going to, but I cut him off. I had just found out about Suzanne and I wanted to talk to Harry about it. That was more important at the time."

"I hope things work out between you two," Noley said.

"So do I."

They drove in silence as the night nestled into the mountains. When Noley pulled into Guy's parking lot, she glanced at Lilly. "Remember, hurry. I don't want to be here longer than necessary." She parked next to Lilly's car. There were two men talking not far away, near the entrance to the bar. Lilly got out and reached into her coat pocket for her car key.

"Hey!"

Lilly looked up, startled. She whipped her head around to see who was talking. One of the men was advancing toward her. A wave of cold sweat swept over her and she held the car key so it was sticking out between two of her fingers in case she needed to defend herself. She could hear Noley's car door open.

"Oh, it's you again. I'm glad you're finally getting that thing out of here." The man stepped closer and gestured toward Lilly's car. It was Guy.

Noley had come to stand next to Lilly. "She was just cleared today to drive again or else we would have been here sooner." She sounded defiant, as if she expected Guy to tell Lilly he was charging her for parking.

"Good. I don't like cars here overnight. Liability, you know," he said, his voice gruff.

"What about the liability of someone being attacked and injured on your property?" Noley challenged.

"Noley, it's okay. Let's go," Lilly said quietly. Suddenly their roles seemed reversed. Noley was gearing up for an argument and Lilly wanted to leave. Her head was starting to hurt.

"Just get outta here before I call the cops and report you," Guy said in a menacing voice.

"Report us for what?" Noley asked.

"Just get out!" Guy bellowed. "I don't need no one gettin' hurt again."

Was that a threat?

CHAPTER 44

"Noley, we need to leave. Now," Lilly said. Noley turned and got into her car, still glaring at Guy through the windshield.

"I don't want to see you back here," Guy spat at Lilly. "You're nothing but trouble."

Lilly didn't answer. She slid behind the wheel of her car, started the engine, and pulled out as swiftly as she could without hitting anything. Noley circled around behind her and tailgated her all the way back to Juniper Junction.

When Lilly pulled into her driveway, Noley pulled in, too. She rolled down her window when Lilly walked over to her car.

"I'm sorry about my outburst," Noley said. "That man is the worst."

"He is," Lilly agreed. She shivered, but not from the cold. "And we were standing right next to him. If he was the one who killed Suzanne and kidnapped Alice…." She couldn't finish her sentence.

"I don't think he was the one," Noley said. "He's got a business to run, and both women were an important part of that."

"But sometimes people let their emotions make decisions

instead of their brains. It would have been good for business if Hassan and I could have gotten a drink while we were there, too, but he threw us out. That's bad for business."

Noley acknowledged the logic with a nod. "Well, I'm going to head back to my house. Are you sure you'll be all right tonight?"

"We'll be fine, I promise," Lilly said. She leaned down and pecked Noley on the cheek. "Thanks for going with me tonight. You made me braver."

"I'm afraid I let my emotions make my decisions," Noley answered wryly.

Lilly laughed. She wouldn't have been able to laugh just thirty minutes before, but the stress of being at Guy's Place was beginning to wane.

"See you later," she said. Noley drove away and Lilly went into the house.

"Laurel!" she called out. No answer. Lilly went to the bottom of the stairs and called again. And again, there was no response.

Thinking Laurel might be wearing earphones, she went and tapped on her bedroom door. Nothing. She tapped more loudly and opened the bedroom door, peering around it to see if Laurel was there.

The room was empty. *I wonder what 'grounded' means to her,* Lilly thought. She had returned Laurel's phone to her, so she pulled out her own cell and texted Laurel

Where are you?

She waited several minutes for a reply, and getting none, she called Laurel. The phone went right to voicemail.

Now Lilly was mad. She made more noise than she should have in the kitchen while she made dinner, then eventually sat down by herself to enjoy the cold, limp tuna salad sandwich she had slapped together. Barney didn't beg for a single bite—even he didn't find dinner appealing.

She was finishing her sandwich when her cell phone rang. She snatched it up, expecting a barrage of excuses from Laurel over why she had violated her punishment.

But it was Bill.

"Lilly," he began.

"Is it Mom? I haven't even had a chance to go over there yet. I swear I'll go over after dinner. Is she all right?"

"Mom's fine, as far as I know. I'm calling about Laurel."

Those few simple words turned the tuna sandwich in her stomach to cement.

"What about her? Is she okay?" Lilly asked quickly, her breath caught in her throat.

"She's okay, but she's been brought in again for vandalism. Different type of property damage, same friends."

Lilly set her elbow on the table and supported her head in her hand. "Oh, no. What did they do this time?"

"Spray painting the back of one of the stores on Main Street."

"What is wrong with that kid?" Lilly wondered aloud.

"I don't know, but she needs a ride home. I can't take her right now because I'm so busy. Can I call Noley to come get her?"

"The doctor cleared me to drive today. I'll be down in a couple minutes. You should probably put her in a cell for her own safety, because she's going to need it when I get there."

Bill chuckled. "The cells are full this evening. That's why I'm so busy."

Lilly was back in the car just a few minutes later, speeding down to the Juniper Junction police station.

Laurel was in big trouble.

Lilly stalked into the building, her blood boiling. She told the desk sergeant why she was there and he asked her to take a seat. She fumed in one of the plastic chairs for several minutes, trying to breathe through her mouth so she wouldn't smell the odors of garlic, coffee, and sweat that wafted in the air around her.

Presently Bill came into the station lobby. Lilly stood up expectantly, but he motioned for her to sit down.

"Now, I don't have any kids—" he began.

"Don't," Lilly interrupted him. "Whatever you're going to say, don't. I am furious with her."

"She's really upset this time," Bill said. "I think there's more to the story than I've heard. Just remember that when you're yelling at her."

Lilly slowed her breathing a little bit. "I heard her talking to Noley the other day when she didn't know I was there. She was afraid that when Mary Louise attacked me and broke the shop window, it was karma's way of getting back at Laurel for the acts of vandalism she was responsible for. It surprises me to learn that she's at it again."

"It surprises me, too. She's a good kid, Lil. I got the sense that she learned her lesson the first time. Maybe you can find out what's going on."

Lilly rubbed her eyes. "This has been a long day. I'll take her home and we'll talk about it. Can you bring her out here or do I have to go back there?"

"I'll bring her out." Bill stood and went back into the precinct offices to retrieve his wayward niece while Lilly waited less impatiently than before.

It only took a minute for him to fetch Laurel and bring her to the lobby. It was clear from her puffy eyes and streaked cheeks that Laurel had been crying.

Lilly clenched her teeth, bracing herself for anything—the truth, a pack of lies, a teary outburst full of excuses.

But what happened surprised her. Laurel ran to her, hugged her, and repeated "I'm so sorry" over and over again. Lilly hadn't been prepared for an apology. It disarmed her completely. She looked at Bill for guidance that she knew he wasn't in a position to give. He looked around, focusing on everything but her face.

She held Laurel away from her. "We need to have a talk. Let's go home and you can tell me everything." She thanked Bill, then turned and walked out of the station. Laurel followed a few steps behind.

"Have you eaten?" Lilly asked when they pulled into traffic outside the station.

"No. I'm not hungry."

"Okay."

Neither one spoke until they were home. Lilly pulled a chair out from the kitchen table, sat down heavily, and motioned for Laurel to sit down opposite her. Laurel sat.

"Tell me what happened today," Lilly began.

Laurel took a deep breath. "Karley and Bella and I were hanging out in study hall today and they told me they were headed to Main Street after it got dark. They went shopping the other day and I guess one of the salesladies was rude to Bella. So they were going to take some paint and splash it over the back of her store."

Lilly said nothing, so Laurel took another deep breath and continued.

"They picked me up once it started to get dark outside. I told them I was grounded from the last time I went with them, but they said as long as you weren't home, you'd never know I was gone. So I went, and Bella had a can of spray paint because she couldn't find any regular paint in her garage. I didn't do the actual spray painting. I was just there while they did it."

Laurel stopped talking and Lilly presumed she had reached the end of her explanation. But there was something that confused her.

"Why didn't you just tell them to bug off?" Lilly asked. "Surely you tried telling them *no*."

To her surprise, Laurel started crying all over again.

"Because they said they would start a rumor about me at school if I didn't go with them." Laurel was crying harder now, dragging in short breaths between sobs.

"So they *bullied* you into going?" Lilly asked. She was horrified. These girls were monsters.

Laurel nodded, weeping too forcefully to answer with words.

Would being a parent ever get easier?

CHAPTER 45

"They made up some horrible things about me, Mom. They said they'd tell everyone, starting with Nick," Laurel cried.

Lilly got up and put her arms around Laurel. "Things have been pretty awful for you lately, haven't they? And I haven't helped matters because I've been so preoccupied with trying to find Alice. I'm sorry you've had to learn about false friends the hard way. Karley and Bella are no friends of yours."

"I know," Laurel sniffed. "But what's to stop them from spreading rumors about me?"

"I am. I'm going to stop them. I'm going into school first thing in the morning and talk to anyone who will listen to me. Don't worry about this. We're going to solve it."

Laurel swallowed hard and covered her face with her hands. "You can't do that. Everyone will say I'm a snitch." She groaned.

"Okay, then I have something else in mind."

"What?"

"The less I tell you, the better. But no one will know you or I have anything to do with it."

Laurel gave Lilly a skeptical look. "Whatever you're thinking, don't. I'll end up paying for it somehow."

"No, you won't. Now go upstairs and get some sleep. You've had a long day, and so have I. Things will be better tomorrow."

Laurel kissed her mom goodnight and went upstairs. Once Lilly had satisfied herself that Laurel was in her own room with the door closed, she took out her cell phone and called Bill.

"Bill, there's something I'd like you to do for me."

* * *

The next morning when Lilly got to the store Harry was already there. He looked terrible.

"Harry, is there anything I can get for you? Coffee? Something to eat?" Lilly asked in concern. It looked like the stress of Alice's disappearance and Suzanne's death were getting to him.

"There's nothing," Harry said dully. "I couldn't eat if I tried."

"Then how about a milkshake? I can go get you one."

"Maybe I'll have one later," he said. Lilly wondered if he said that just to get her to stop nagging him. He gave her a tired smile as if he knew what she was thinking. "I'm serious. I might have one later."

They busied themselves getting the shop displays ready for the day. Harry's cell phone rang as Lilly was walking to the front door to unlock it.

She returned behind the counter as Harry hung up the phone. He seemed agitated.

"That was David," he said. "He called to ask whether I knew Suzanne. I guess the police told the family about her death so they wouldn't hear it on the news and think the dead woman was Alice. Just like you did for me."

"Why does he want to know if you know Suzanne?" Lilly asked.

"Because he and his crazy parents still think I have something to do with Alice's disappearance, even though the police said my alibi checked out."

"I suppose they're even more worried now that Suzanne has been a victim, too."

"I suppose so. But do they have to be so obvious about thinking I did it?" Harry grimaced. At least the phone call had brought some life to his voice and some color to his cheeks. Lilly didn't worry about him as much when she knew he could muster up some emotion other than fear or doubt. Anger wasn't always such a bad thing.

Lilly was heading out around lunchtime to grab something to eat when Bill came into the shop. Lilly looked at him and cringed. She didn't know whether to expect news about their mother, Laurel, Alice, or Suzanne.

"I was just down the block, so I thought I'd come in to tell you that the bar owner, Guy, has been cleared in Suzanne's death," he said. Harry, who had been listening with an anxious expression, let out a long sigh. His shoulders slumped.

"I was hoping they caught the person who killed Suzanne," he said. "I can't help but think that whoever did it also took Alice."

"You may be right," Bill said. "But they're working hard to find out who killed her. Hopefully they'll get a break and catch the person very soon."

"Thanks for coming by," Lilly said to Bill. "Any other news?" She arched an eyebrow at him.

"I did what you asked me last night," he said. "I don't think there will be any problems."

"Thanks," she said with a smile.

Harry watched the exchange with interest. Lilly suspected he wanted to know what Bill was talking about, but he didn't ask.

Lilly went to Armand's bistro to pick up something for lunch, and she grabbed a sandwich for Harry, too, even though he had said he couldn't eat. She figured the scent of the warm baguette with Brie and honey would do the trick.

And she was right. He didn't eat the whole meal, but he managed to eat over half of it.

"Thanks, Lilly," he said. "I guess I was hungry, but I feel like I shouldn't be treating myself while Alice is God-knows-where doing God-knows-what."

"I get that," Lilly said, "but you can't starve yourself, either. We don't want Alice to find you emaciated when she gets back."

Harry frowned. "I hope she comes back."

Lilly shook her finger at him. "Of course she's coming back. Don't talk like that."

She hoped she was right.

That afternoon Noley called to see how Lilly was feeling.

"I'm doing all right."

"I thought I'd bring dinner over tonight," Noley suggested.

"That sounds good. Thanks."

Now she had something to look forward to. She wondered what Noley would make.

"Do you want to join us for dinner, Harry? I'm sure Noley wouldn't mind."

"Thanks, boss, but I'll pass. I just want to go home after work."

When Lilly got home that night Laurel was in the kitchen, rummaging through the fridge.

"I've got good news," Lilly said. "Noley's bringing dinner. How was school?"

Laurel straightened up and shut the fridge door. "Yum. I wonder what she'll make. School was actually fine. Karley and Bella totally ignored me and I don't think they told any lies about me because no one said anything about it today." She was smiling.

"Good. See? I told you everything would work out."

Laurel gave her mother a suspicious look. "Did you go into

school? Did you say anything to anyone?"

"I might have planted an idea in someone's ear, but it's nothing that would be traced back to you."

"Mom, what did you do? Who did you talk to?" Laurel's voice was rising and she clenched her jaw.

"I—" Lilly began. But there was a knock at the back door and Laurel went over to let Noley in. She held two big bags over her arms and carried a baking dish with potholders.

"Who's hungry?" Noley asked.

"Me," Lilly said, hoping Laurel would let the other matter drop.

"Me," Laurel said. She took the baking dish from Noley and Lilly lifted the bags and put them on the countertop.

"Put that dish on the table," Noley directed Laurel. "Lilly, there's salad and bread in the bags." Lilly took the contents out of the bags and set them on the table, too.

"These look interesting," she said.

"I'm trying my hand at Latin cooking," Noley said. "I audited a Latin cuisine class in cooking school and every so often I get a hankering for it."

"Ooh, these look good," Laurel said, lifting tin foil from the top of the baking dish. A homey, spicy aroma filled the kitchen. "What's auditing?"

"It's when you attend classes and learn everything, but don't take tests. So you don't get credit for the class, but you don't have to pay for it, either." Noley pointed at the casserole dish. "Those are chicken *tamales*," she said, then she pointed at the things Lilly had brought to the table. "Those bread balls are called *pan de yuca* and the salad is made of jicama, hearts of palm, and avocado."

Everything was delicious. "Noley, I wish I could cook like you," Laurel said after dinner.

"Do something else," Noley advised with a laugh. "Something more lucrative."

CHAPTER 46

*D*inner with Noley had been just the distraction Lilly and Laurel needed. After Noley left, Laurel went upstairs to finish her homework and Lilly sat down to rest her eyes, grateful that Laurel hadn't asked any more questions about what Lilly might have done to help the bullying situation. After a little while she called Tracy to see how she was doing.

Tracy was not doing well. She was grief-stricken over her best friend's death, and she was terrified to go to work. She and the other dancers had made a pact. They asked Guy to reserve parking spots for them off to the side of the bar, and they all parked in the same area. After work they would all leave together and get into their cars at the same time. They figured there was safety in numbers. It would have been nice if Guy had hired a security guard, or at the very least, a bouncer, but he had refused. He said it would be too expensive and he couldn't afford security with the financial beating he was taking after Alice's disappearance and Suzanne's death. It seemed patrons were beginning to stay away from the bar for fear of getting kidnapped or, worse, killed.

But Lilly suspected it wasn't the patrons who were in danger. The dancers were the ones who needed to worry.

She went to bed that night wondering what Hassan was doing in Washington, then scolding herself mentally for thinking of him right before bedtime. The last thing she needed was to start feeling sorry for herself again.

The next morning there was no additional news about Suzanne's killer, so whoever did it was still on the loose. When Harry got to work, it was clear to Lilly that every day was harder than the last for him. He missed Alice terribly. And though he didn't think Alice's family missed her much after finding out about her "secret" job, Lilly was sure they must be sick with worry over her disappearance.

She called Bill midway through the morning. "Any news about Alice? Anything at all?" she asked in a quiet voice. She was in the office and knew Harry couldn't hear her, but she didn't want to take any chances.

"Nothing yet. A couple of the detectives are going around again and asking questions to some of the same people they've talked to already."

"Will they be coming in to talk to Harry?" Lilly asked.

"I don't know. Don't tell him, just in case."

"Why not?"

"So he doesn't freak out."

"Okay. Have you talked to Mom or Nikki?"

"No. You?"

"I called Nikki this morning on my way to work. She said Mom has had some good days mentally, but that she's still a little unsteady on her feet."

"That's concerning," Bill said.

"I agree. Maybe the next step should be to move her bedroom downstairs so she doesn't have to leave the first floor," Lilly suggested.

"That's probably a good idea. We'll need to talk to someone to have a shower installed in the downstairs bathroom."

"I can talk to Nikki about it tonight. I told her I'd be by to see Mom. Nikki might have some other ideas, too."

"All right. I'll meet you there if I can, but no promises. I have to work tonight."

"No problem. Bill, what did you say to Karley and Bella the other night?"

"They were in separate rooms at the station, so I talked to each of them before their parents came to pick them up. I told each of them that I knew what was going on with the bullying and that I would be checking with the school every week to make sure they weren't getting into trouble. And if they did anything that looked like bullying, I'd see to it that the shop owners in town might change their minds about bringing up charges against them for the acts of vandalism. So far the merchants have been pretty good about it because they're kids, but I told them it wouldn't stay that way if word got out that they're bullying other kids, too."

"Thanks, Bill. Don't tell Laurel what you did. She'd kill me."

Bill chuckled. "I won't say a word. She'd kill me, too."

When Lilly left the office to join Harry in the front of the store, he gave her a look of utter dejection.

"Harry, I just talked to Bill. No news yet."

"Thanks anyway, boss."

Lilly had to fight the urge to contravene Bill's order by telling Harry that the police might be questioning him again, but as Bill had pointed out, she didn't want Harry to worry any more than he already did.

The police didn't show up that afternoon. Lilly couldn't help but think they were missing something. There was something ... something that was just out of reach ... that she wanted them to know.

But, as hard as she tried, she couldn't grasp that thought and hold it.

* * *

The next morning Harry reported that the police had, indeed, questioned him again at his house when he arrived home from work the night before.

"Did they just ask you the same questions they asked before?"

Harry nodded. "They threw in a couple new ones, too. They asked me about my friends, the ones who know Alice. Do you think they suspect one of them?"

"I don't know. They need to cover every possibility, though. They need to start building more leads. Maybe one of your mutual friends knows something and doesn't even realize it."

Harry shrugged. "That's possible. I can't take much more of this waiting. I feel like I'm going crazy."

"I'm sure that's completely normal, Harry," Lilly said with a sympathetic nod. "It's the not knowing that makes it so hard."

"It is," Harry agreed.

"Have they questioned Mary Louise again?" Lilly asked. She would love to be a fly on the wall for that interview.

"I don't know. I haven't talked to her or anyone else. Mary Louise has kept her distance since she freaked out and threw that stool through the window."

"You haven't talked to any of your other friends?"

"Not very much. People are weird since Alice went missing. They don't know what to say to me, so they don't say anything. They stay away, especially now that I don't need anyone spending the night at my house anymore."

"What about Mack and Wayne and Stu and all those people who were at your house the night I brought over the macaroni and cheese? They haven't all abandoned you, have they?" Lilly was incredulous.

"I wouldn't say that," Harry said. "But they're definitely not coming around as much as they were. They all have their own lives to lead." His eyes betrayed the sadness behind his words.

"Harry, you're coming to my house for dinner tonight," Lilly said. "And that's an order. If I had known you're going home and sitting there by yourself every night, you would have been eating all of your meals at my house."

"I appreciate that, boss, but I don't mind being by myself. It gives me plenty of time to think. And I want to be there in case anyone calls about Alice."

"They'll call your cell. You're coming over." Lilly's tone brooked no disagreement.

"Okay. Thank you."

The day passed quickly. Lilly found herself wondering two or three times what Hassan was doing in Washington, but she quickly pushed those unwelcome thoughts out of her head. There were more important things to worry about—a missing woman and a murder, for example.

Lilly called Laurel at home after school to ask her to set the table for three and to make sure dinner was heated up by the time she got home from work with Harry.

Harry followed her home late that afternoon. Lilly was pleased to see that Laurel had prepared not only the tamales, but a salad, a pan of cornbread, and fruit for dessert.

They talked about anything and everything except Alice and Suzanne over dinner and dessert, and when Harry left later that evening he was wearing a smile and his shoulders and neck didn't look as tight as they had been recently. The night out did him good.

Lilly shooed Laurel out of the kitchen as a thank you for putting together such a nice meal for Harry, and then she did the dishes herself. She let her mind wander while she worked, even allowing herself to think about Hassan. She wondered what would happen when he returned from Washington. He had said they needed to talk—was he leaving her for good, or did he want to try again?

She and Laurel watched television for a little while before Lilly let Barney out one last time. Then they went upstairs. Considering all that had happened, it was a relaxing evening and Lilly wished all her evenings could be like that.

She had made a little area for Barney to curl up by her feet and was just snuggling down under the covers when all her drifting thoughts came together in a flash of crystal clarity.

"That's it!" she exclaimed.

CHAPTER 47

She kicked the covers off, startling Barney with the suddenness of her movements. He barked once while she fumbled in the dark for her cell phone. When her hand closed around it, she picked it up and hurriedly dialed Bill's number, dropping it twice in her haste.

"Hi, Lil. What's up?"

"I've got something," she said breathlessly. "Harry came over for dinner tonight. We had leftover tamales that Noley made. I got thinking about how Noley was saying the other night that she audited a Latin cuisine class when she was in school, and—"

"Lilly, does this story have a point?" Bill cut in.

"Stop being nasty and I'll tell you," she snapped.

"All right. I'm sorry. Now what do you have?"

"You mentioned that the detectives checked with the community college administration to see who was enrolled in Alice's classes. But they probably didn't ask if there was anyone auditing those classes. Usually a school will make a student pay for an audited class, but I've heard of professors allowing students to listen in to classes without registering, particularly in large lectures. If that happened in any of Alice's classes, only the professors would be able to give detectives a complete picture of who was in each class." Lilly let out a long breath.

"So you're saying that someone, unbeknownst to the college, might have been in one of Alice's classes," Bill said. There was just a hint of something in his voice. Was that excitement?

"Exactly. And if the detectives didn't talk to the actual professors and only questioned the administration, they might not know about extra students in the room."

"You might have something there," Bill said. The cadence of his words had picked up. "Let me make a call. I'll get back to you." He hung up without another word.

Lilly lay back against her pillow. Barney cocked one ear and tilted his head, probably wondering what was going on and why they couldn't just go to sleep.

"Soon, Barn," she said. "I'm waiting to hear back from Bill."

She lay there, fretting, until Bill finally called back about fifteen minutes later.

"You were right. No one asked Alice's professors who might be auditing the class without the college's knowledge. Someone's going to head out there first thing tomorrow morning to start asking questions."

"Even though tomorrow is Sunday?"

"Yes. They'll visit the professors at home if they have to."

"Will you let me know what they find out?" Lilly asked.

"It depends. I'll try," he said. "How's Mom?"

A pang of guilt began to tighten Lilly's shoulders and neck. "I didn't talk to her today. I'm the worst daughter, I swear. I'll call her tomorrow and let you know. I guess you didn't talk to her today either?"

"No. If you're the worst daughter, then I'm the worst son."

"Once all this is over, I can spend much more time with her," Lilly said.

"All right," Bill said with a sigh. "I'll call you later."

Lilly lay back once again. Barney seemed to sense that the

excitement was over for the evening and turned in several circles on the bed before collapsing into a heap at Lilly's feet.

I wish I could sleep the sleep of a happy dog, Lilly thought. She didn't know how long she lay there, hoping her suggestion to Bill would bear fruit. And as so often happens in the darkness, all her recent decisions flooded her mind to roost so she could spend the next several hours examining her conduct in each and every situation, wondering what she could have done differently.

And in particular, she thought about Hassan. Though lying about her trip to Guy's Place had seemed a good idea at the time, she now knew she had made a grave error in judgment. There was nothing she could do about it but apologize again, and she fervently hoped he would accept her apology. She had learned her lesson. But as comforting as it was to promise herself that she wouldn't lie to him ever again, she wondered if she would ever get the chance to prove herself. Not knowing what he would say to her when he returned from Washington was beginning to eat away at her.

She woke up grumpy the next morning, and was still grumpy when Harry called her cell phone.

"Lilly, they found something."

Lilly was instantly on alert. Could the detectives have talked to the professors already?

"What?" she asked eagerly.

"They were able to pull a partial license plate from the video footage at Guy's Place, but it wasn't enough to narrow down the suspect list enough to shave significant time off their search. They're running the numbers against anyone who might be related to the case. They wanted to know if I recognized the number." Harry paused. "Who memorizes all the license plates they see? I told them I would have to visit everyone I know and write down their license numbers. I'll do it, but it'll take some time."

"I feel like we're getting closer to finding Alice," Lilly said. She told him about her idea about talking to Alice's professors about students who might be auditing their classes without registering for them.

"That's great," Harry said. "Maybe they'll find something. I hope you're right—maybe we *are* getting closer to finding Alice!"

Lilly didn't want to get his hopes up only to have them dashed if nothing came of her suggestion to the police, but she figured that feeling of hope might give him a little lift he so badly needed.

"I'll let you know if I hear anything," Lilly said.

Harry took a deep breath. "I hope they find something."

But Lilly didn't hear from Bill that day. She knew he would call her the minute he knew something, so she didn't pester him by phoning. Instead, she and Laurel went over to Bev's house and told Nikki to take the day off. Then they spent several relaxing hours chatting, looking through old photo albums, and playing cards with Bev.

* * *

It was just before lunch on Monday, three weeks after Alice had gone missing, when the little bell over the front door jingled and Lilly looked up from a receipt she was writing for a customer.

Hassan stood there, his suitcase next to him on the floor.

She inhaled sharply and dropped her pen. The customer turned around to see what had caused such a reaction from Lilly, and Hassan smiled slightly. Lilly's heart skipped a beat at the sight of that familiar smile. She finished filling out the form with fingers that trembled just a bit, then the customer left.

Lilly walked toward Hassan.

"How was your trip?" she asked, suddenly at a loss for words.

"Fine. How is your concussion?"

"Fine. What's going on?" *It's painful, talking like this*, she thought.

"I thought, if you're not busy, we could grab something to eat at the bistro," he said. *He looks as nervous as I feel.*

"Let me check with Harry and see if it's all right if I leave him alone for a little while."

Harry had gone into the office to look up something for another customer. She ducked her head into the office, where he sat frowning at the computer.

"Do you need help with anything?" she asked.

"Nah, I'm just trying to find something for the woman out there," he said, gesturing with his head toward the front of the store. He stood up and walked toward her.

"Do you mind if I go out to get something to eat?" she asked.

"Not at all," he said. "I'll get something when you come back." He preceded her into the front of the shop and went to talk to his customer.

She followed him with some trepidation, realizing that she had been hoping he would say he needed her help for something. She wasn't sure she was ready to talk to Hassan.

"He'll be okay by himself," she told Hassan. "We can go." She grabbed her coat from behind one of the counters.

"Can I leave my suitcase here?" Hassan asked.

"Sure." She took the handle and pulled the suitcase behind another counter.

He held the door open for her and they left. She noticed that Harry was watching them with a smile. She hoped it was warranted.

They walked in silence to the bistro, where Hassan again held the door for her while she ducked under his arm to get inside. It was warm and the aroma of French food was enticing. Lilly knew just what she wanted—the *flamiche* with leeks and cream.

She had ordered a small *flamiche* and Hassan had ordered a *jambon-beurre* when Lilly's phone rang.

"Sorry," she mumbled. "I meant to silence that." She looked at the caller ID. It was Harry—she hoped everything was okay at the shop.

"Hi, Harry."

"Lilly, can you come back? Right now," he said in a strange voice.

"What's the matter?" The tone of his voice had raised the hackles on her neck.

"Please hurry."

CHAPTER 48

"I'll be right there." Lilly hung up and turned to face Hassan, who had been listening to her side of the call.

"I'm sorry to have to run, but Harry needs me at the store. Something's wrong."

"Do you want me to go with you?" Hassan asked. He reached for his wallet to pay for his sandwich.

"It's up to you. But I have to go now." Lilly grabbed a ten-dollar bill from her wallet and handed it to Hassan. "Will you pay for my lunch with this? If it's not enough, I'll pay you back. I'm not hungry anymore."

She turned and hurried out of the bistro and up Main Street to the jewelry store. She burst into the store and found Harry pacing.

"What happened?" she asked breathlessly.

"Bill called," Harry answered tersely. "The detectives talked to all of Alice's professors. They found out that there were two people auditing Alice's classes."

A cold twisting feeling began in the pit of Lilly's stomach. She didn't know what was coming, but it couldn't be good.

"And?" she prompted.

"And one of them was Mary Louise."

"That doesn't surprise me," Lilly said. "I've had my suspicions about her from the beginning and—"

Harry cut her off.

"Stu was the other one."

Lilly stood there, dumbstruck.

"Stu, as in your friend Stu?" she finally asked. Harry nodded grimly. "I can't believe it," she said. "How did we not know this before now?"

"No one ever mentioned it," Harry said.

"So what are the police doing now?"

"They didn't say, but I assume they're going to question Stu."

"I need to call Bill," Lilly said. She pulled her cell phone out of her pocket and was dialing her brother's number when Hassan came into the store carrying a paper bag. He held it up and pointed to it, looking at Lilly. She gestured for him to wait.

"Bill? Harry says his friend Stu is auditing one of Alice's classes." Lilly didn't stop for niceties, but got right to the point of her call.

"That's right," he answered, a determined edge to his voice.

"So what happens now?" she asked.

"They're on their way to Stu's workplace right now to talk to him," Bill said.

"What if he's not there?"

"Don't worry about that. They're detectives. If he's not there, they'll figure out where he is."

Lilly let out a shaky breath. "Stu is Harry's friend," she said quietly.

"He may not be the friend Harry thought he was," Bill said. "I'll call you as soon as I know anything. They're keeping me posted because they know Harry works for you."

"Thanks."

They hung up and Lilly turned to Harry. "Bill will let us

know as soon as he can. They're on their way to Stu's work right now."

Next she turned to Hassan, who was still standing in the middle of the shop in his overcoat, holding the paper bag.

"I brought lunch from the bistro," he said simply.

"Thank you. I don't know if I can eat, though," Lilly said. "I'm so nervous about what the detectives are going to find. Harry, do you want my *flamiche*?"

"There's no way I can eat right now," he said, wringing his hands. "I'd throw up."

Lilly looked inside the bag. "I'll try to eat some of it," she said, then looked at Hassan. "Do you mind if we eat out here? I want to be here for Harry."

"That's fine," Hassan said. They placed the food on a countertop and ate while standing up. Lilly couldn't have eaten sitting down anyway, such was her rising anxiety. Harry continued to pace back and forth across the front of the shop until a customer came in to drop off a necklace for a clasp repair. Harry glanced at Lilly.

"I'll take care of this," he said. He squared his shoulders and led the woman to another counter where he examined the clasp closely. Then he wrote up a receipt for her and put the necklace in the office after the woman left.

"I wish more people would come in," he said. "It helps me to relax a little when I'm working."

"If it would help, why don't you clean something?" Lilly suggested.

"I'll polish the countertops," he said, "even though they're already clean. Can't hurt, right?" He gave a nervous laugh.

He went back into the office and returned with a cloth and glass cleaner. He had bent down to clean the front of the case closest to the door when the bell jingled and the door opened. All eyes turned toward the person in the doorway.

It was Stu.

Harry looked at Lilly, who looked at Hassan and back to Harry.

"What's up, Stu?" Harry asked. His attempt to sound light was mangled by his tight, tense voice.

"Nothing. What's up with you?" Stu asked. He was taking one slow step at a time further into the shop.

"Just working. I haven't seen you in a few days. How have you been?" Harry asked. Lilly and Hassan stood still, watching the two young men talk.

"Can I talk to you in private? Stu asked, ignoring Harry's questions.

Lilly found her voice.

"Actually, I need Harry right now. You're welcome to talk to him in here." Harry threw her a grateful glance.

"I guess you didn't hear me. I asked to talk to him in private." Stu's words hung in the air, clearly challenging. Something clicked in Lilly's brain. How dare this little thug talk to her like that?

"I heard you just fine. He's working now and I told you that you can talk to him in here." Lilly's hands were balled into fists at her sides. Hassan placed his hand on her arm.

"Easy," he said quietly.

Stu stared at Lilly for several seconds; she stared right back at him. She hoped he wouldn't realize how badly her legs were quaking.

Harry spoke up. "Whatever you need to say, Stu, you can say it in front of Lilly and Hassan. They're friends of mine."

Stu swallowed. His Adam's apple bobbed up and down in a slow, jerky motion. He turned around and walked to the front door, locked it, and turned back to his captives. Lilly moved forward with a start, but Stu held up his hand.

"I gave you a chance to leave. You blew it. Now you're going to stay in here." He nodded toward the office door. "All of you, get in there."

Lilly, Hassan, and Harry all looked at each other. Lilly was pretty sure she knew what they were thinking because she was thinking the same thing. Did they dare try to overpower Stu? Three against one were pretty good odds.

But before any of them could make a move, Stu reached into his pocket and drew out a switchblade. He pushed a button on its hilt and a lethal-looking blade sprang out.

"I told you to go in there," he growled, gesturing with the knife toward the office door. Single file, Lilly, on legs that felt like jelly, led the way into the office, followed by Hassan, Harry, and Stu. Once in the office, Stu locked the door behind him and leaned against it. Lilly, Hassan, and Harry stood in the middle of the cramped space, wondering what would happen next.

Stu shook his head in mock sadness. "Tsk, tsk, tsk. I wish I didn't have to do this. I was only trying to talk to Harry alone." He pushed himself away from the door and glared at Lilly.

"Whatever you have in mind, you should know that my brother is a cop and he's on his way over here," Lilly lied.

"Then he'll have something to do when he gets here." Stu sneered. He gazed at the knife blade, running his thumb along its sharp edge.

"I'm sure we can talk this through," said Hassan. "Stu, is it? You don't want to do something you'll end up regretting."

"I won't regret it, believe me," he said, now switching his gaze to Harry.

"Stu, if this is about Alice, just tell me what's going on. I want to help you," Harry said. His voice held a pleading edge.

"I don't need or want your help, you sonofa—" He stopped and took a deep breath, as if he were trying to calm his own nerves. Or preparing himself....

In an instant, he had knocked Harry down and was on top of him, trying to thrust the knife blade into Harry's chest. Hassan sprang into motion, leaping onto Stu's back and trying to pull him off Harry. Harry was twisting this way and that, trying to avoid the knife. Blood smeared on the floor where Harry was writhing, and he let out a roar.

"You think this is bad?" Stu shouted, panting. "Just wait until I go home and try it on Alice!"

Lilly had been rooted to the spot, but once Harry let out that primal yell and she heard Stu's shocking response, she jumped into action. She scrabbled for the closest object she could get her hands on, a metal tray that held the outgoing mail. She lifted it with both hands to bring it down on Stu's head, but he moved suddenly and Hassan was squarely in her line of fire. She jerked her arms down and yelled to him to get out of the way.

"Hassan! Move!" she screamed. He broke his concentration only for a moment to see what she was doing, then immediately rolled out of the way so Lilly could have a clear path to Stu's head.

Harry had twisted sideways and was attempting to scramble to his feet to gain the advantage over Stu. Stu, though, raised his knife and was plunging it down into Harry's ribcage when Lilly, with a scream of exertion, swung the metal tray and hit the side of Stu's head.

CHAPTER 49

A fraction of a second later, Stu slumped over Harry's torso. Blood streamed from his head and Harry, with a cry of alarm, shimmied out from underneath his former friend. He stood up, but had to bend over with his hands on his knees to catch his breath.

"Did you hear what he said?" he panted. "Alice is at his house!"

Hassan had managed to get to his feet, too, and was pulling out his cell phone when a loud knocking sounded on the back door of the office.

"Lilly? Are you in there? Lilly!"

It was Bill.

"Bill!" she shouted. The door handle was rattling and she bounded around her desk to open it.

When Bill stepped inside, he was greeted with a bewildering sight: Harry, bleeding from his chest and still gasping for breath, Lilly, tears streaming down her face, Hassan, standing in the middle of the office with a look of shock on his face, and Stu, unconscious on the office floor.

"What happened here?" he asked.

Lilly took a deep breath. "Stu came in here and attacked Harry. Hassan and I were trying to stop him. Bill, listen. He said he was going to go home and do the same thing to Alice!"

Bill's eyes widened. He reached for the radio on his shoulder and moments later had requested that a phalanx of officers go to Stu's house and break the door down, if necessary.

Then he called an ambulance for Harry, who was sitting on the floor, wincing in pain and holding his side.

"I'm okay," Harry panted. "I just want you guys to find Alice."

"We'll get her," Bill said grimly. "But you're going to the hospital. We'll let you know the second we find her."

Lilly had run to the front of the shop, where her purse still sat on the countertop. A lone woman stood on the sidewalk, peering into the store and checking and double-checking her watch. Lilly unlocked the front door long enough to tell the woman there was an emergency and to return the following day, then she locked the door again and sprang for her purse. There was a scarf in there that she hadn't worn that morning, so she whipped it out and carried it back into the office.

"Harry, hold this against your side," she instructed. He did as she told him to do, grimacing with the effort.

"Lilly, are you all right?" Hassan asked. She nodded, too overcome with emotion to say anything.

It wasn't long before the jewelry store was swarming with police officers and paramedics. Two of the paramedics stabilized Harry as quickly as they could and whisked him away to the hospital, promising Lilly and Hassan that they would take good care of him.

Stu woke up to find an officer standing over him. He looked dazed, then Lilly could see that the reality of the situation had dawned on him. The officer guarding him noticed, too.

"Don't move!" he barked.

Stu slumped down onto the floor again while the paramedics turned their attention to him. Two officers watched him closely while he was strapped onto a stretcher, then one of them joined him in the back of an ambulance while the other followed in a police car. Lilly had no doubt they would keep a careful watch on him at the hospital.

Two other officers were questioning Lilly and Hassan separately. They wanted to know everything from the moment Lilly received the call from Harry while she was in the bistro to the moment Bill arrived at the back door of the shop.

When they had asked all their questions, Lilly went over to where Bill was standing, talking to another officer. Bill nodded and the officer walked toward the front of the store.

"How are you doing?" he asked Lilly.

"Okay, I guess. Do you think Harry will be okay?"

"I think so. A stab wound is serious, but I've seen much worse and those people survived." His radio began to squawk. "Excuse me," he said. He walked a few feet away and listened, then answered briefly.

"They've got Alice. She's okay."

"Thank God!" Lilly cried. It was then that the stress of the day came crashing down and she collapsed into her desk chair, sobbing. The police went on with their work, moving around her, while Bill and Hassan just let her cry.

Finally, several minutes later, she wiped her eyes, blew her nose, and stood up.

"Sorry about that," she said. They both smiled gently at her.

"That's okay," they said in unison.

"Do you know anything about what happened to Alice?" Lilly asked Bill.

"Nothing yet. I'll let you know when I hear something. If you're all right, I'm going to head down to the station. I need to start writing this up," Bill said. "These officers will be here for a little while." He nodded in the general direction of the officers who were left.

"Thanks, Bill," Lilly said.

"Bill, you should have seen her," Hassan said. "If she hadn't hit Stu with that metal tray, he would have sunk that knife right into the side of Harry's chest. She probably saved his life."

Bill looked at his sister.

"Don't tell Mom," she said.

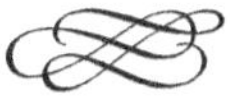

CHAPTER 50

*A*fter Bill left, Lilly sat down again at her desk. She tried to get some work done, but all she could do was stare at the wall, her body numb with shock. She wanted to leave, but she had to stay until the police left so she could lock up the store.

Hassan sat in the office, too, not saying anything. Eventually he roused himself and went to the front of the store, then returned wheeling his suitcase.

"I'm going to head home," he said. Lilly didn't know if he was referring to his home in Minnesota or his home in Juniper Junction, and at that moment she didn't even care.

"Okay," she said flatly. She couldn't summon any more emotion for him.

"Can we still talk?" he asked.

"Yes, but not today." She ran her hand over her tired eyes.

"I'll call you in the next few days," he said. She nodded and he went out the back door. When he was gone she slumped back in her chair, tempted for a moment to indulge in a little bit of self-pity, but she sat up again and squared her shoulders. She was going to plow through some work until the police left, then she was going to go to the hospital to see how Harry was doing. If he didn't already know the good news about Alice, she planned to tell him. Then she was going to go to her mother's house and check on her, then she was going to go home and have dinner with Laurel. Then she was going to bed.

It was after the normal closing time when the police officers finally left, but it wasn't too late. Lilly locked up and hurried over to the hospital, where she found that Harry had been admitted with a stab wound. They wanted to keep an eye on him overnight. She was his first visitor, though he had received a phone call from Bill. *Leave it to him to steal my good news*, Lilly thought with a grimace.

"They have Alice!" Harry exclaimed weakly when he saw Lilly. "She's okay." He was beaming tiredly, despite the bandages and the IVs and the exhaustion that was evident on his face.

"I'm so happy," she replied, taking his hand in hers. Then she had a thought. "I'll be right back, Harry."

She went to the nurses' station and waited for someone to come along and help her. When she had asked her question and received confirmation, she returned to Harry's room.

"Are you all right? Where did you go?" he asked.

"I'm better than all right," she said, thinking *Take that, Bill. You can't steal all the thunder.*

"What do you mean?"

"I mean, Alice is just two floors down from you. You can go see her!"

His mouth hung open. "She's here? Are you sure?"

"Positive. I just went out and asked a nurse to check for me. She's here for observation."

Suddenly Harry looked nervous. "Do you think she wants to see me?"

"Why wouldn't she?" Lilly asked, incredulous.

"Because I didn't find her," he said. "I didn't look hard enough. I should have known it was Stu when he stopped coming around. He never wanted to stay overnight at my house, either."

"No one could have known that," Lilly scolded "Now do you want me to wheel you down there, or what?"

He swallowed. "I guess so, if you think that's the right thing to do."

"It's not my call, Harry. It's yours."

There was a knock at the door. Harry glanced up and his face went white. Lilly whirled around and stared.

Alice stood in the hallway, smiling timidly.

In two steps Lilly was at the door, flinging it open to let Alice come in. She wrapped Alice in an embrace, her tears mingling with Alice's, and then stepped away so Alice could approach the bed. The young woman walked slowly, trying to move her IV stand with her, and Lilly reached out to help so the tubes wouldn't get tangled.

By the time Alice reached the bed, Harry had swung his legs over the edge and was trying to stand up.

"Don't try to get up," Alice told him. "Let me come to you. I'm stronger."

He reached out and she leaned into him, tubes and all. When Lilly tiptoed out of the room, they were laughing and crying and holding onto each other for dear life.

* * *

After Lilly left the hospital, her cheeks still damp with tears of happiness for Harry and Alice, she stopped at her mother's house.

"Haven't seen you in a while," Bev remarked sharply when Lilly walked into the living room.

"It's been crazy, Mom," Lilly said. She was simultaneously relieved to see that her mother's moxie hadn't dimmed and annoyed that her mother greeted her that way.

"Is everything okay?" Nikki asked. She gave Lilly a meaningful look, letting Lilly know that she had been worried.

Lilly smiled her appreciation for Nikki's thoughtfulness. "Yes, I think everything is fine now."

"What are you two talking about?" Bev demanded. "What's fine?"

"Everything," Lilly said simply. She sat down next to her mother. "Tell me what you've been up to today."

* * *

Lilly spent the next hour talking to her mother and Nikki. It was just as if the past three weeks hadn't happened. They didn't talk about anything but happy times and happy memories, and by the time Lilly headed home, exhausted, Bev was in a much better mood.

Nikki walked Lilly to the door. "Lilly," she began. Her tone was wary. Lilly was on alert immediately.

"What is it?" Lilly asked.

"It's just that Beau and I are planning that getaway weekend that he gave me for Valentine's Day. I'm wondering if I can get a few days off to go. We're planning on—"

"No details," Lilly said, holding up her hand and cutting off Nikki's train of thought. "Of course you can have days off. Just tell me when, and Bill and I will arrange our schedules so one of us can be here all the time. We really need to concentrate on getting someone else in here so you can have a life again. But I don't need to know what you and Beau have planned. Please." She smiled and Nikki blushed.

"Thanks, Lilly. I'll let you know when we have the dates finalized."

Lilly couldn't wait to get home and slip into her pajamas. She was starving, too. It felt like she had choked down that *flamiche* days ago.

Laurel was waiting for her when she trudged into the kitchen.

"Mom! What happened? You look terrible."

"Thanks," Lilly said wryly. "It's been a long day. They found Alice. She's going to be okay."

Laurel's face broke into a broad smile. "That's great! Where was she? What happened to her?" She peppered Lilly with questions while they made dinner and sat down together to eat.

Lilly told her everything she knew, but there were still things she wondered about. She would talk to Bill in the morning. First, though, she needed sleep.

"I have news, too," Laurel said with a sly smile as they finished the dinner dishes.

"Oh? What news?" Lilly asked.

"I'm going to prom," Laurel said.

"You are? With whom?"

"Vanessa," Laurel said excitedly. "Her boyfriend dumped her! Can you believe it? So we made a pact that we wouldn't go with any boys. We're just going to go together and have fun."

"That's my girl," Lilly said, gathering Laurel into a hug. "We can go shopping for a dress this weekend, if you'd like."

"Definitely. We can go with Vanessa and her mother," Laurel suggested.

"You got it."

After Laurel went upstairs Lilly let Barney out and then went upstairs herself. She couldn't wait to crawl between the covers.

But before she could even get in bed, the phone rang. It was Hassan.

"Can we talk?" he asked. "I know you wanted to wait, but I have to get something off my chest. Is this a bad time?"

"It's okay," she said, suppressing a sigh. She longed to be asleep.

"I want to apologize for everything," he said. "I was wrong to react the way I did when you didn't tell me the truth about everything that happened at Guy's Place. I thought about it and you a lot when I was in Washington and I know you were just trying to keep me from worrying. I tend to see things in black and white, and that wasn't a black-and-white situation. I'm truly sorry."

"And I'm sorry I lied to you," Lilly said. "If I had to do it over again, I wouldn't. I should have known it was better to tell you the truth and let you worry." She managed a chuckle.

"Do you think we could try that lunch again tomorrow?" Hassan asked.

"I doubt it. Harry's going to be fine, but he' still in the hospital and I won't be able to leave the shop," she said.

"Leave it to me. I'll bring something in."

She could hear the smile in his voice and she smiled, too.

"It's a date," she said.

CHAPTER 51

The next morning Lilly was at work early when her cell phone rang. It was Bill.

"I called to tell you what we learned last night when we questioned Stu," he said.

"Tell me everything." She sat on the stool, the one Mary Louise had thrown through the window, while she listened to the story.

"Well, you know that Stu was auditing a course with Alice," he began. "He knew her through his friendship with Harry, and when he found out she was a student at the community college where he was also a student, he decided to audit one of her classes just to be closer to her. Essentially, what started out as a serious crush turned into an ugly obsession with Alice."

"Did Alice realize it?"

"Apparently not at first. But she left campus to go to work at Guy's Place one night and he followed her. He didn't know she was a dancer there, but he found out pretty quickly. He watched her dance and when it was her turn to waitress, he started hitting on her. He figured she was loose if she was a stripper, but she made it clear to him that she was committed to Harry and that she only danced because it was good money and since her parents weren't helping to pay for her classes at the community college, she needed the cash."

"We figured that, knowing her personality," Lilly put in.

"Right. Needless to say, she's quit that job."

"Good."

"Anyway, he kept returning to the bar and bothering her, and she just kept on rejecting him. It triggered something in his head. The next day was Valentine's Day, and he knew Harry was going to pop the question. He followed Alice to Guy's Place that afternoon when she went to get her paycheck, and when she left the building he grabbed her from behind and took her to his house."

"Oh, my God." Lilly closed her eyes. She didn't know if she wanted to hear the rest.

"He kept her in the basement. He didn't touch her, and she confirmed that. He just wanted to look at her and he didn't want Harry to have her. It was that simple. Twisted, but simple."

"So how did he keep her there?" Lilly asked.

"She was chained to the wall. But he fed her and gave her water to drink and let her use a crude bathroom he had set up in the basement. Under supervision, of course. She was just biding her time, waiting for a chance to escape, when everything hit the fan at your store and the police found her."

"What about Mary Louise? Was she involved at all?"

"It doesn't look that way. She's just weird. She had a thing for Harry and she wasn't going to let something like a serious girlfriend get in her way."

Lilly shuddered. "How did you happen to be at my shop when Stu was there?"

"I was in the neighborhood, talking to one of the merchants about some petty shoplifting. I had just heard that Stu's license plate was a match to the partial plate they found on Guy's security footage, so I decided to stop by and tell Harry in person.

When the front door was locked and there was no sign in the window explaining why, I knew something was wrong. So I went around back."

"Thank you."

"Stu is the one who attacked you in the parking lot at Guy's Place, too. And he killed Suzanne. He's as good as confessed to both," Bill said quietly.

"I'm glad to know you've caught Suzanne's killer. I assume he did it because he was afraid she would recognize him and be able to identify him to police?"

"Exactly," Bill said. "He attacked you for the same reason. He knew you had seen him in the bar that night."

"I think he must have been in line waiting to use the restroom. That's the only thing I can think of. I didn't even recognize him. It was too dark in there."

"Well, he recognized you." Unspoken words hung in the air. Lilly was lucky to be alive.

There was a knock on the glass window of the shop. Lilly looked up and smiled when she saw Noley standing there, holding up a paper bag. That meant homemade muffins.

"Bill, Noley's here. I'll catch up with you later. Thanks for everything," she said. "I owe you."

"You could never repay me," he said with a laugh.

Lilly opened the door to let Noley in, then locked it again. She started the coffee maker in the office while Noley unpacked her bag. There were two ham and egg breakfast sandwiches, along with blueberry muffins. They were Lilly's favorite.

They gabbed for a half hour, until it was almost time for Lilly to open the shop for the day. Lilly told her all about what had transpired the day before and everything Bill had told her just minutes earlier.

Noley sat dumbstruck. "How come you didn't call me last night?"

"I was so tired, I just couldn't. Plus, I knew we would talk today. And I have more news." She told Noley about her phone call with Hassan.

"He's bringing lunch in today."

"I'm so happy for you. And Harry and Alice and Hassan, too," Noley said. "It sounds like everything has worked out."

Just then Lilly's phone buzzed with a text. She looked down. It was from Harry.

She said YES!

Lilly couldn't stop the grin that spread across her face.

"Well," she said. "It may not have been the perfect Valentine's Day engagement that Harry hoped for, but there's going to be a happy ending. We have an engagement party to plan, after all."

THE END

LILLY'S MACARONI & CHEESE

12 oz. macaroni, uncooked
6 T. butter
6 T. flour
3 c. milk
12 oz. grated Cheddar cheese
Salt and pepper
Seasoned breadcrumbs
Prepare macaroni according to package directions. Drain.

Preheat oven to 350 degrees. In a large saucepan, melt butter over medium-high heat.

Add flour, whisking to make a roux. When flour is incorporated, cook, whisking constantly, for one minute. Gradually add milk and whisk until combined and smooth. Cook until mixture begins to thicken. Add cheese and whisk until mixture is smooth. Add cooked macaroni to mixture and stir to coat.

Pour entire mixture into greased 3-qt. baking dish. Sprinkle top generously with breadcrumbs. Bake, uncovered, for 30-35 minutes.

LILLY'S ZUPPA TOSCANA

1 lg. onion, diced

1 lb. sweet or hot bulk Italian sausage, depending on your heat preference (a mix also works)

3 lg. potatoes, peeled and diced into bite-sized pieces

2 cloves garlic, minced

4 c. chicken broth

1 c. heavy cream

3 c. baby spinach

Salt and pepper

In a Dutch oven cook onion and sausage over medium heat, breaking up sausage with a spoon until crumbly, until onions are soft and sausage is no longer pink. Add potatoes, garlic, and chicken broth. Bring to a boil.

Reduce heat and simmer for 12-14 minutes, or until potatoes are tender. Stir in heavy cream and bring mixture to a boil. Boil for 1 minute. Remove from heat and stir spinach gently into mixture. Serve with Italian bread and olive oil for dipping.

BUTTERSCOTCH PUDDING

½ c. brown sugar
2 T. plus 2 t. cornstarch
Dash salt
2 c. milk (do not use skim)
2 egg yolks, lightly beaten
1 T. butter
1 t. vanilla

In a medium saucepan, stir together brown sugar, cornstarch, and salt. Gradually add milk and egg yolks, whisking to combine. Cook over medium heat, stirring constantly, until mixture comes to a boil. Continue cooking and stirring for 2 more minutes or until mixture is thickened.

Remove pudding from heat; add butter and vanilla and stir until butter is melted.

Divide pudding into four ramekins and press plastic wrap on the surface of each to prevent a skin from forming. Refrigerate until chilled.

THE WORST NOEL

THE JUNIPER JUNCTION HOLIDAY
MYSTERY SERIES: BOOK ONE

Lilly awoke hours before dawn to the sound of her alarm clock going off. She flung her hand in the general direction of the nightstand to find the snooze button and stop the incessant ringing, but only succeeded in knocking the clock to the floor.

"Ugh," she groaned. She leaned over the side of the bed and clawed the floor, trying to reach the clock. When she found it, she turned it off and sat up groggily, wiping sleep from her eyes and yawning. Barney, the family's Soft-Coated Wheaten Terrier, lifted his shaggy, brindle-hued head and stretched across the foot of the bed.

"I hate Black Friday," she said to Barney. The biggest shopping day of the year brought a level of anxiety that gave her nightmares the other three hundred sixty-four days. She peered into the bathroom mirror before heading downstairs. Her brown hair was tangled from sleep and her eyes, normally bright hazel, were hooded and sported bags.

She needed coffee and lots of it. She went downstairs to find that the kids had left the kitchen light on all night again. "Good," she muttered to herself. "I was hoping to give the electric company a nice fat check for Christmas." She switched off all the lights but one and started the coffeemaker. Before long the kitchen was filled with the aroma of ground Arabica beans and Lilly's senses started coming alive.

After showering, dressing, and grabbing a quick breakfast, Lilly poured herself a travel mug of coffee and slipped out the side door without making a sound. Normally Barney followed her downstairs for breakfast, but it was too early for him.

The car didn't even have time to warm up during the short drive to Juniper Junction Jewels. Lilly drove along Main Street, smiling at the Christmas lights that hung from the shop fronts and the street lamps. She loved this festive time of year. And since this was Colorado, there were several inches of freshly-fallen snow on the ground to make the lights seem even prettier. At the end of the block, she swung her car around the back of the row of shops and pulled into one of the parking spots allocated for her jewelry store. Each store got two parking spots so employees wouldn't have to go searching for spots when Main Street got really busy, as was often the case in the upscale Rocky Mountain resort town.

It was so early the plows hadn't even been out yet, so Lilly stepped carefully when she got out of the car. Shifting her shoulder bag from one arm to the other and holding her coffee, she reached for the doorknob at the back of the shop.

It was unlocked.

Lilly's stomach lurched; her body stiffened. This was a shop owner's worst nightmare, made even more horrible when the shop sold precious stones, expensive gems, and custom jewelry. Lilly turned the knob slowly and pushed the door open, peering around it to make sure there was no one waiting for her in the back room.

She didn't see anyone, so she closed the door softly behind her and set her bag and coffee down on her desk. She had been the last one to leave Wednesday afternoon and the shop had been closed for Thanksgiving Day; she shuddered to think that the shop had been unlocked for thirty-six hours. She wracked her brain trying to remember locking the door behind her on Wednesday, but she couldn't. She couldn't remember setting the alarm, either, but that obviously hadn't gone off because the alarm company had her home number and her cell number.

Quickly walking over to the vault where she kept her inventory when the store was closed, she stopped short when she saw that the door to the vault was slightly ajar. She put out one finger to push the door open a bit farther; wave after wave of nausea swept over her when she saw that one of the sliding shelves that held the jewelry had been moved. She stepped into the tiny vault and pulled the shelf out a bit further—there was a necklace missing. A pearl necklace. She frantically pulled out all the other shelves in turn, not daring to breathe until she satisfied herself that nothing else had been taken. She backed out of the vault and strode to her desk, where she leafed quickly through the papers littering the top. Nothing else seemed to be missing.

She pushed open the sliding barn door that led to the interior of the shop.

Lilly prided herself on making Juniper Junction Jewels a homey, rustic place that looked like someone's living room. As such, the lighting inside the store was provided mostly by lamps set strategically around the shop rather than cold, sterile fluorescent lights.

She turned on the lamp closest to the office. She didn't notice the body lying on the floor behind one of the glass cases until she tripped over it.

Please visit https://www.amymreade.com/newsletter to sign up to receive monthly news, updates, promotions, contests, and recipes.

ABOUT THE AUTHOR

Amy M. Reade is a cook, chauffeur, household CEO, doctor, laundress, maid, psychiatrist, warden, seer, teacher, and pet whisperer. In other words, a wife, mother, community volunteer, and recovering attorney.

She's also the *USA Today* and *Wall Street Journal* bestselling author of the Juniper Junction Holiday Mystery series, The Libraries of the World Mystery Series, The Malice Series, and three standalone books. She lives in southern New Jersey, but loves to travel. Her favorite places to visit are Scotland and Hawaii and when she can't travel she loves to read books set in far-flung locations.

Her days are split between writing and marketing her books, but uppermost in her mind is the adage that the best way to market a book is to write another great book.

www.ingramcontent.com/pod-product-compliance
Lightning Source LLC
Chambersburg PA
CBHW021104110726
47900CB00007B/2020